Clear and Convincing Evidence

Clear and Convincing Evidence

The Arcadia Chronicles

H. C. Helfand

Book Two

This book is a work of fiction. References to real people, events, establishments, organizations, or locales are intended only to provide a sense of authenticity and are used fictitiously. All other characters, and all incidents and dialogue, are drawn from the author's imagination and are not to be construed as real.

Copyright © 2022 H.C. Helfand
All rights reserved.
ISBN: 979-8-3608-4716-8

To my family

Justice, justice shall you pursue, that you may thrive and possess the land . . .

Deuteronomy 16:20

Table of Contents

ABBY 1
ABBY 3
ABBY 5
ABBY 9
ABBY 11
ABBY 15
DAVID 16
ABBY 18
ABBY 21
ABBY 24
ABBY 26
ABBY 29
ABBY 33
ABBY 36
ABBY 39
DAVID 41
ABBY 42
ABBY 45
ABBY 49
ABBY 51
ABBY 54
ABBY 56

DAVID	59
ABBY	60
ABBY	62
ABBY	64
ABBY	66
ABBY	68
ABBY	71
DAVID	73
ABBY	74
ABBY	76
ABBY	78
ABBY	80
ABBY	82
ABBY	84
ABBY	87
ABBY	90
ABBY	92
ABBY	95
ABBY	97
DAVID	99
ABBY	102
ABBY	105
ABBY	106
ABBY	110
ABBY	114

ABBY	116
ABBY	118
ABBY	121
ABBY	123
ABBY	126
ABBY	131
DAVID	133
ABBY	135
ABBY	138
ABBY	141
ABBY	143
ABBY	145
ABBY	149
DAVID	151
DAVID	152
ABBY	155
ABBY	157
ABBY	161
ABBY	162
ABBY	165
ABBY	168
ABBY	171
ABBY	173
ABBY	175
ABBY	177

ABBY	180
ABBY	182
ABBY	185
ABBY	187
ABBY	189
ABBY	191
ABBY	194
ABBY	197
ABBY	199
DAVID	202
ABBY	204
ABBY	207
ABBY	210
ABBY	213
ABBY	216
ABBY	220
ABBY	222
ABBY	224
ABBY	226
DAVID	230
ABBY	233
ABBY	236
ABBY	238
ABBY	240
ABBY	242

DAVID	245
ABBY	246
ABBY	248
ABBY	253
ABBY	254
ABBY	256
ABBY	258
ABBY	261
ABBY	264
ABBY	266
ABBY	269
ABBY	271
DAVID	273
ABBY	274
ABBY	276
ABBY	278
ABBY	280
ABBY	283
DAVID	285
ABBY	287
ABBY	289
ABBY	291
ABBY	293
ABBY	297
ABBY	299

ABBY	301
ABBY	304
ABBY	308
ABBY	310
ABBY	311
DAVID	315
ABBY	319
ABBY	321
ABBY	324
ABBY	327
DAVID	328
ABBY	330
ABBY	332
ABBY	336
ABBY	339
ABBY	341
ABBY	344
DAVID	346
DAVID	348
ABBY	350
ABBY	353
ABBY	356
ABBY	357
ABBY	358
CODA	360

ABBY

July 1998

I swore I would never go to law school.

Most of the lawyers I knew were either morons or crooks. Or broke or dead. I could conjure an honorable handful, but they were few and far between. Dan Hutchinson was one of the few.

Three years ago, Dan, crafty and strategic, helped me secure a pristine parcel of land in Arcadia, on the western edge of Baltimore County. Together we exposed a contemptible fraud and restored the land to its rightful owner, my estimable partner, David Armacost. The land drew me to David, and his dream created The Gleanings, a community farm. It became our home, our pastoral paradise, our unsullied sanctuary.

My former world of title searching had crumbled like a timeworn scroll. Now I spent my days engulfed in an administrative haze arranging programs, visits, and maintenance for the farm. For a while, every day at The Gleanings thrilled me, yet no more. My love for The Gleanings would never die, but the boredom was killing me. I slid into a pattern that afforded ease but little growth and craved a next step.

Ever since I met Dan, he tried to convince me to go to law school. Dan persisted, and, as I languished, my resistance shrank to an undetectable speck. My motive still eluded me. Was it because David was so highly credentialed? A noted mathematician and professor, he had more degrees than I had toes.

Every stupid lawyer in the world made it through law school. If they could do it, so could I. That was a motivator. Abigail Fischer, Attorney-at-Law. It had a certain ring, didn't it?

I surrendered. Now law school loomed, and I drowned in second thoughts. I bet David I wouldn't last a day. He warned me never to bet against myself, especially when I had something to prove. We doubled the ante and awaited the result.

Who would win?

ABBY

David won.

On Dan's recommendation, I enrolled in night classes at the Baltimore School of Law. It was not the most prestigious law school in town, but many of its alumni held high positions and local judgeships. Because I had no tangible ambition it did not matter to me. But Dan's opinion did, and that was the one I followed.

Step One: Find the right building. Check.

I lumbered three flights up, straining under the weight of my ancient L.L. Bean knapsack filled with the heaviest books I ever bought. Briefcase-toting hyenas sped past me on the left, elbowed me, and nearly knocked me down.

Step Two: Find the right room. Check, with a wobble.

Class was even worse. The professor sadistically called on people. By name. And surrounding me, the hyenas were raising their hands! Finding no hole in the floor from which to escape, I prepared myself for humiliation.

Which never came. Lucky me. It was unintentional, but I couldn't have picked a better seat. The student seated directly ahead shielded me with shoulders the width of a football field. Scrunching gave me further invisibility. So far, it worked.

I survived my first night of law school. Maybe I would come back.

ABBY

I did.

And much to my surprise, I liked . . . okay, tolerated it.

I never got used to the Socratic method, which I considered veiled torture but managed to hold my own. My initial Pavlovian response to "What do you think, Ms. Fischer?" was to feel the vestiges of my dinner approach my throat. In time though, I managed to squeak out an answer, occasionally right.

What I liked best were the nooks and crannies of the law. The exceptions to the rules, creative interpretations, and conditional clauses, like the one that brought me to The Gleanings. I learned how lawyers mined those crevices and found openings and arguments where none existed before. It was a different way of looking at things. Through a glass, sideways.

Eventually, I forgave Dan. Maybe going to law school wasn't the worst idea in the world. Learning was its own reward; I didn't have to be a lawyer when I graduated. Except I guess that was the point. And Dan's next crusade.

Dan and I met in Towson for dinner every couple of months. We caught up, joked, and mocked other lawyers. Dan's specialty was professional malpractice defense. He once taught a legal ethics course at law school, a class he nicknamed "Hey Dummies, Don't Do This." Dan's syllabus overflowed with cautionary real-life examples.

"Want that?" Dan asked before he seized the last Avocado Roll. "Any after-graduation plans?"

I strained to take him seriously. Dan was a Civil War reenactor and came to dinner straight from the battlefield. Tonight, he was in Union garb. With his handlebar mustache, he looked authentic but out-of-place eating sushi dressed like General Grant.

"No," I said. "Should I?"

"Why don't you consider coming in with me? I could use an associate."

"You're kidding, aren't you?"

The last thing I wanted to do was to make excuses for bad lawyers.

"I'm perfectly serious," he answered. "I'll train you myself—you'll be magnificent."

Dan tended toward hyperbole. Magnificent? Maybe art or literature, not law and lawyers. That technique might work on juries, not on skeptical me.

"Dan, aren't all your clients lawyers who screw up?"

"Well, yes. But there's never a lack of business. Have you seen my car?"

I had. He drove a Ferrari. He also lived in a mansion on Charles Street. Okay, so there was money in malpractice. But that wasn't my goal.

"Look," I said. "Thank you for your confidence, but I'm not ready to commit. I think I might want to do something more public-service oriented if I want to practice law at all."

"Sure, Abby. Sounds like too much of David's do-gooderism rubbed off on you. Perfectly fine, though. Go forth and save the world."

"I wouldn't go that far. The world's a big place." I jangled the keys to my old Honda.

The waiter came by with his pad. "Ready for the check, or should I send it to Gettysburg?"

Dan grabbed it. "Smart ass," he said, and handed the waiter two twenties. "Keep the change."

Out the door, we shared an awkward hug. The medals on his chest scratched my chin.

"Thanks for dinner and the job offer. I'll think about it."

"Any time you're ready." Dan waved and held up two fingers. "Peace, Abby. See you at Appomattox."

ABBY

Law school and I reached a truce. If it didn't kill me, I would stay. Eventually, it had to end.

And faster than I thought, it did. I took some day classes too, trying to speed it up. Night school, day school. Day school, night school. A mechanical wind-up legal toy; crank me for more, get me through.

By the time I finished my third year, I had enough of torts, contracts, and evidence. Only one more semester to go. Because I'd complete my law degree in December, I could take the bar exam in February, even though I wouldn't officially graduate until May of 2002.

In June 2001, this was my plan.

ABBY

It wasn't exactly a Robert Burns mice and men moment, but my best-laid plans hit a glitch. A big one.

I missed my period in July. At first, I didn't give it much thought since I wasn't regular. But when August came with a repeat, I knew something was up. My breasts swelled to mini soccer balls and chafed at the touch. I wanted to heave the moment I woke. Uh oh.

I married Ted Fischer when I was twenty-one, unthinking. We split after nine years. No children, no regrets. David and I, partners since 1995, successfully avoided discussing marriage or children, presumably content with the status quo and reluctant to upset the balance. We thought we evaded conception by conventional means. We weren't idiots.

But maybe we were since we failed. Planned or not, reality struck. This was a balance disrupter and had to be faced.

How would he take it? I wasn't entirely displeased; at thirty-eight, I might not get another chance to have a child. It hadn't been a concern before, but now confronted with the possibility, I heard my reproductive clock ticking away.

My deepest fear, at the core of my being, lingered. For a long time, I doubted my ability to love. David assuaged that suspicion, and I believed I loved him as much as I could love anyone. Children, long avoided, were another story. Did I have the capacity to stretch that love? To someone completely dependent and from whom I could not escape? The uncertainty gnawed at my gut. Which, ironically, sat physically proximate to where a child now likely lay implanted in my womb.

That morning, I took a home pregnancy test. Seeing the thin plastic stick turn pink made it real. I closed my eyes and gulped. The phlegm rocketed down my throat, and I willed myself into acceptance. If lucky, this child would be more like David. Patient and kind, with a strong sense of who he was and what he wanted in life. Unlike me.

I kept the news to myself all day, debating the reveal. How should I frame it? "Guess what?" with a big smile or a somber "We need to talk?" Recalling his warmth with other people's kids, I leaned on the expectation of David's happy reaction. But what if I were wrong? Did he admire them from afar but not want any of his own?

Damn, why didn't we ever talk about it? How naïve were we? I stewed all day, my stomach in knots, trying to plan for a reaction I couldn't predict. I mindlessly munched on pack after pack of saltines to soothe myself, but that didn't cure my queasiness. Was it the baby or my nerves? After pacing the soles of my shoes thin, I needed to get it over with.

Let the chips fall where they may.

ABBY

Easing my mind was hopeless. Maybe a move outside would still my jitters.

The mossy hills in the distance carpeted the barely clouded sky. A chickadee hovered over the cherry trees. Crickets in a choir rubbed their wings in song. Glorious, but not enough. The novel I took for diversion was a bust, too. After having to reread every paragraph for a few pages, I gave up.

The front door squeaked open and banged shut. David. He would have made a terrible spy with his heavy gait. Bonk, bonk.

I already staked my claim in a chair on the patio. My fingers involuntarily thrummed the cast-iron table. Zero hour. The screen of the sliding door gave me a partial view of the kitchen. David entered, looked around, and called, "Abby?"

No escaping now.

"I'm out here." I floated a half-hearted wave.

He reached into the fridge and pulled out a beer. "Want one?"

"No, thanks."

The patio faced his garden. August had been cooler than usual that summer, and we often ate outside, the days still long and lazy.

He joined me, and I pointed to some ripe tomatoes on the vine. "Why don't you pick some for dinner? How about Caprese salad?"

"Good idea." He pulled some and lined the bursting red globes in two short rows on the table. "Think that's enough?"

"Sure," I said.

That wasted a couple of minutes.

David sat, took a few sips from his beer, and stretched his legs. Resting the long-necked bottle on the table, he asked, "How was your day?" A hank of hair flopped over his forehead. Though gray, it gave him a boyish air.

I took a long breath and slowly exhaled. "Umm." I should have prepared a better answer.

David's eyes narrowed. "Something wrong?"

"No, not really."

He scooted closer. "What is it?"

I steeled myself. Just tell him.

"I'm pregnant."

David's eyes fluttered, and he emitted a high-pitched breath. He placed his large farmer's hand on mine and stopped the movement of my twitching fingers. The small creases alongside his mouth deepened, a sign of his pleasure. His gaze shifted from our hands to my eyes.

"That's it," he said. "We're getting married."

"Why? Because I'm pregnant?"

"No." David lifted my hand to his lips and kissed it. "Because I love you."

"Are you sure?"

"Absolutely. I've wanted this ever since we met."

"But we never . . ."

"I wasn't sure you wanted to do it again. And I didn't want to risk ruining a good thing."

His eyes misted. "But a baby—oh, Abby." His voice trailed off to an audible breath.

I swallowed hard. "Okay. But let's do it soon. I don't want to look like a bride at a shotgun wedding."

He snorted. "No shotgun, I promise. This is love, not necessity."

Then reality struck. My twitching resumed.

"But I have school, work, the bar exam. How can we do this?"

"Breathe, Abby. I will take care of everything. You'll just have to show up."

"Just one thing. I do not want to get married at the Court House. I did that once—and once was enough."

I kicked the table leg. My first wedding was an experience best forgotten. No way I wanted a repeat of that debacle.

David barely took a moment. He tilted his hand toward the scene before us.

"We'll have it here in a few weeks and invite some friends for a small ceremony."

He was right. Summer-lush hills encircled our home, and deer lapped at the still pond. Even in a month, David's garden would be exploding with marigolds and zinnia.

Maybe we could pull it off. I'd be useless, but when David put his mind to something, it happened.

David flushed, a hot pink descending from the tips of his ears to his throbbing throat.

"Good God, what's wrong with me? How are you? When is the baby due?"

"I'm fine," I said. "By my calculation, the baby is due in the middle of March, which is quite considerate of him or her. I should be able to take the bar exam in February and then have some time off."

David took a long sip of his beer and, by now glowing, shook his head back and forth and smiled. And smiled. And smiled.

I gripped the edge of the metal table and twitched. And twitched. And twitched.

ABBY

What just happened?

I sent David inside to fetch me a glass of water. I needed a few seconds alone, and stared at the horizon, reeling.

The tsunami rushed toward me—wedding, law school, bar exam, baby. Hey, David, how about some vodka instead? Straight. Not that I didn't love him or want to marry him. Of course, I did. But now?

And I had to get pregnant for him to ask?

I would have married him years ago, but I thought he was the reluctant one. Talk about missed signals. And my own mixed emotions.

I could have suggested it, too. I had a mouth. I never stood on ceremony when it came to any other topic. Why this one?

And it didn't matter now, did it? David's delight at the news sent motes of happiness glinting in the air. I grasped for one to share. He sauntered back to the table with my water, still sporting that blissful grin.

Live in the now, I repeated to myself, trying to identify the earworm penetrating my brain.

What was that stupid song?

Oh Christ, that's what it was.

Here Comes the Bride.

DAVID

Abby's news sparked a charge that roiled his bones. From almost the moment they met, he wanted to marry her. But she already had one unsuccessful marriage. What if she didn't want to try again?

They may as well have been wed. They were legal partners in everything else: The Gleanings, their home, and all their possessions. Marriage might be unnecessary, yet it gnawed at him. All right, he was a throwback, but why shouldn't they make it official? But he was also a bit of a coward. He would never forgive himself if his misstep drew them apart.

This time he did not hesitate. In fact, he didn't even ask her. Not like him at all. But he blurted it out—his heart overruled his head. If ever there was a time for boldness, this was it.

And a child. By now, he didn't expect parenthood to happen to him. But if marrying Abby gave him joy, the prospect of a child made him overjoyed. Before meeting Abby, he lived alone for a long time. Solitary years. He tried filling time with constant projects and diversions. Despite them, none ever erased the loneliness. Not even the bottle, which too often offered succor. He longed for a family but accepted his life would be different. Then Abby appeared. Now, this.

He knew her tastes; not fancy, but simple, with a graceful note. The wedding would be small. They had no family, only an intimate circle of friends. What better place than overlooking the sweeping vista of their farm?

He inhaled with satisfaction. From the start, he wanted to spend the rest of his life with her. Every day she surprised and delighted him. Even on a rare bad day, she made him laugh and feel loved. Now he could not imagine living without her; marriage would seal their bond. It had taken six years, but she was worth the wait.

ABBY

The guest list proved easy; some of David's colleagues and friends from Boston and a few of mine from my old job at the Court House. And, of course, Ted, my former husband, and Raoul, his partner. Although our marriage was a disaster, Ted and I enjoyed an affectionate truce. He and Raoul became our chosen family.

It would not be a religious ceremony. I'm half Irish Catholic and half Jewish, and David was raised a nominal Protestant if anything. Religion was not part of our lifestyle or vocabulary. David asked his friend, Rami, who taught at Princeton, to be our officiant. He promised me Rami would keep it short and sweet.

That settled, David ordered some food and drink, and I found a flowy beige dress. I didn't want anything strikingly bridal, and although I'd not yet gained weight, I wanted to guarantee nothing showed. Not that it much mattered, but maybe I was more conventional (or vain) than I thought.

I hadn't bought a dress in years and wasn't even sure of my size. I'm so small I can sometimes fit in children's clothes. That search failed. No appropriate dresses there unless I wanted puffed sleeves, ruffles, and a bow. Which I did not. The shift I found was loose enough to conceal but not consume. I twirled and liked the way it rippled and flowed.

I pictured Eileen, my mother, standing beside me, nodding. She died when I was seventeen and never saw me wed. What would she think now? Law school would have made her proud; she always stressed my independence. Even so, she'd consider David quite a catch. He would have charmed her from the start.

David returned from picking up the marriage license. Whistling, he handed me the envelope. I pulled it out, David reading over my shoulder.

I glanced back at him. "Who is Kiran Kumar?"

"Oh, that's Rami. I had to list him as the minister since he got his mail-in ordination. Rami is his nickname. It's a math thing—after Ramanujan, a famous mathematician."

"And what was your nickname? Einstein?"

"No, nothing clever for me. Just David. And he was a physicist."

"You mean it's not the same thing?"

"Ahh, no."

I knew that, didn't I?

David listed me as Abigail Robins Fischer. Robins was my father's name. I was not attached to it, since my father abandoned me when I was young. The last time I saw the jerk was when I was about eight years old. Then nothing. I stayed Robins but later stuck it in the middle. Fischer was Ted's name, which I never bothered to change.

My finger stopped at an entry. "You have a middle name?"

That was a surprise.

"David MacLaren Armacost?" I swatted his arm. "Where did that come from?"

David twisted his mouth in a half-hearted smile. "It was my mother's maiden name, but I seldom use it. I never met her family; I think they were estranged."

"Why?"

"I'm not sure. It may have been because she was pregnant when they got married."

"Really? How do you know that?"

"Well," David said, "I was born six months after their wedding and weighed almost ten pounds. I doubt I was premature."

I gulped. "Ten pounds, yeesh. Should I be worried?"

David gauged me—all ninety pounds of me. "Maybe."

"So, we're following a family tradition," I quipped, then regretted it.

David's eyes bulged with a look he reserved for when I said something outrageous. I had no other questions.

ABBY

Sunday, September 9, a perfect late summer day. David pulled off everything in a month. The weather cooperated, cirrus clouds patched over a full sun. A tender breeze whispered above the ridge, accompanied by the dulcet tones of a Peabody string quartet.

Dressing was easy. I grabbed the silky dress and threw it over my head. Trying to up my game, I splashed on a blast of eau de something and ran a comb through my hair, wavering over a sparkly barrette to secure one side. Too frou-frou?

Oh, why not? I bought it, didn't I? I slipped it in and turned to admire myself in the mirror. Not bad for a pregnant woman working on a farm. It was my wedding day.

David corralled me in the hall and held out a large, square box.

"What is this?" I hoped it wasn't a gift; I had nothing for him.

"Open it." Those little mouth creases of his, so sweet.

I raised the lid to find a bouquet with lacy greenery, lavender thistles, and white roses, its soft fragrance rising as I inhaled. I hadn't even thought about carrying flowers.

David lifted it from the box and handed it to me. "A bride should have a bouquet."

I covered a smile with my hand. He was so much more sentimental than I. He sported a boutonniere that matched, pinned to the lapel of his tan poplin suit. David left his shirt unbuttoned at the collar. I had never seen him wear a tie and didn't think he owned any.

The valley, still verdant, framed the scene. Rami wore a white linen tunic and looked like an impish yogi. As I strode down the grassy aisle, I focused on David, who faced me, riveted. His hair shone silver in the streaks of sun, and behind his rimless glasses, David's sky-blue eyes glistened. I joined him at the makeshift altar and took his hand.

Rami read a poem by Rilke and spoke a few words about the mathematics of love. I tried to follow him but couldn't concentrate. Anything about math flummoxes me. No matter. David laughed at the right times, and I couldn't take my eyes off him. David fished in his pocket and pulled out two rings. His face beamed brighter than the day as we exchanged vows and the matching gold bands. I stood on my toes to reach him for a kiss and startled when he lifted me off the ground, his sturdy arms encircling my waist.

In the garden, we toasted, ate, and drank with our friends. Despite some early queasiness, I sampled the food and even took a few sips of champagne. David had chosen well: savory frittata bites, canapés with smoked salmon and capers, carpaccio, and crudités. Instead of a cake, he found elegant petit fours and had them artfully arranged on rustic plates adorned with lemon leaves.

I scanned the small crowd and spied Ted refilling his flute of champagne. I strolled over and squeezed his arm.

"Sorry, Ted, but this definitely eclipsed our Court House wedding."

Ted smirked. "I hope so. Ours was pretty weak, as I recall."

The beginning of our fiasco was as unmemorable as it could be. But it never failed to amaze me that Ted and I were closer now than when we were married. Ted was the only other person I told about my pregnancy.

Hearing my name, I swiveled. David, standing with Raoul, waved.

"Go ahead, Abby," Ted said, patting me lightly on the butt. "Number two needs you."

"Love you, too." I kissed Ted on the cheek and slipped away.

ABBY

That night, we made a beeline for the bedroom. Other than a ceremony, we were the same couple we had been the day before.

Yet it was different. We made a commitment we wanted to believe was inviolable. Because of my experience, I knew otherwise. Nothing lasts forever. But despite our familiarity, my heart still swelled when David entered a room. Sometimes, I would be doing nothing and catch him gazing at me with that loopy look. What would it take to make this last a lifetime?

As we slipped into bed, I asked, "How does it feel to be a husband?"

David faced me, grinning. "As good as it gets." He lightly ran his finger from my earlobe to the base of my shoulder. "And you? A wife, I mean."

"Even better than the first time, but don't tell Ted."

"I wouldn't dream of it. But is it all right now?" David tentatively lowered his hand. "The baby?"

"Of course—but I promise not to get too rough with you," I teased, knowing how gentle a lover he was.

With that, I eased my body atop his, nibbling his shoulders and neck. David spanned his large hands across my bottom, and as we merged our bodies, he closed his eyes, his mouth framed with creases of delight.

ABBY

Two days later, on September 11, terrorists struck New York, Washington, and Pennsylvania, and the world changed. We remained safe in our cocoon but mourned the loss of innocent life and the comfort of unappreciated security. One of David's acquaintances from Boston had been on the flight that struck the World Trade Center North. David turned inward and spoke little the next few days.

I resumed working and law school. It was a light final semester for me; only three courses and then I was done. David was scheduled to speak at a symposium in New York in December. If it went forward, maybe we'd tack on a few days. I hadn't been to New York in years. Who knew when we would get a chance once the baby came?

In early December, the phone rang around 10:00 on a Sunday morning. David was out running an errand. Immersed in studying for my last law school exam, I considered ignoring the call. But I didn't. My concentration was already interrupted.

"Hello. I'm looking for an Abigail Fischer." Male voice, clipped. New York accent.

"I'm Abby Fischer. And you are?"

"My name is Eitan Rabinowitz, and I believe we are cousins."

That was unexpected but not unbelievable. My father, whom I had not seen since I was a child, was named Mark Robins. My mother suspected his family name was originally Rabinowitz.

"Really? How did you find me?" I asked, my skepticism aroused.

"My aunt—our aunt, Nina. Nina Soresman, in Westchester. She's into genealogy and recently found your name. Your father is Mark Robins, right?"

I grunted, still suspicious.

"Nina is your father's and my father's sister," he explained. "She found your number and gave it to me."

I still had no idea who he was or what he wanted.

"Look," I said. "I don't know you, but I haven't seen my father in almost thirty years. I know nothing of his whereabouts and frankly have no interest in finding out." I tried not to be rude but was getting impatient.

Eitan persisted.

"I live in Jerusalem. My daughter, Miri, is in Baltimore. Unfortunately, she's in the hospital. We can't be there and hoped a relative could visit her. She's on her own and scared. Do you think you could do this?"

As I was about to become a parent, Eitan's request pulled at my heartstrings.

"I can," I said. "Where is she?

I was busy but not too busy for this.

"Good Shepherd Hospital. Do you know it?"

I did. Good Shepherd was one of Baltimore's oldest psychiatric hospitals. My mentor, Jack Warfield, who suffered many demons, had been a frequent patient and cynically referred to Good Shepherd as his vacation home. This was not the hospital visit I envisioned.

But what else could I do? Poor girl, all alone. Eitan did not have much information and asked me to call Aunt Nina, who could fill me in. Without pleasantries, we hung up.

I was still staring into space when David returned.

ABBY

David ambled into the kitchen carrying a bag from the hardware store, followed by Ridgely, our Golden Retriever. Ridgely was the only one who would ride with David and had accompanied him to the store.

A notoriously slow driver who was easily distracted, David hated driving. When we went out together, I was always at the wheel. That's why I was surprised when he bought a bright red pickup. Once in a while, David, a serious man, had a flash of whimsy. The truck was one of them.

I looked up from my reverie. "Guess what? I got a call from a guy in Israel."

David drew his brows together. "About what?"

"He claimed to be a long-lost cousin. From my asshole father's side. He said his daughter is in Good Shepherd and he wants me to go see her. I never heard of the guy."

"Could it have been a prank?"

"I don't think so. At least, I hope not—I told him I would. He said to call an Aunt Nina for details. It was weird, but he didn't sound fake."

"Maybe you should," David said. "It's not like we have any other family to speak of. Call Aunt Nina."

I rolled my eyes. "I have no idea who these people are."

"But you told him you'd visit his daughter, didn't you?"

"Yeah, I did." Me and my big mouth.

David handed me the phone. "Make the leap, Abby. You've done it before."

He was right. That was how I found him, and that changed everything.

I dialed the number Eitan gave me, and Nina picked up on the first ring. How should I address this relative I never met?

"Nina? This is Abby Fischer. I just spoke to Eitan Rabinowitz, and he told me to call."

"Abby! It is wonderful to hear your voice!"

Without skipping a beat, Nina rapidly recited the history of the Rabinowitz clan. I strained to keep up. A mile a minute was but a fraction of her speed. Nina's parents, presumably my grandparents, Chana and Meir Rabinowitz, emigrated from Russia to America in 1913. Settling in New York, Meir changed the family name to the more Americanized Robins.

Nina was the youngest of Chana and Meir's three children. Her brother Phil, Eitan's father, died several years ago. My father, Mark, was the middle child.

And there were more cousins than I could imagine. Eitan adopted the family's original surname and moved to Israel. He and his wife, Esti, had seven children, the oldest of whom is Miri. Seven children! That fact alone floored me. I was still trying to grasp the prospect of having one.

I tried adding up the number of relatives Nina mentioned in mere minutes, but my addition skills failed me. Astounding. Nina was the steadfast keeper of the family flame.

Nina's tone quieted. "Abby, when was the last time you saw your father?"

A long time ago. Big reach.

"I'm not sure, maybe 1972." I had little memory of that brief visit.

"Abby, you probably never knew this, but your father suffered from illness all his life—mental illness. He has spent the past thirty years or so in and out of hospitals and clinics."

Really? I thought he was just a shitty father. Had I misjudged him my entire life?

Nah, probably not.

"He had drug problems, too." Nina wavered a moment. "I am so sorry we never reached out to you, but the truth is, we only came across your name earlier this year. When Eitan told me about Miri, I remembered something about a relative in Baltimore and found your information. I'm about to go away this week, and can't make it down to see her. Your visit would mean so much to all of us. If Miri suffers from the same condition as your father, we would do anything to have her avoid his fate."

What was his fate?

Acid singed my gut. "It's been years. I figured he was dead."

"Your father is alive, but not really with us," Nina said. "He has dementia and lives in a facility not far from me. I try to visit every week or so, but he barely recognizes me. I like to think it gives him a bit of comfort simply to know someone is there."

This information was far too much to absorb. The burgeoning family was one thing; my father's existence was another. My resentment for him often outweighed my indifference.

"Abby, I'm sure this is shocking, but please consider trying to come and see him sometime. He is a lost soul."

He was certainly lost to me. And he could stay lost, as far as I was concerned. But Miri was another matter.

"You've given me a lot to think about," I said. "For now, I'll visit Miri and call when you get back."

"Thank you, dear. I know it's a strange way to welcome you into the family, but we really appreciate it. Take care."

Strange? Understatement, Nina.

David stuck his nose past the Sunday New York Times. He's not an eavesdropper, but I could tell he was interested in my conversation. I gave him as many morsels as I could recall.

"So," David reflected, "you have this enormous Jewish family, and your father, whom you thought was dead, is in a nursing home with no idea who anyone is?"

"That's about right."

David shook his head. "Abby, you are living proof that life is full of surprises."

That was true. Finding David had been a major surprise.

His eyes wandered to the ceiling. "I guess they're my relatives now, too."

"Yup." I twisted my mouth. "What's mine is yours. Please tell me we're not going to search for the MacLarens anytime soon."

David shifted his gaze to me. "Not a chance. One revelation at a time is enough."

ABBY

I called Good Shepherd to inquire about visiting Miri. That was the first step. I gathered my wits for the next.

I drove into Towson and approached the gothic stone gatehouse that guarded the hospital drive. Was that witchy spire quaint or foreboding?

The russet main building stretched along an expanse of lawn. I took my time walking toward the entrance. Rows of windows lined with shades stared at me. Some lowered; some rose. Were they winking? I shook the thought out of my mind.

I heaved my shoulder to shove one of the hefty wooden doors and entered a reception room. Plush velvet couches rimmed patterned carpets. Soft classical music wafted from speakers hidden from view. I sniffed a hint of bleach in the air. Clinically posh?

I asked the receptionist about visiting a patient and sank into one of the couches, awaiting a response. My knee bounced in staccato time. After a few minutes, she directed me to the third floor, where Miri was currently meeting with her lawyer.

Hmm, interesting. Even though I spent the past three and a half years in law school, I had no idea why Miri needed a lawyer. Had she been arrested?

Jesus, what was I getting into?

I tried a metal door past the elevator, but it wouldn't budge. The only place to sit was a sleek modern couch; stylish, but much less comfortable than the one downstairs. I sat, my eyes darting from one hallway to the other, waiting. About twenty minutes passed when a woman carrying a briefcase emerged from the locked door of the unit beyond the waiting nook.

At first, the woman rushed out, her heels clicking on the vinyl floor. After noticing me, she approached.

"Are you here to visit Miri?" the woman asked.

She looked about forty-five or fifty, with blonde curls, askew, framing her face. Dressed in black, she wore a multi-colored scarf artfully tied about her neck.

The woman held out her hand. "I'm Marta Hansen, Miri's attorney."

"I've never met Miri, but I'm her cousin," I said. Marta raised an eyebrow, so I gave her the shorthand behind my visit.

"So why is she here?" I asked. "Is Miri in trouble?"

"No." Marta shook her head. "I can't tell you details because of client confidentiality, but I'm an assistant public defender and I represent patients in involuntary commitment hearings."

That was new to me. I must have missed that course in law school.

"But," Marta said, "Miri isn't having a hearing because she is voluntarily staying in the hospital. I went to see her today to confirm that."

"I see. I'm a law student, but I'm completely unfamiliar with this area of the law."

"Really? How far are you in school?"

"I'm almost done. I take the bar in February."

"Interesting." Marta handed me her business card. "Look, I have to go see another client. Call me after the bar exam. We're always looking for baby lawyers."

Marta dashed down the hall, her curls bouncing in tandem with her steps. I sat back against the rigid sofa and resumed waiting. But I filed Marta's card and our conversation away for due consideration.

ABBY

No one emerged for another ten minutes, so I tapped the buzzer beside the locked unit door. An aide answered and held it open. It clanged shut behind us.

He led me to a room with a safety window facing a nursing station, and I sat on one of the wood-framed chairs. I shifted my weight, and when the chair didn't move, I rose and tried to jiggle the leg. Damned if it wasn't bolted to the floor. As was the rest of the furniture. I didn't expect that but maybe I should have.

A few minutes later, a small woman, barely an adult, entered. My mystery cousin.

Miri's long dark ringlets in no way resembled my straight brown bob. She assessed me with thickly lashed chocolate brown eyes, so unlike mine, wide-spaced and green. Miri wore a prim white blouse and denim skirt that almost reached her ankles. Not exactly my style. But I sensed a connection I couldn't define.

Miri raised a delicate hand to me in a welcoming gesture. She had a sweet, soft voice with a trace of an unfamiliar accent. In perfect English, Miri asked, "So, you're my cousin?"

"I guess I am," I said. "Apparently, my father and your grandfather were brothers. Or something like that."

Miri poured forth with unexpected candor. "Okay, cousin. This is what happened. I came to Baltimore a few months ago. My parents suggested spending a term at Bais Sarah. It's a women's religious school. I liked it, but it was hard being away from home. I couldn't cope. I was up all night and couldn't eat or focus. I was frightened all the time."

Miri's slim fingers fluttered as she spoke and added an element of drama to her tale. I followed them like a cat stalking a bird through a window.

"How did you get to the hospital?" I asked.

"For three awful days, all I did was cry and act like I was out of my mind. I can't even remember everything. I think one of my teachers brought me here. It's not bad. They're giving me medicine, talking to me, and I'm starting to feel like myself again. The doctor said I should be discharged in a few days, but I'll stay as long as I need to get well."

I hadn't known what to expect, but for someone in a psychiatric hospital, Miri sounded remarkably sane.

Impressed by Miri's insight, I pursued my inquiry. "Do you want to go back to Israel now?"

Miri shook her head. "No, no. The school will take me back, and I want to return. I'm going home in the spring, and I think I'll be okay at school until then. I'll take the medicine and see a counselor. I just want to get back to my life."

Miri pointed to my middle. "How about you, Abby? Do you work? When is the baby due?"

I gave her the condensed version since I was here to see her, not gab about me. And we talked on and on.

Someone knocked on the door and interrupted our conversation. When I looked at my watch, I was surprised we had been chatting for over an hour. But not unhappy I came. In less than a week, I went from having no family to diving into the unknown depths of a sea of relationships. I wasn't used to feeling close to people in general, let alone those with familial ties. It was new; simultaneously uncomfortable and comforting. Having opened the door, I realized it was a contradiction I couldn't escape and might as well accept.

So far, the theme of my life was to expect the unexpected. Why should this be any different?

ABBY

David peppered me with questions about Miri. I reached for the words to describe our meeting.

"There was something there, despite our differences. Some indefinable level of ease. And it wasn't her appearance. We don't look at all alike. I know it sounds weird, but I felt close to her."

"I understand," he said. "Now with no one left, I miss that trust and connection. I guess you don't appreciate it until it's gone."

That must have prompted David to bring up the subject of my father, which I had been trying to avoid.

"I know it's not my place, but you should consider visiting your father. What if he didn't mean to abandon you? Maybe he was so ill he had no sense of reality or memory of you and your mother. Now it sounds like he barely exists."

I grimaced. "And what am I supposed to say to him?"

David placed his hand on my arm. "You don't have to say anything. Just forgive him."

"I'm not sure I can do that." I couldn't look at David and stared at the floor.

He lifted my chin with his finger. "Can you try?"

David had a point. Seeing Mark wouldn't erase all the hurt, but it would round out his story and give it finality.

I could try.

DAVID

If only Abby had grown up with a family like his. She might have been less guarded, less wary. His parents may have been taciturn, but he always knew they loved him and Maggie. He and Abby would raise their child with the love and security he knew when he was young.

It wasn't that Abby was incapable of love. Not at all. Everything she did showed how deeply she cared for him. If only she could discard the shell she placed around herself. Maybe squaring the circle of her relationship with her father would help.

Why wouldn't she be nervous? Abby had a lot on her plate—work, law school, the bar exam, the baby, and now, her father. When the baby came and everything else resolved, maybe she could relax.

Of course, he wasn't the best example of limiting himself. He always piled too much on. Now, though, he was mostly teaching, and his other projects, The Gleanings and The Numbers Game, were practically running themselves. Oh, and his book. He'd been working on a biography of Erdős, an eccentric mathematician, for years, and it was time for it to be done. For a minute, he forgot about that. He had a call with the publisher scheduled for next month. Maybe that could wait, too.

ABBY

Did the phone even ring on her end? I dialed and immediately heard, "How's Miri?" before I had a chance to say hello.

"Much improved," I reported. "She's quite a remarkable girl." Nina urged me to add details of my visit. I described Miri's candor, intelligence, and willingness to seek treatment.

"Wonderful, wonderful," Nina cheeped. "And how about you?"

"Fine, thanks," I said. "David and I are coming to New York. We'll be there for a few days. Maybe we can meet."

Nina's outburst filled the heavens. "Fantastic! Tell me everything!"

"I don't know that much about it, but David is speaking at a symposium at Rockefeller University, and we thought we'd come up a few days early."

Nina normally spoke at twice the speed of most people, but this was Nina on overdrive. "What a coincidence! If I'm right, I think Bill will be there, too."

"Bill?" I asked.

"Oh, that's my husband. He's involved with everything these days. At least this venture is close to home. Most of the time I can't keep track of where he's going next. Let's take advantage of this opportunity."

I sensed the wheels turning in Nina's head. She gave the impression of a master planner and wasted no time devising an agenda.

"Would this work? I can pick you up in the City in the morning. We'll come back here if you want to see your father. It doesn't have to be a long visit. Even a few minutes will do. But it will mean something to him."

"Okay . . ." I gulped.

Nina wasn't done. "Then we can go back into the City and all meet for dinner. How does that sound?"

Good," I said, uncertain what I was agreeing to and afraid I might overdose on Nina. "How about if I take the train to meet you? Why should you have to drive into the City twice?"

"No, no," Nina cooed. "I don't mind."

"Really, Nina. I can take the Metro North and meet you around noon."

"All right," Nina acceded. "But let me know if you change your mind. I'll come right down."

When I told David about our plans and the coincidence, he paused.

"What is her husband's name?"

"Bill. I think their last name is Soresman."

David took a moment. "William Soresman? If that is who I think he is, he's a top-notch scientist and a business genius. Quite an influential person."

"Do you know him?"

"I've never met him, but he's a legend. He's a physician who started a small biotech firm a number of years ago. From what I understand, he sold it to a huge corporation, and the sale was rumored to be in the hundreds of millions of dollars. I think he does a lot of consulting now."

I took a few seconds to figure out the possible relationship. "So, he could be my uncle? And he'll be there, too?"

"Could be. Let me check." David found his conference material and picked through the pages.

"Well, what do you know?" David handed me the schedule and a short bio near the front of the brochure. "One and the same."

I pointed at him. "See," I said. "You're an influential person, too."

David waved his hand in dismissal. "I'm just a minor cog. Bill Soresman is a big wheel."

"But now, you're related, thanks to me."

David swallowed a laugh. "Abby, I always said you were full of surprises."

ABBY

New York. Magical, even after the pain of 9/11. Central Park, Metropolitan Museum, two plays, and delectable meals.

We supped at Ethiopian and Romanian cafes and lunched on Finnish lohikeitto and Szechuan dim sum. With Viennese pastry in between. The weather was brisk and clear, and we walked for miles, working off some of the calories.

Thursday morning, David made sure I left the hotel room and didn't chicken out. Not that I wasn't tempted. Once on the train, my fate was sealed. On arrival, I mounted the steps to my destination as if meeting the firing squad instead of Aunt Nina.

"Abby!" a high-pitched voice rang behind me. I turned around. A small woman standing aside a massive Mercedes sedan waved both hands in the air.

As soon as she saw me, full-frontal, Nina was abject. "Oh honey, I am so sorry. You didn't say you were pregnant. I never would have let you take the train."

"No, it was good." I pointed to my belly. "The baby liked the ride."

Nina must have been at least sixty but appeared much younger. Being small myself, I knew how that worked. But more than that, Nina's dark hair was perfectly coiffed, not a lock out of place, her complexion clear and smooth. She needed a small pillow behind her back to reach the pedals, just like I did. Nina's diamond studs and enormous pear-shaped solitaire blazed in the light.

Nina only wanted to know about me, how I felt, and what I needed. She exuded a rush of mother love, one I hadn't known for such a long time.

We drove about fifteen minutes and arrived at a sprawling, single-story building with a broad red awning. A large sign read "Pleasant Ridge Assisted Living and Memory Care Center." My stomach filled with mordant dread; tiny beads of sweat edged my face.

Entering the lobby, I did a 360-degree turn. This place was more like a five-star hotel than any nursing home I had ever seen. No unpleasant smell, no zombified elders slumped in wheelchairs by the door, no shredded carpet or worn lobby furniture. How in the world did a bum like Mark land in the Four Seasons of nursing homes?

Everyone seemed to know Nina, and she greeted them all by name. As I followed her down a hallway, I passed double doors bearing a plaque engraved "Soresman Auditorium." I asked about the signage. Nina said Bill's mother had lived here, and when she died, the family wanted to show their appreciation. I peeked into the cavernous room; it must have been a sizeable gift. I presumed Nina and Bill also paid for Mark to live and be cared for here.

We reached a sunny atrium, and Nina led the way to the back. There, facing a window, sat a hunched, thin man in a wheelchair. Wispy white hair barely covered his stippled scalp. Dressed in a short-sleeved blue shirt and gray cuffed pants, he had an argyle cardigan folded over the arm of the chair. Unscuffed leather slippers covered his feet.

Nina tapped the man on his shoulder. "Mark, look who's here to see you!"

My only memory of my father was of a slight, but dapper man with dark hair and a ruddy complexion. On his last visit, he brought Danish pastry and called me "sweetie." Odd that I remembered that. This man was pale, his arms nearly translucent. Although he probably wasn't much older than Nina, he looked as if he could have been her grandfather.

He smiled at us without recognition. I wouldn't have expected him to recognize me, but what about Nina, who visited him every week? David was right—this was pitiful.

In a cheery, singsong voice one might use with a young child, Nina motioned toward me. "This is Abby, your daughter. Isn't she beautiful?"

Mark gave no sign of understanding, but Nina continued. "And she's going to have a baby! Isn't that the best news?"

Mark looked through us as if we weren't there. But he kept smiling, so I had to believe he was not unhappy.

Nina chirped, "Isn't it almost time for lunch?" and pushed his wheelchair out of the room. She guided it down the hall to a well-lit, seasonally decorated dining room with wide windows facing a garden. An ornament-studded Christmas tree and a giant menorah shared a corner display.

Nina placed Mark at a table with other residents and arranged a napkin around his collar. There was a glass of water by his plate, and she lifted it to his mouth. Mark took a few sips and licked his lips. Nina gently blotted them with the napkin. I desperately hoped we would not have to stay and feed him. Part of me regretted the selfish thought; the rest of me wanted to run.

Fortunately, a dining aide appeared, whom Nina knew by name. She spoke to Mark in a soothing voice and described the menu for lunch. Nina gave me a glance that signaled it was time to leave. Remembering David's advice, I reluctantly touched Mark's bony hand and mouthed, "I forgive you."

I turned to leave but found myself immobile as if mired in quicksand. I couldn't look back, afraid I might turn into a pillar of dung or something equally abhorrent since I felt like shit. What was I supposed to do? Show affection for someone so absent in my life? It was hard enough for me to love anyone, and he scraped the bottom of my list if he made it at all. Had my father ever loved me? Maybe he couldn't love and that was my inheritance. Was I following in his footsteps by abandoning him now?

Nina grabbed my hand and pulled me free, rescuing me from my crippling ambivalence.

"Hungry?" she asked, still gripping me as we headed out the door.

"Uhh." It was all I could manage.

"Good. Let's have lunch."

ABBY

Nina chose a small bistro not far from Pleasant Ridge. By the time we arrived, most of the business crowd thinned out, and we had a corner of the restaurant to ourselves. I remained quiet, still processing the visit with Mark.

After we ordered, Nina thanked me. "I'm so grateful you came today. You did a mitzvah in coming. I know it was difficult, and even if Mark could not understand, you did a great service to him and to me."

"And to me, I suppose." I stared, unseeing, at the table. "All those years, I thought he was a rotten father who never cared. I had no idea."

Nina sighed. "Many times, he was his own worst enemy. God knows we all tried but could never get through. He desperately needed help, but it was impossible getting him to accept it. It's all water under the bridge now. I like to think he's finally in a place of peace."

I wasn't so sure I could look at it that way. Being in that state, like Mark, had to be the deepest circle of Hell.

"And more thanks, Abby, for going to see Miri. We need to make sure she doesn't end up, God forbid, like your father."

About that, I had good news.

"You'll be happy to know Miri's doing well," I said. "I picked her up when she was discharged and offered to bring her to our house, but she wanted to go back to school. We talk often and she knows she can come over or call any time."

I truly meant it. Meeting Miri brought me into this family. I was grateful, too.

ABBY

After my initial introversion, I opened up to Nina and told her about our wedding, The Gleanings, my jitters over the bar exam, and lack of plans afterward. Nina's dark eyes focused on every word I said.

Nina said Bill admired David and his work and was eager to meet him. I concurred; the feeling was mutual. We had a 7:00 reservation for dinner in the City at Le Marais, a Parisian-style steakhouse. I couldn't help thinking what a relief it would be after seeing Mark. A drink or two, just this once, wouldn't hurt the baby. I had a good excuse.

With several hours to spare, Nina suggested we stop by her home. I had the feeling Nina wanted me to see it. Not in a boastful way, but because she was proud of it.

Nina's sedan snaked up the long drive lined with mature trees. Because it was December, the trees were bare, but I pictured the lush canopy that guarded the path every other season of the year.

The house stood at the end of the drive. Long and rambling, with shingled wings sprouting from each corner, it went on for a mile. A wide veranda swathed the front door. I gazed at the pale blue ceiling and imagined lounging in an Adirondack chair, sipping lemonade on a summer day.

Nina gave me a brief tour of the central wing before we sank into velvet armchairs in a family room that faced a wall of windows. From where I sat, I could see the Olympic-sized pool, bordered by a Japanese garden. In the distance stood massive free-form sculptures that seemed to sprout from the earth.

The home oozed comfort, especially the family room, decorated in warm beige with touches of forest green. Original paintings covered walls opposite floor-to-ceiling shelves brimming with books.

Nina handed me a cup of tea and offered a plate of sugar cookies. I had picked at my lunch, so I did not decline. She pointed out clusters of framed photographs gathered on the tables nearby.

"Bill calls this my gallery." Nina's face shone as she identified each one.

Silver frames held sepia photos of Nina's parents taken in Europe when they were young. I searched their faces for a smidgen of me. Beside them was a professional shot of Nina and Bill's wedding. Nina wore a satin gown with long sleeves and a portrait collar draped over her shoulders in the fashion of the time. I assessed my gracious host; Nina did not look much different today.

Nina adjusted a faded picture of a family at the beach and pointed out her parents, brothers, and herself as a child. Mark was the one in the middle who looked like he couldn't stand still. Nina, wearing pigtails and a big grin, held a fluffy swirl of cotton candy wrapped around a paper cone.

"That was in Atlantic City," Nina reminisced. "We went there every summer." Nina gestured at the array. "These are the story of my life."

On other tables sat photos of Nina's kids and grandkids. Some looked taken in exotic places, others at the pool in view beyond the comfortable room. All happy times.

I tried not to think about what I missed. No if onlys. Mark was Mark; nothing could change the past. I shooed away my childhood longing for the grandparents, cousins, uncles, and aunts everyone else seemed to have. At least I was part of a family now.

Before we left, I followed Nina into the spacious kitchen. Outfitted with every imaginable high-end feature and adjacent to a pantry fit for a palace, it exuded class. I tried not to gawk. Nina must have noticed and sought to minimize the visual effect of their wealth.

"Abby, believe me, it has not always been like this for us. We have been so blessed. Both Bill and I came from modest, middle-class families. I was a French major, of all things, and taught high school while Bill got his M.D./Ph.D. Later, we had our three children, and I stayed home with them. I am so grateful I was able to do that but have some regrets I never pursued more of a career. I think what you're doing is wonderful. I'm sure you'll make an excellent lawyer."

Glad she thought so; I had my doubts. I didn't know if I even wanted to practice law. Maybe Nina's confidence would rub off on me. I'd settle for getting through the bar exam.

ABBY

Nina drove us into the City and handed the car and keys to a valet, who addressed her by name. When we entered the restaurant, I had to adjust my eyes to the dim light. Illumined by burnished brass lamps, the paneled walls shone like polished leather.

The maître d' greeted Nina warmly. "Good evening, Mrs. Soresman. So good to see you again. Dr. Soresman and the other gentleman are waiting in the bar."

Seated at the end of the long marble bar, Bill and David engaged in lively conversation. I was glad to see they hit it off. And did they. David stood up and introduced me as "his beautiful wife." This effusiveness was uncharacteristic—how much had he had to drink? We completed the pleasantries as David and Bill continued to energetically bond.

After Nina and I ordered drinks, Bill said, "How unexpected is this? David and I have long known each other by reputation but never met. And now we found this connection. Who could have guessed?"

David chortled as we toasted. "Bill introduced me to everyone as his nephew."

Bill joined in. "All of these people who've known David for years told me, 'I didn't know David

Armacost was your nephew.' I told them neither did I until last week."

David and Bill dissolved in laughter. Nina side-eyed me, and we shared a where-did-this-come-from? look.

I got a better look at Bill as he and Nina led the way to the table. They made a well-matched pair. Like Nina, he was slim and fashionable. Certainly, his subtly checked suit was bespoke. Bill had short, graying hair and a trim beard and wore a watch that probably cost more than my car.

Our meal was nirvana. I hadn't eaten steak in months and the tournedos melted in my mouth. Bill pronounced the frites better than the ones in Paris; the Bordeaux was out of this world. I couldn't imagine how much it cost. Two bottles, too.

The wine relaxed us, and we lingered for several hours, laughing and talking. Despite only having met Bill and Nina that day, it was as if I had known them for years. Nina and Bill treated us like family. And, I suppose, now we were. It was a new feeling for me and cautiously, I enjoyed it.

ABBY

It had been an impossibly full and emotional day for me and, by his account, busy for David, too. By the time we reached the hotel, too exhausted to examine the day's events, we fell into bed. The next day on the train home, David and I dissected the observations we made of our new-found relatives and my reevaluation of Mark.

"Well, I did it," I said. "As you predicted, he was pathetic. All that resentment I had slid into pity. I despised him for so long, but how can I keep hating a man reduced to diapers and drool?"

"It's all your fault, too," I admonished him. "Your kindness is seeping into me too deeply. You'd better promise to shoot me if I ever end up like Mark."

David quirked a short laugh, but I wasn't kidding. To me, that would be a fate worse than death. He'd never do it, though. David would probably be wiping my spittle like Nina did for Mark.

God, what a grotesque thought.

But if it weren't for David's compassionate urging, I might still be left with bitterness toward a man who likely lived a life of despair. I had to admit it; he was right.

The yin to that yang was our rapport with Nina and Bill. The couple's goodwill and generosity were staggering.

"I've never seen anything like it," I said. "On our way into the City, I noticed at least three hospitals with signs for a Soresman Wing or Pavilion."

"I know," David agreed. "I'm familiar with several research institutions funded by their foundation. Abby, we try our best with our little patch of land, but their largesse is astounding."

David dozed the rest of the trip home. I pulled out a paperback I brought but couldn't get Mark out of my mind. The prodigal father I would try to forgive.

I shivered as soon as I entered our home. Small puffs of my breath floated by like filmy welcoming clouds. David started a fire for warmth. He had spent the past weekend commandeering a cord of wood for the winter. I stood in front of the fireplace and raised my hands to catch the heat, the crackling flames a calming symphony.

We readied for the night. Earlier that month, the baby began actively exploring the boundaries of my womb. It became so flagrant and frequent that I could identify the assaultive body parts—an elbow, a knee, a foot.

I perched on the side of the bed, my legs dangling over the floor as I removed my clothes. Undressing, I sat topless for a minute, my anticipation of sleep interrupted by a sharp, low bump. I glanced down and massaged my burgeoning middle. Another thrust and the outline of a heel protruded from my lower torso. David faced me, captivated.

He stared, wide-eyed. "There's really someone in there!"

"Yes!" I bared my teeth and formed my hands into claws. "I am truly possessed."

David placed his large hand over my pregnant belly and kept it there for the next few kicks.

"Amazing." He closed his eyes. "Simply amazing."

DAVID

The short trip energized David. What an honor it was to speak at the conference! All of the other presenters were so much more accomplished than he. His education wasn't lacking, but his work paled compared to the others.

Equally thrilling was meeting Bill Soresman and finding their connection. He had long respected Bill from what he read about him over the years. Bill's successes were manifest. And what a warm and generous man. There was so much to admire.

Bill seemed quite taken with him, too. The attention Bill showed him was almost embarrassing, especially when they were surrounded by so many more talented and credentialed scholars. Before dinner, Bill shared some long-range plans. Could there have been a feeler included, possibly for a future arrangement? Bill's remarks gave off a distinct vibe. But maybe he was wrong. He should probably keep it to himself.

ABBY

And then it was done. Over. Finito. For good.

I finished law school with little to no fanfare and moved on to studying for the bar. Some days, I barely ventured out of the house. A mid-December snowstorm shut everything down for almost a week. Even David, never fazed by the weather, stayed home when classes ended.

We didn't celebrate Christmas, and I'm still not sure why. During our first year together in Arcadia, I brought home a fresh fir from a local tree farm. Its scent transported me to past winters in New England. I loved stringing popcorn and cranberry garland and winding it through the branches. A funky angel ornament purchased from a shop in Hampden teetered on the top. Even without religious meaning, the tree gave me a feeling of warmth and contentment. When I lived with Ted, we spruced up the house a little at Christmastime, but living in the country made me want to go all out.

After that, the practice fell away. The next year, I brought it up, but David kept putting me off. So, I dropped it, though puzzled by his reluctance. I got a strong sense it was deeply personal, and I was not inclined to probe. David's birthday is the 25th of

December, so that became our seasonal observance. He didn't like making much of that, either.

I invited Miri for a subdued birthday dinner. David was keen to meet her, having heard so much from Nina and me. Miri and I had been speaking on the phone regularly. To my relief, she was readjusting and doing well in school.

To be safe, knowing Miri's religious bent, I served a vegetarian meal with rice, eggplant, and aromatic spices. And topped it off with carrot cake, David's favorite.

After dinner, Miri helped clear the table and asked, "How do you feel about having the baby in a few months? Are you ready?"

"No, and I'm absolutely terrified," I said. "I was an only child and know nothing about babies or childrearing. I have no idea about feeding or how to change a diaper. I bought a book, but that scared me even more."

"Don't look at me," David added. "I'm a complete ignoramus."

Miri giggled. "Not to worry. I'm the oldest of seven and an expert. My youngest sibling is still in preschool. I can do everything but breastfeed. Diapers are no problem. My mother says I can get any baby to go to sleep. She couldn't do it without me."

David and I shared stares. Did we strike gold?

Miri smiled with Israeli confidence. "Call me anytime. I'll tell you what to do."

"Oh, don't worry, Miri," I promised. "We will."

ABBY

The countdown began on New Year's Eve. Studying for the bar exam seized my life, a raging demon that possessed my soul. It never let up. All day. Every day. Failure was unthinkable; I was determined to only have to take it once.

Nina and I spoke occasionally. Nina and Bill spent part of the winter at their seaside apartment in Israel near Herzliya and were almost ready to leave.

Nina assumed the role of my surrogate mother. She wanted to make sure I was well and David and I had everything we needed for the baby. Nina made us promise not to buy anything yet and implied she and Bill had it covered. Not having had a mother for so long, I took Nina's boldness for affection and appreciated it.

Especially now, preoccupied with trying to remember everything I learned the past three-plus years in law school. How much civil procedure could I extract from the recesses of my brain? I prayed not to mix up the ninth and tenth amendments to the Constitution, in case the examiners tortured us with minutia. If they asked anything about the Uniform Commercial Code, I was dead.

The first day of the two-day bar exam arrived. I barely slept the night before. It probably didn't help that the baby bounced on my bladder non-stop. That, and my nerves, did me in. When I decided to get up for good, David called to me from his side of the bed.

"I'll drive you downtown. Conserve your energy; you'll need it. You won't have to worry about parking."

God, I hated David's driving. He was so slow, it made me crazy. But maybe I could squeeze in a few more minutes of studying before the exam.

I blew out a stream of air. "Okay. But let's leave soon." I knew he would take twice as long as I would to get there.

In the car, I balanced the heavy bar review book atop what used to be my lap and tried to go over my notes. Thinking I could study now was a foolish expectation. There was no way I could concentrate. When we arrived, I dashed out of the truck before David could wish me well.

ABBY

I left the exam feeling worse than I did when I arrived. What a bust. I was sure I failed and descended into doom when David met me afterward. He tried to cheer me by telling a joke he heard at work that day. Forget it. We ate a quiet dinner and, unable to study one moment longer, I dropped into bed.

The next day's test was multiple choice, another screaming failure. To me, every answer looked right. Or wrong. But I made it through and was relieved it was over. All I could think of was taking a long, soothing bubble bath as soon as I got home. Maybe David would scrub my back. Ahh.

My fellow test takers looked as shell-shocked as I. I stood in line at the table to turn in my test sheet and only wanted to shove it from my life forever. The proctor ignored me when I placed the paper in his outstretched hand. As I turned, something inside of me twitched. Wetness seeped between my legs. Then . . . Whoosh! I stood there, mortified, in a puddle of amniotic fluid.

"Oh my God!" the person behind me shouted. I put my head in my hands and wanted to disappear.

Someone sat me down. My due date was in two and a half weeks. It was a little early, but not dangerously so. Still, this was not part of my plan.

"Where's your car?" one of the proctors asked.

I shook my head from side to side, in shock. "No car. Got a ride."

He offered to take me to the hospital and call David to meet me there. I was delivering at Mercy Hospital, only a few blocks from where I took the exam. I accepted the offer and kept my legs crossed the entire ride.

ABBY

I arrived at the hospital in ten minutes. The examination revealed I was fully effaced and more than halfway dilated.

I sat propped in bed with an IV dripping into my arm when David entered, biting his lower lip. I had heard him clomping down the hall.

"What's your problem?" I asked. I probably should have been more sensitive, but I was the one in labor, not him.

David gritted his teeth. "The nurse asked if I was your father."

This error usually amused him, but not today. Redness edged upwards, creeping from his collar to his unsmiling face. He thwacked his fingers against the rolling table by the bed.

Geez, he should be used to it by now. Even though we're only a few years apart, I'm small and always mistaken for someone younger, and David, prematurely gray (though less prematurely as time went on), was often thought to be older.

I laughed it off. "Get over it, Professor. We're having a baby."

As his pique subsided, David settled himself. He adjusted his frame in the chair by my side and patted my hand.

Around the middle of my pregnancy, I had amniocentesis due to my age and because David's sister, Maggie, had Down syndrome. Not that a similar discovery would have mattered. We simply wanted to be prepared to raise our child the best we could. The test did not reveal any chromosomal issues. So other than this day arriving slightly earlier than expected, we had few worries about the child who was about to emerge.

ABBY

Hard labor burst on the scene, shattering any peace we may have pretended we had. We sporadically attended Lamaze classes and had some idea of what to do, but when things got intense, our schooling failed us. I tried to concentrate on breathing. It was futile. My uterus, exploding in its effort to rid itself of its contents, set my teeth on edge. David, not ordinarily squeamish having grown up on a farm, winced sympathetically at every hard contraction.

Raucous laughter echoed outside the labor room. I was not in the mood for hilarity.

I glared at David. "Go find out what's so fucking funny." My sense of humor had evaporated quickly with the onset of pain.

He ducked his head into the hallway, then stepped out and closed the door behind him. He returned a few minutes later. Another contraction cemented my ill temper.

I glowered. "So?"

"I'm not sure you want to know," David said.

"Of course, I do. What was it?"

"They're taking bets."

"Who? About what?" Pain swirled, and I started to huff.

"The residents—about you." David focused on the floor, clearly uncomfortable with the conversation. "Someone put a note outside your door: Caesarean in situ."

"What?" I snapped between breaths.

David cringed. "They're betting on whether you need a section. You know, you're so small and the baby's big."

"Assholes! There's no way I'm having a section after going through this." Tensing with the apex of the contraction, I squeezed my eyes shut and shouted an extended "F U C K!"

David eased me through it as the doctor entered to check my progress. The OB held up an index finger—one more centimeter to go.

After a few more episodes of abject agony, I made it into a delivery room. David gowned up and joined me. One last push and the contents of my womb poured into the doctor's waiting arms, followed by a high-pitched wail and the announcement that the baby was a boy.

The doctor invited David to cut the cord, which he did, carefully. The bluish snake-like cable fell, flaccid and done. United for months, the baby and I were now entities unto our own in the continuum of life.

I raised my head to catch another glimpse of my former tenant. Hearing him was insufficient; I needed visual proof and peeped, "Can I have him?" Someone placed the gooey baby on my chest, and David hovered over us, lightly fingering the baby's downy arm.

A nurse whisked the baby away for vitals and clean-up, and, after expelling the afterbirth, I lay there still. The pain was gone. I recalled a line from Richard Brautigan. Silent, like deer tracks in the snow.

David followed me to recovery, and after a while, someone brought the baby to my arms. Swaddled in a blue and white striped flannel blanket, he wore a white toque with a pompom on his head. I giggled. I knew the little hat was regulating his temperature, but he looked ridiculous nonetheless, like a tiny, capped troll. He had blotchy red skin and ten fingers and toes and was, of course, perfect.

ABBY

Jordan Elliott Armacost. Maybe the name was too grown-up for a little guy, but someday it would fit. We named him for David's father, John, and my mother, Eileen. Neither would ever know him, but their memory would live on in what we hoped would be his good, long life.

Coming home from the hospital, we found our front door blocked with packages containing every conceivable piece of baby furniture and paraphernalia. It took us hours to unwrap the massive shipment. There was a souped-up stroller that could have competed in the Indianapolis 500, along with baby clothes, blankets, and enough diapers to last until Jordan was toilet trained. Nina had thought of everything.

The first days were a blur. Why bother getting dressed when Jordan latched onto my breasts constantly? David changed a few diapers, but that was about all he was good for. I thought we were managing, but no one could prepare us for the sheer exhaustion and my hormonal upheaval. Sleep was as treasured as gold and having an actual meal but a dream. David and I coped, taking turns doing the things new parents have done for millennia. We would survive, but some help wouldn't hurt. Then came Miri—blessed Miri.

Near the end of the week, the phone rang. I had been ignoring calls in favor of living undisturbed but fortuitously answered.

"Abby, it's Miri. I'm done with school. Do you need any help?"

I fell to my knees.

Not too proud to beg, I yelped. Within minutes, I sent David to pick her up and waited, ear to the door, for them to arrive. My prayers were answered. Upon entering the house, Miri took charge. David and I, almost middle-aged, worshiped at the feet of our experienced, barely more than teenaged, cousin.

Miri—the godsend, the baby whisperer. She knew instinctively what Jordan needed and when he needed it. I could eat, sleep, bathe, and do almost everything else other humans do.

Nina and Bill called to hear about the baby, and we thanked them profusely for their overabundant gifts. Nina, ever gracious, politely shrugged it off.

"This is what we did for our daughter and would do for any of our children. Your parents aren't there to help, so we're happy to step in."

I remained floored; it was all too much. "I still don't know what to say. If not for you and Miri, I don't know how we would have managed. Thank goodness she's staying another week or two."

The phone crackled with Nina's delight. "You see," Nina said, "that is what families are for. You helped Miri when she needed you, and now she is returning your kindness."

That I had a family at all was a surprise. That it was this family—that was a miracle.

DAVID

David leaned against the bedroom door, bone weary. How astounding that babies were so time-consuming! How did other parents do it? And here, Abby was nursing, and he barely had to do a thing. What happened to his supposed stamina? Now gone, if he ever had any. An illusion to be tossed out the window.

Every time he gazed at Jordan, his heart nearly burst. Did his own parents, gone almost twenty years, feel this way when they looked at him and Maggie? Could this have been how much they loved him? Maybe you had to be a parent to understand.

And Abby. She was so small and, without damage it seemed, carried this wailing, vital, wiggling human being with unlimited potential. What a marvel. Of course, creatures have been doing this since the beginning of time. But their love produced this child and, at this moment, that was everything.

ABBY

With Miri around, we began to resemble ourselves again. Time to reenter the world. I called Ted to let him know we were ready for visitors.

In an hour, the doorbell chimed, and I shouted, "It's unlocked!"

"We're here!" Ted announced.

He strolled in. Raoul followed, struggling with a massive box wrapped in colorful paper pattered with cars, buses, and trains. He plopped it on the living room floor.

Straightening after depositing the box, Raoul flashed a wide smile revealing his blinding, perfect teeth. He shook his head to fling thick black hair from his eyes. His amazing turquoise eyes. My stunning reminder of life's ironies. Leave it to Ted to find the most gorgeous man on the planet.

Miri sat in a rocker holding the baby. I introduced Miri as my Israeli cousin. Ted glanced sideways at me. "Since when did you have Israeli relatives?"

"Since now. I'll give you the whole story sometime." I knew he couldn't wait to hear.

Ted and Raoul greeted Miri, and Ted identified himself as my former husband. Now it was Miri's turn to look surprised. I told her I would explain it later, too.

"Can I hold the baby?" Raoul asked, and Miri passed him over. Raoul and Ted cooed and bounced him.

Ted pointed to the box on the floor. "Open it, Abby."

It was almost as big as the ottoman in front of the sofa. I couldn't lift it, so I pushed it with my foot. What in the world did they bring?

"I hope you didn't buy him a car—he's still too young for that."

"Don't worry," Raoul purred. "We're saving that for his first birthday. Go ahead. Make sure to check out the card."

I eased it from under the cherry red bow. The card overflowed with cuteness and was signed "Love from your favorite uncles, Ted and Raoul."

Inside, I found a collection of children's books, including every classic. There must have been a hundred of them: Goodnight, Moon; everything by Dr. Seuss; books on shapes, colors, and letters; story books and animal books. Knowing Ted and Raoul, they probably hand-picked each one.

"Keep looking," Ted said. "There's something else in there."

I probed around and found monogrammed bookplates in the same adorable pattern as the gift wrap.

"You guys thought of everything."

"Of course, we did." Raoul grinned. "He's the first baby in our family."

We moved into the kitchen for brunch, also brought by Ted and Raoul. Miri set the table, and David, beaming, opened a bottle of Prosecco. Clinking our glasses, we raised a toast to life.

ABBY

After another week, it was time for Miri to go home. David and I struggled to let go; we had all grown close. But Miri needed to return to her parents, siblings, and friends. I had David take her to the airport. I was a wreck and couldn't bear to say goodbye.

I developed a routine. Feeding, changes, and naps took on a rhythm as spring approached. Jordan, who emerged over eight pounds, grew bigger each day. When we first came home, David, with his large farmer's hands, could practically hold him in his palm. Now Jordan took up a hand and a half, maybe two.

Having never had a father's presence, I was overcome watching them. Besotted, David read quietly to himself in the evenings, balancing Jordan in the crook of his arm. Every so often, he would shift his gaze from his book to the sleeping baby, followed by a far-off look and a wistful sliver of a smile. I used to question my capacity to love. Seeing them together melted my stony core and reassured me.

What did I want to do next? I still popped into The Gleanings now and then. Winter was our slow season, and Raoul, as director, managed well enough without me. Raoul and I also considered hiring an associate who would take up some of the clerical and administrative slack if I permanently left.

But now, I finished law school, and this would be as good a time as any to move on. To what, I was unsure. Then I remembered the first time I met Miri and my conversation with the lawyer Miri didn't need. At the time, the work seemed intriguing. I searched for the lawyer's card and found it at the bottom of a purse I hadn't used for months. Marta Hansen, Office of the Public Defender, Chief, Mental Health Division.

ABBY

No pickup, so I left a message on the answering machine. I doubted Ms. Hansen would remember me, but it was worth a try. A few hours later, the phone rang.

"This is Marta Hansen. I'm returning a call from Abigail Fischer."

"Ms. Hansen, I'm Abby Fischer, the law student. We met at Good Shepherd. You said to call after the bar exam."

"Right—you came to see the Israeli girl."

"Yes, that was me."

"Weren't you pregnant? Did you have the baby?"

"I did, almost during the bar exam." I tittered and told Marta the sordid tale about my water breaking on the scene.

"Jesus Christ! That must have turned a few heads."

"Yeah," I said, glossing over my abject indignity. "I was a little embarrassed."

Marta guffawed, then turned serious. "So, when do you hear about the bar?"

"In a few weeks, I think."

"Call me back then," Marta said. "I'm going to assume you passed. You sound smart. Let me know what happens, and we'll talk."

I hung up the phone, worried I may have called Marta too soon, but glad she remembered me. Jordan's waking cry interrupted my thoughts and set off tingling in my bursting breasts. I had much to think about, even as I sprinted into his room, racing to avoid a sodden shirt.

ABBY

I stared at the mailbox all morning. I could see it from the house and couldn't take two steps before checking again. Come on, come on. U.S. Postal Service, hear my plea.

And there it was. The bar results. I hesitated a few moments before opening it. It was just a letter, but my fate teetered in the balance. I was sure someone could hear my heart thundering miles away.

I swallowed, took one swift rip, and praised be to God, even one I barely believed in, I passed. Relief showered me in a cleansing cascade. No more bar exams for me.

The single-page letter fell to the floor. Giddy, I scooped Jordan from his playpen and we waltzed in a loop around the room. He sensed my delight and started giggling, the tweet of a tiny bird.

I called David, exultant and ignited with energy over my liberation. "Guess what?" I could barely croak it out. "I…I…"

Choke, Choke. "Passed! I fucking passed! Can you believe it?"

David's pride coursed through the phone. "Of course, I believe it. I knew you would."

I was glad he did; I certainly had my doubts. Heavy ones. I thanked him for his confidence and for encouraging me from the beginning. Now though, I had a lot more to consider, like whether I wanted to be a lawyer at all.

David counseled patience. "Don't worry about it now, you'll figure it out later. Enjoy the moment." He had a gentle way of focusing on the present.

And I did.

David brought home a chocolate and vanilla ice cream cake to celebrate. With rainbow sprinkles. My mouth watered so, his cheek glistened from my kiss.

Oh, David, you devil.

Because Jordan was too little to have any, David and I each had an extra piece in his honor. Even after the second piece, I scraped the plate with my spoon, seeking every last sweet, melted drop.

"Well, Counselor," David teased, as he rubbed my shoulders. "Who are you going to rescue next?"

ABBY

In May, though I had not yet officially graduated from law school, I was sworn in and admitted to the Maryland bar. In a grand courtroom, seated with the other proto-lawyers, I raised my hand as a red-robed appellate judge administered the oath.

Afterward, with Jordan ensconced in his fancy stroller, David and I ambled along the cobblestone streets of Annapolis. Baskets of May flowers adorned the doorways of narrow homes built centuries ago. We bought crab cakes at a market stall, along with a yellow tin of Old Bay spice for home, and ate a peaceful lunch on the dock overlooking the harbor. Sailboats glided by and seagulls swooped and cawed. A soft breeze carried the whiff of salt water and spray. Hours may have passed. Lulled by the white-tipped waves, we could have been the only people in the world.

A few weeks later, I graduated with my class. The hall filled with the group's worried buzz about the bar exam in July. Nerves sizzled in the air. I kept quiet about my reversed sequence.

I did not expect to find Ted and Raoul waiting for us in the auditorium. Raoul held a bouquet of mixed roses.

I turned to David. "How did they know? Did you invite them?"

"Of course, I did, Abby. They're family. We're all so proud of you."

I waved to Ted and Raoul and skipped to my seat. Leave it to David to share his pride.

The formalities concluded with claps and cheers. On my way out, I caught up with some of my classmates. Everyone wanted to know about the baby. I pointed to where David, Ted, and Raoul stood. Ted was holding Jordan, and I couldn't resist. "He's over there, with my husbands."

No one asked for an explanation, but there were a few curious looks. I bid my classmates luck on the bar exam and joined my family in the hall.

ABBY

I would be lying if I said I didn't find Marta Hansen more than a wee bit intimidating. If there were a dictionary of clichés, Marta's picture would illustrate no nonsense. She was blunt, profane, and unflappable. And scared the bejesus out of me. If I thought working for Jack Warfield, resident lunatic, was tough, Marta was fearless and expected you to match her in intellect and grit. Everyone worshipped her.

    I found the public defender's office, located on St. Paul Place in downtown Baltimore. I parked in a seedy garage because it was cheap. The garage elevator was broken and rushing down six flights of concrete steps, I scuffed the only decent pair of shoes I owned. When I entered the office, Marta eyed me up and down. Marta was effortlessly stylish and, as I later learned, considered me a fashion as well as a training challenge.

    At first, I thought I was simply meeting with Marta to learn about the unit. I didn't realize until Marta started talking that it was a job interview.

    I hadn't been on a job interview since 1984, and it showed. After having worked at The Gleanings for the past six years, my wardrobe lacked certain professional garments, such as anything other than jeans and tees. Somehow, I managed to find an old skirt and jacket that mostly matched stuffed in a trunk. Miraculously, even after having a baby, they fit. I added a barely worn pair of ballet flats. Even though I wasn't certain about the nature of my visit, I still wanted to create a good impression.

I had no resume or credentials to offer. Marta didn't seem to care. She quizzed me about law school, my previous jobs, and what I knew about the public defender's office. Which was nothing.

"I run the public defender's mental health unit," she said. "We had six attorneys, and one was recently appointed to the Baltimore City bench. So, we have a vacancy. I'm losing someone seasoned, but I always start fresh."

Marta peered at me over cat-eye reading specs. "I don't care what you've done before. I prize inexperience. That way, I don't have to clean up anyone else's shit. I'm going to train you my way—the right way."

"Here's what we do. We primarily represent individuals at risk of being involuntarily committed to psychiatric hospitals. The hearings are held right in the hospital before an administrative law judge. The clients' conditions vary. They range from floridly insane to mildly insightful. It's the job of the hospital to prove that the patient, due to mental illness and dangerousness, needs institutional care."

"Look, I'm not going to lie. It can be very challenging. Some of these hospitals are real dumps. They're old, gloomy, and poorly maintained. You'd be shocked. Or maybe not. Some of my staff have been injured by patients who've lost control. There are risks."

"But the reward is sweet." Marta looked me straight in the eye. "These are some of the most vulnerable people in the world. We are defending their liberty and to me, there is no greater cause."

"Plus." Marta winked. "You will meet some of the wildest fucking people you've ever seen."

I was sold.

Marta said the office had to wait until the next fiscal year, which would start in a week or two, to make an offer. She expected someone new would start in August and asked whether that fit my schedule.

I hadn't expected the meeting to get this far but didn't want to hesitate. I probably should have waited to talk to David, though he already understood I was ready for something new.

I winked back at Marta.

"Count me in," I said, and took the plunge.

ABBY

Despite my lack of hesitation, I did have reservations. Leaving Jordan and starting something utterly new was a big step. Other excuses plagued me.

Of course, I had already agreed, so unless I wanted to look like an idiot, I was stuck.

I sought David's advice. Being a mathematician, he methodically reduced my options to a statistical chart. On graph paper, no less. He had me list all of the pros and cons, with color-coded symbols and numerical values. Greek letters, too. Which, of course, were all Greek to me. But he patiently explained the process and after his painstaking guidance, I confirmed my decision.

Then I heard from Marta with a reprieve.

"Sorry, Abby. Good news first. You've got the job. Here's the bad news—we can't bring you on until November. It's the fucking budget; I have no control. Do you still want it?"

This wasn't bad news to me. I appreciated the extension of time. By November, my childcare plans should be in place, and I could also brush up on that area of the law. I would feel ready by then.

"Of course," I said, trying to find the right balance between confidence and relief.

Marta, not one for extended pleasantries, ended the conversation with a brisk "Great—see you in November!"

David, Raoul, and I had discussed my transition from The Gleanings to a career more suited to my legal education, and now it would become a reality. In preparation, we hired Peter Fitzgerald with my eventual departure in mind.

Pete had been David's student at MIT and later worked for The Numbers Game, the program David started that brought him to the attention of the MacArthur Foundation. Pete ran the Chicago office and he and David kept in frequent contact.

Pete was not your typical MIT student. He and David made an uncommon pair. David, so conventional with his clipped gray hair and professorial mien, was Pete's antithesis. Pete's perpetual smirk, bristly sapphire 'do and tattooed sleeves were more punk than mathematician. But he was an acolyte and only wanted to work with David. David returned the admiration. Even as Pete tried to hide his talent behind his rough facade, David saw through it. I knew how much he respected Pete's intellect and humor.

Pete, a lifelong Bostonian from Southie, punctuated every sentence with "wicked" something or other. His accent reminded me of Eileen's, steeped in the old neighborhood. Southie was one of the few New England working-class enclaves in which we hadn't lived. Eileen had some distant Shanahan relatives there, so I wasn't a complete stranger to the close-knit crowd. Heck, maybe Pete was another long-lost cousin, just like, but totally unlike, Eitan Rabinowitz.

Pete was also the bearer of good news. His girlfriend, Sandy, was an aspiring writer and English major who recently graduated from Northwestern in Chicago. She wanted to spend a year or two writing before applying for an MFA and had taken a job as a nanny for the summer. Pete urged her to move to Maryland so they could be together. Sandy could write anywhere.

    Hearing my dilemma, Pete suggested Sandy could care for Jordan when I started my new job. It would give Sandy time to write and add to her portfolio without having to look for a less flexible position. A perfect solution. All impediments removed, I prepared myself for the next step.

ABBY

I couldn't say it was out of the blue. Nina and I spoke occasionally, so I was not surprised when she called one Monday evening in September, a few weeks after our first anniversary.

Nina's voice was somber, and she barely prefaced her remarks. "Abby, I have some bad news. I'm so sorry, but your father passed away today."

After visiting Mark, I frankly had little thought of him. I wasn't sure how to react. Seeing him had been profoundly sad, but I had no real connection to him. His absence in my life, notwithstanding his many limitations, left him a void to me.

But Nina had been so kind, and I knew Mark's death had meaning for her, even though he meant nothing to me. I wanted to be sensitive without sounding false.

"I'm so sorry, Nina," I said. "I know it's a big loss for you. What can I do to help?" I hoped that was good enough.

Nina didn't even sound like Nina. The chirp was gone, and her voice lost an octave. "There's a graveside funeral on Wednesday and I'll be sitting shiva at home for the rest of the week."

I knew little about Jewish funeral practices but thought there might be some custom for a quick burial followed by a period of mourning. I felt an obligation, not to Mark, but to Nina, to go. Being present for Nina, who so warmly welcomed me, seemed the only appropriate choice.

"I'll be there," I said.

Nina urged me to bring David and Jordan, too. She said the presence of children always lightened the mood at a shiva house. Besides, everyone was eager to meet us. I wasn't sure who everyone was but wanted to please Nina and agreed.

After the conversation, David entered the kitchen as I sat, cross-legged, blank-faced. I looked up at him.

"Well, now I'm really an orphan. Nina called. Mark's dead. The funeral is on Wednesday." My monotone betrayed my indifference.

"Oh, that's a shame, Abby." David draped his arm around my shoulders.

"Is it?"

"Yes, it is," he said. "We'll all go."

I nodded, and there was nothing more to say.

ABBY

On the morning of the funeral, David buckled Jordan in his car seat, and we set off. Of course, I drove, as David read and napped. Even though David was an awful driver, he wasn't a bad navigator, and we arrived at the cemetery without detours or delay.

We parked near Nina's car and walked toward a small area covered by a green canvas awning balanced on metal poles. A light wind rippled the canvas; the poles shook ever so slightly. Under the awning, next to a newly dug grave, two short rows of folding chairs held court over a casket perched above the void.

Nina and Bill stood under the awning, talking to a few people, including a young couple and a woman wearing a head covering. As we approached, Nina called to us.

"Abby, David, thank you for being here." She held her hand out to her companions. "This is our daughter Caren and her husband, Ben. And this is Rabbi Bienstock, who will be conducting the service." Caren hugged us and everyone cooed over Jordan.

Rabbi Bienstock faced me. "I'm very sorry about your dad, Abby." After a pause, she pointed to the chairs in the front row. "The first two are for you and Nina, the mourners."

Was that what I was now? I hadn't considered that being part of the equation. I'm sure I looked confused; a burning hollowness filled my chest. Rabbi Bienstock must have noticed the wary expression on my face.

She took me aside and placed a light hand on my back. "I understand how odd this must be for you," she whispered. "If you are not comfortable, please don't feel obligated to assume that role. No one will mind if you want to stay in the back."

"No," I said. "But thank you for asking. I can do this."

I appreciated it would be important to Nina. She was the only reason I came. I found my place next to Nina in the front row. David stood with Jordan in the back to distance themselves in case the baby fussed. David and Bill had been talking and when the service began, Bill took the other seat beside Nina.

The Rabbi recited some Hebrew prayers and made a few remarks, mostly about Mark's childhood with Nina, Phil, and their parents. She called me his beloved daughter and, with difficulty, I suppressed a sardonic laugh. Nina took my hand and gave it an affectionate squeeze.

I watched as the metal apparatus lowered the coffin into the grave. Mark's final home was a plain wooden box, unadorned. A fitting end to an anonymous man.

My vision clouded. I barely heard the wind as my body shrank into a rough piece of rock. What was I doing here? Pretending to mourn a man I neither knew nor wanted to know? Dust to dust, the Rabbi said. My rock shattered and then I was dust, scattered to the wind.

When the service concluded, all present formed a line and shoveled dirt from a large mound into the grave. David handed Jordan to me and tossed a generous clod of earth that spread over the coffin. I hadn't noticed before, but someone must have handed him a black skullcap that he placed on his head.

After returning Jordan, I walked ahead, safely encased in my icy bubble. Or so I thought. My ankle shook and, as I started to slip, David upped his steps and grabbed my elbow with his free hand.

"Slow down," he said. "I've got you."

ABBY

Once back in the car, I followed Nina and Bill to their home. Dozens of vehicles lined the driveway. A throng packed the front hall and spilled into rooms as far as I could see. I knew no one.

Nina found me and took me aside. The people were their friends. She told them the funeral would be private, but they were welcome to stop by afterward. I sought a corner to avoid the swarm and lost track of David. A short while later, Caren and Ben arrived with their two young sons. She spotted me and waved. I wandered from my safe spot and surveyed the landscape.

Nina's massive Queen Anne table groaned under trays of smoked fish, salads, bagels, and blocks of gourmet cheese. Stations for coffee, tea, juice, and sodas sliced the corners of the room. Some of the men, including David and Bill, downed shots of schnapps. The living room transformed into a giant dessert cart, tables laden with bone china platters holding pastries and cakes. Everything looked luscious, but I had no appetite.

Nina told me in advance she would have a crib set up for Jordan in a bedroom, so after showing him off as much as he could stand, I placed him on the mattress, and he quickly fell asleep. I returned to the crowd and tried to mingle as best I could.

Caren came to my rescue. She was slight, like her parents, and had reddish brown hair cut short. She handed me a glass of orange juice and insisted I drink it. Caren had Nina's warmth and candor, and I clung to her as if she were a lifeline thrown into an ocean of sound.

ABBY

The crowd dribbled away. I poked around to look for David, and Nina asked, "Would you be able to stay for the minyan?"

When I looked confused, she smiled at me to explain. "It's a brief service and Rabbi Bienstock is coming to lead it. It should start around six and last less than a half hour."

"Of course," I said.

What're another few hours?

Around four o'clock, more food arrived. Aluminum pans piled high like silver building blocks, filled with meat, potatoes, vegetables, and countless sides, covered the marble kitchen counters. Enough for a regiment. White cardboard boxes followed, bearing more cake. Who could possibly eat this much?

"Don't worry. We're not going to eat it all today," Nina said. "I'll put it away. Our friends sent it—it's a mitzvah."

Interesting religion. No fire and brimstone, just food and more food.

David and Bill spent the afternoon huddled together, while Nina, Caren, and I relaxed by the pool. Every so often, my eyes fluttered. I apologized for my inattention. Nina and Caren, engaged in conversation, took no offense and urged me to rest. Knowing I had the long drive ahead of me, I complied.

No one was hungry for dinner before the service. Friends, including Rabbi Bienstock, started arriving about a quarter to six. Nina was right; the service was short.

At the conclusion, as at the funeral, Rabbi Bienstock had Nina and me recite the mourner's prayer, repeating the words after her. When it ended, Rabbi Bienstock turned to us and said, "May you be comforted among the mourners of Zion and Jerusalem." Before today, I never would have considered myself part of that assemblage. Now I wasn't sure.

Driving home, I was glad I nodded off in the afternoon, giving me a second wind. Traffic was light, too, and David and Jordan mostly slept. Before he dozed, David told me how meaningful the day was to him. His own parents' funerals had been austere, and when Maggie died, only he and a few of her caretakers came to grieve.

He touched my shoulder. "You have quite a family."

"Don't forget," I reminded him. "They're your family now, too."

DAVID

David had never seen such an enormous cemetery. A zip code in itself, with acres and acres of manicured lawn and paved paths. Uniform headstones; granite, gray, and square. A designer graveyard, not a pebble out of place.

You would need a map to find your loved one. Over there, coordinate B-345. Were the stones in alphabetical order? Following Abby, he passed by Cohen, Feinberg, Miller. And then Rabinowitz. This must be the right row.

She barely said a word the entire ride to New York. Of course, he slept most of the way, so she didn't have much chance to talk. It wasn't intentional; he simply couldn't stay awake in a moving car. But she probably wouldn't have said much anyway. At least not today.

He stood at the edge of the awning with Jordan, more of a spectator than a participant. Which was fine with him. When he ducked under the awning, an older man in a dark suit handed him a black skullcap and a bobby pin. He noticed the other men wearing them and stuck it on his head. When in Rome.

The service couldn't have lasted more than ten minutes. A few gentle words and what must have been an ancient psalm. Abby, next to Nina, rose to repeat a prayer. He didn't want to stand on the edge anymore and wished he were closer to her. She looked so small.

He joined the queue behind the others lined up to fill the grave. How much was he supposed to shovel? The old men ahead of him could barely lift a scoop of dirt. If he had to, he could finish the job. He was no stranger to digging and filling holes. Then he realized it was symbolic. He handed Jordan to Abby and grabbed the shovel from where the last man left it in the pile. The fill of it hit the coffin with a thud.

Nina and Bill's house was party central. Finnegan's wake without the corpse. He'd never seen so much food in his life. All delicious, too. He joined Bill for shots of the most potent schnapps he'd ever had. Shame it was a funeral; he could get used to this.

The later service quieted the festivities and had a spoken musicality that touched him. He did not expect to be moved. He was a man of science and considered most religion just so much hocus-pocus.

There was barely any religion in his home growing up. His Armacost grandparents attended a local church. He may have gone with them once or twice, but did not remember much. Hard pews and his grandmother asking him not to wiggle.

When he was young, David heard murmurs that before his parents met, his father was married to a woman who died. There may have been a child. He wasn't sure and never asked. One didn't back then. His mother was estranged from her family and probably her church. That could explain it.

Something about the funeral service affected him, though he couldn't quite put his finger on it. David never knew anyone Jewish until he went to college. He didn't understand a word of Hebrew and had no idea what the spoken prayers meant. For all he knew, they were hocus-pocus, too.

Maybe it was Abby's embracing family, but there was also a warmth and comfort in the words and rituals that struck him. Did Abby have the same feeling, or did it mean nothing to her? She hadn't mentioned anything, but then, she tended to keep a lot to herself. Sometime he would have to ask.

ABBY

I bustled in the kitchen, preparing for a visit from Pete and Sandy. This was our introduction to Sandy, and I wasn't sure who would be interviewing whom. After washing the same dish three times, I decided to stop. There was nothing to worry about. It's not as if we would be leaving Jordan with a complete unknown.

Pete confessed that Sandy's family was not too keen on him. Sandy and her parents moved from Jamaica to New York when she was a child. Sandy's mother was a surgeon and her father taught engineering at NYU. Pete was white, Irish, and from South Boston, and, despite his degree from MIT, not exactly up to their standards. I suspected his spiky blue hair and tattoos didn't help.

Sandy's parents weren't thrilled with her career choice either and were even more disappointed she was spending her time taking care of kids while she added to her writing portfolio. Moving to Maryland to join Pete was not the ideal life they planned for their talented daughter.

We welcomed the couple and led them to the patio. The leaves tipped into scarlet and gold and lit the horizon. The remnant warmth of late summer wouldn't last much longer, but today the air was still and held a grassy scent. Sandy waved to Jordan, who was sitting in David's lap. David handed Jordan to her, and Sandy spoke to him softly. Jordan grinned, his one tooth visible, and mewed.

A vestige of Jamaica lingered in Sandy's lilt, and I wondered whether it was carefully maintained. If so, it was a good choice, so musical and sweet. I, on the other hand, sounded like Pete growing up and quickly discarded my accent when I came to Maryland. Just like Eileen, I had a strong one. If we had owned a cah, we could have pahked it in Hahvahd Yahd. I half-smiled at the memory.

I described my new job and told Sandy when I would be starting work. Sandy said it was perfect. Sandy asked if, in the interim, she could come by once in a while so Jordan got used to her. Perfect again.

I tried a new recipe for grilled chicken with cilantro, which Pete pronounced "wicked good." Corn on the cob, roasted with cotija cheese, and broccoli salad rounded out the meal. Sandy and Pete brought blondies for dessert, which we warmed and topped with David's homemade ice cream. And there was beer, Corona with lime and Sam Adams—plenty of beer.

"I hear you're a writer," I said. Couldn't I come up with something less trite? Oh well, blame it on the beer.

Sandy's dark eyes shined. "In progress. I'm working on a novel about life in eighteenth-century Jamaica. So far, it's mostly research, but I have an outline and a few chapters of a first draft."

"I'd love to read it. Former English major; former aspiring writer, you know."

"It's pretty rough right now, but I'll be happy to share it when it reaches some level of . . ." Sandy hesitated for the right word. "Competence? But, I'd value your opinion."

Even if she was only being polite, it worked. I was flattered.

More talk, more smiles. Warm feelings swirled and shared. I winked at David; this might work out.

ABBY

D-day arrived and drew me back to my start at Dependable Title years ago. It took me twenty minutes to decide what to wear and I didn't even have that much to choose from. I almost walked out in my clogs instead of the kitten heels I bought.

This morning, Sandy drove in with Pete and arrived around 7:00. I was up and ready to go; David was taking his time. I didn't want to prolong my departure, so I gave my guys quick kisses and shot out the door. Leaving was easier than I thought. No tears at all. Maybe this arrangement wouldn't be so bad.

Driving in, I bounced with a guilty liberation. Should I feel worse about leaving a nine-month-old? David went to work every day—he didn't seem to be torn apart. I turned on the radio, loud, and sang along.

ABBY

My canvas briefcase bulged with training material I picked up earlier in the week. Poring over it was law school redux plus. Everything was new to me, which was exciting. And terrifying.

I arrived early at Good Shepherd and waited for Marta in the lobby. Eyeing the door every few minutes, I tried to read a New Yorker through my nerves. No such luck.

At 8:30 on the dot, Marta breezed in. She carried a Louis Vuitton briefcase and a Birkin bag. How did I know this? From our encounters, I intuited Marta's high fashion quotient and sought to self-educate on the topic. I was, of course, starting at the bottom. But I read and learned something, so when I shopped for a suitable work wardrobe, I concentrated on what I hoped was tasteful and chic. No Birkin bag, though. Not on my new salary. Or the old one, either.

Almost ashamed to say, I even had my hair cut (and highlighted, per the stylist's suggestion—something I never considered before). David asked whether I'd be working in a courtroom or on the runway. I took it as a compliment.

So, appearance-wise, I was confident. Workwise, not so much. I followed Marta down the hall, and an aide accompanying us unlocked a door with one of her many keys. My stomach fluttered as I braced myself for my first shot as a lawyer. Breathe, Abby, breathe.

The cramped conference room's air vent emitted a low buzz. Windows covered one wall and filled the room with light. Marta directed me to a chair on the right side of an oblong Masonite table. Our client, the patient, flanked by an aide, would be sitting with us, and the hospital's presenter and witnesses would face us on the opposite side. The judge would preside at the head of the table, farthest away from the patient. We were pawns in a chess game, lined up atop the board, ready to execute legal moves.

I paged through the list of patients and counted twenty-five. How on earth could we possibly represent them all in one day?

As if she could read my mind, Marta said, "It looks like a lot, but we'll probably have four hearings, at best. Most will be discharged or agree to stay voluntarily. We'll postpone the rest."

Only patients unwilling to stay despite the hospital's recommendation for further treatment would need a hearing. The hospital bore the burden to prove by clear and convincing evidence that the patient required involuntary commitment.

"Clear and convincing," Marta underscored. "Greater than a preponderance of the evidence, but less than beyond a reasonable doubt."

I must have looked perplexed. Marta reached for a sheet of paper in her designer briefcase and handed it to me. "Here is the case law. See if it makes sense to you."

The page contained some notes, including a quote from a Maryland appellate court with the crucial words highlighted. "To be *clear and convincing*, evidence should be *clear*, in the sense that it is certain, plain to the understanding, and unambiguous and *convincing* in the sense that it is so reasonable and persuasive as to cause one to believe it."

I looked up after reading the passage, still foggy.

Marta pointed a red-lacquered nail at the passage. "It's not just a hunch or even a likelihood. Their case has to be solid. Crystal clear. And we do our damnedest to force the hospital to meet that standard."

I nodded to convey my aspirational understanding.

Marta waved the page in the air and handed it to me. "Keep this—it is the key. Someone's liberty is at stake, and that is what we are defending. Do not lose sight of your role. You are the voice of the patient. It doesn't matter if you think it would be better for the patient to stay in the hospital. You can privately try to persuade your client to accept more care, but if they adamantly want to leave, you must present that case. Believe me, that is the hardest part of the job."

I reflected on her words, remembering Miri and picturing Mark, who bounced from hospital to hospital for years. Ours was a delicate professional balance, where instinct and emotion had to be overridden by legal obligation.

"You have to find potential flaws and defects in the hospital's case and carefully comb through the patient's records to analyze the hospital's evidence for inconsistencies and errors," Marta said. "But never forget. It is their burden."

Marta's seriousness magnified the responsibility of the job. I hoped I would be up to it. Law school was one thing; real life was another.

I checked my watch every few minutes. Breathe, just breathe.

Knock, knock, knock. Someone was at the door, signaling the first patient was on their way. That was our cue.

ABBY

The parade began when the hospital presenter, a middle-aged woman wearing an ID badge on a lanyard, entered the room. The judge followed her and arranged recording equipment at the head of the table. Marta was familiar with both and greeted them warmly. She earlier explained to me that Good Shepherd had four presenters who rotated each week and one of at least fifty judges could show up on any given day.

Marta never knew until the hearing which judge would preside. But having done the job for so long, she knew them all, some better than others. There were several she considered good friends, but you wouldn't know it after the hearing began. Then it was strictly business.

Marta and I stepped into the hallway to meet our client. She was a young woman named Bree, gaunt, with choppy hair and scarred hands. Marta spoke to Bree for a few minutes and confirmed she wanted to attend the hearing. We returned to the room with Bree, an aide at her side.

As we were seated, an older man carrying a binder arrived and sat next to the hospital presenter. Marta whispered to me that he was Bree's treating psychiatrist and would be testifying on behalf of the hospital.

The judge started the recording and gave a brief introduction to the case. His speech was hurried, and I strained to catch it all.

The doctor paged through Bree's chart. "Bree believes God speaks to her through the radio and demands that she end her life. Last week she tried to slash her wrists with a paring knife. The week before, her mother was able to wrest a bottle of Xanax from her before she downed them all."

He flipped to the next section. "She's compliant with medication here but is unenthusiastic about it. She doesn't want to eat. If she keeps taking the medication, I think she could improve and be discharged to outpatient care. But for now, she's still dangerous. Not to others, but to herself."

Bree remained silent throughout the doctor's testimony, except for a whisper that sounded like a prayer. At one point, she put her head down on the table and covered it with her hands.

Marta looked at her notes from the day before. "Doctor, do you agree Bree is taking her medication?"

"Yes, but..."

Marta curtly interrupted. "Thank you. And, doctor, have you spoken to Bree's outpatient psychiatrist?"

"Not yet, but..."

"Thank you, doctor. No more questions."

Now it was our turn to present Bree's case. Marta turned to the young woman. "Is there anything you would like to tell the judge?" Bree slowly shook her head and repositioned it on the table.

Marta made a brief closing argument. "Your Honor, this young woman has shown improvement, has reliably complied with medication in the hospital, and has displayed no suicidal or dangerous behavior here.

She sees a psychiatrist on the outside and her family is willing to assist her when she goes home. The hospital has not met its burden by clear and convincing evidence that she is dangerous to herself or others and requires institutional care. Therefore, I move for her release."

After only a minute or two, the judge read his decision aloud, found the hospital met its burden, and ordered that Bree be committed for treatment. The entire hearing took less than twenty minutes.

Bree gripped the arms of her chair and slowly rose from her seat. Her shoulders hunched, she faced the floor and shuffled out of the room with the aide. Marta took the carbon copy of the judge's decision to give to Bree in the hall.

Marta beckoned me to sit with her in the waiting area outside the hearing room to briefly dissect the case.

Placing her notes in Bree's file, Marta explained, "This one was fairly typical. Except for a few questions and legal arguments, there was not much we could present. This was one of the cases I was talking about. No question, she needed treatment but didn't want to stay. That's our duty, though, and I had to mount the best case I could for her release."

"Some cases, with procedural errors or poor evidence, are easier to win, but this one was destined for a loss. And, it really isn't a matter of win or lose. The point is to provide the best representation for a client whose rights and liberty are at stake."

"I understand," I said. "But it's still so sad."

Marta raised an eyebrow. "Well, you'd better toughen up. This one was benign. Just wait until you have a case with an abused child suffering from PTSD.

Or someone with severe neurological problems and violent behavior who has to be in isolation. Those are the hard ones."

"Look, this is the job," she said. "You will be cursed, spat upon, and even at risk of assault by our clients. But, there is a reward for doing something for people who cannot help themselves and are at the lowest point in their lives. Don't ask me what it is, but you'll know it when it comes."

Battle scars and a warrior for liberty. She made it sound so noble. Ordinarily, I'm not idealistic, but I had to admire Marta's zeal.

The only other hearing was for a geriatric patient, Max, who did not want to attend the proceeding. Another depressing case, but I needed to get used to that. Max's nursing home sent him to the hospital after he hit another resident and smeared food on the walls. They refused to take him back until he was properly medicated. Which I feared meant sedated.

Marta did not have much to offer on Max's behalf, and he was retained. In our post-hearing hallway debrief, Marta sighed. "Poor guy. I tried all week to contact his family, but no one returned my calls."

She slid his file to the bottom and snapped her briefcase closed.

ABBY

Our day done, I slipped out a side door not knowing where it led and followed a brick pathway. A tidy garden bordered the path. It was unoccupied and drew me in. I wasn't in the mood for conversation. Maybe communing with nature would lift my pall.

I plopped onto a bench that faced a circle of triangle-shaped topiary boxwoods. Globular flowers, pink and purple puffs, separated them. The arrangement reminded me of a crown, the blossoms resembling jewels between the pointed studs.

An oxidized plaque on a post stood next to the floral crown, with a green patina and etching on the metal base. "In Memory of T. Johnson Warfield. Life is a garden."

No. No way.

I teetered and almost fell from my seat. Jack Warfield's garden? It had to be a joke. Jack Warfield's life was an uncontrolled overgrowth.

Jack had been my mentor. A lawyer of questionable sanity, Jack taught me everything I knew about land records and titles. His yellowed files led to finding the deed that brought me to David and The Gleanings. Jack's sister, Evelyn Warfield Bass, must have funded this garden and installed the plaque after his death. She gave me his old Knabe grand piano, which I treasured. Evelyn and David founded the Warfield School for children with special needs. Maybe she seeded bits of Jack's memory wherever he made an impression in life.

That lifted me for about a minute until I considered Jack's experience here. Had he been agitated like some of the patients I heard in the hall? I could almost hear his booming voice, spewing fear and nonsense. Or was he catatonic, oblivious to the woken world? The picture of Jack, so brilliant, laid low and vulnerable, beset me. I knew his history, but being here, in this place, channeled his unseen presence and brought me even farther down.

I left the garden, found my car, and plucked the note stuck on my windshield. "Your rear tire is flat." Jesus Fucking Christ. Really? I trudged back to the hospital to make the call. Waiting for the tow truck, I turned on the car radio but quickly shut it off, no longer in the mood to sing along.

ABBY

David had already relieved Sandy by the time I got home. I went through the motions for dinner and almost let a large pot of pasta boil over. After putting Jordan to bed, I tried to recapture my day for David and describe the emotional contortions I had to control.

"There was almost nothing we could do. I felt so helpless and incompetent. And all I was doing was watching. Maybe this isn't right for me. This is visceral, gut-punching stuff. First, it was this profoundly sad girl who kept trying to kill herself, then it was this pitiful old man whom no one wanted. What's the point?"

David listened without comment, giving me a chance to expel my thoughts.

"And the fucking flat tire. That was the icing on the cake. Is someone trying to tell me something?"

He never took his eyes off me but pulled at his thumbs, something he did when deep in thought. When I ended my soliloquy, he was brief. "It sounds challenging."

Was that it? I glared at him. "That's an understatement. Do you have any gems of advice, Professor?"

"From your description, Marta did her job and put on the best cases possible. Plus, there were positive results. The patients who needed to stay in the hospital will get help. You had a flat tire—that's life, not a message from above. I know how you operate; you'll do the best you can. You can't internalize everything. Ultimately, you'll have to let it go."

I considered his observations. Our clients received due process and treatment. Maybe Marta was right about no winners or losers. It was the justice system in action. Everyone played their roles with seriousness and conviction.

"Besides, Abby, you've been with troubled people before. Didn't you spend all that time with Jack Warfield?"

Funny how Jack came up; I hadn't mentioned the garden. But David had a point. The Record Office was the perfect proving ground for Good Shepherd.

I couldn't bug out after the first day. Compared with other legal jobs, this one had the potential to truly help needy people, unlike conveying land, drafting contracts, and drier areas of the law. Maybe there was a reason I went to law school. Could I make a career out of representing the Jack Warfields of the world?

I propped my chin on my palm, looking at nothing but air. "I guess I'll find out soon enough."

ABBY

My journey took shape as I met my colleagues, traveled from hospital to hospital, interviewed patients, and observed hearings. I learned about mental illness and the most common diagnoses: schizophrenia, bipolar disorder, depression, and a plethora of other syndromes and conditions. I began to represent some patients on my own. No releases so far, but that result could be elusive. Everyone urged me not to lose faith. One would come along.

After three months on the job, I had my first success. I was at Baltimore General, an aging hospital in the city center. It was rundown, with peeling paint and narrow, dim hallways. The elevator shook as I rode it to the fifth floor. Patients wandered in the halls, and I had to walk through an understaffed common area to reach the hearing room.

The room was oddly multi-purpose. Along one wall sat a desk piled with papers and a microwave oven topped with salt and pepper shakers. The round table in the center of the room served as the makeshift court.

My client, Tess, like many of the patients at Baltimore General, was homeless. She had come to the emergency room clothed only on the upper portion of her body. The staff believed Tess's mental status and lack of attire made her vulnerable on the street and certified her involuntary admission. Tess disagreed and firmly refused to stay.

I met with Tess before the hearing and found her story compelling. Tess had a serene and measured demeanor, and I believed she would make a credible witness. Sometimes, we did not encourage patients to testify for fear their delusions would seep through and harm their defense. This was not the case here. Tess would be her own best advocate.

Of indeterminate age, Tess's carriage belied a life of hardship. She held herself as royalty, resolute and erect. Probably a stunner once, with sculpted cheekbones and perfect teeth, Tess retained her air of confidence. I could only speculate what led to her fall.

When it came time for her testimony, Tess looked the judge in the eye and spoke without hesitation.

"Your Honor, I am homeless by choice and know I have a mental illness. I take my pills every day and never skip. Sir, have you ever been homeless? Just try finding a bathroom. I know where most of the public ones are, but that day, I was out of luck. I couldn't get to one in time and peed myself."

Tess stated this matter-of-factly, without shame.

"It was freezing, so I didn't want to be outside, soaked in wet pants. I took them off, wrapped myself in my coat, and came to the E.R. to see if someone could give me some scrubs. That was it, but because I'm on psych meds someone decided I chose to walk around naked. Totally wrong. I only wanted some freaking pants. I've taken my meds every day here and made no trouble. Please let me out of here. I know what it's like to be on the street, and I can take care of myself."

Because of Tess's coherent testimony, my argument was simple. "Your Honor, my client is admittedly homeless, but by her own volition. Homelessness alone does not equate to dangerousness. My client's actions that day were rational. She came to the hospital for the sole purpose of finding dry clothing, something any reasonable person would do. She has insight into her condition and is consistently compliant with medication. Her behavior in the hospital has been exemplary, and even the doctor deemed her a model patient. The hospital simply cannot prove, by clear and convincing evidence, that my client is a danger to herself or others due to a mental illness. As such, we ask for her release."

The judge was persuaded and ruled in our favor. Tess could gather her possessions, if she had any, and leave. She waved to me as the aide escorted her down the hall.

A first victory! I couldn't wait to tell Marta and the others. I was learning.

People could be mentally ill, but as long as they were not hurting themselves or others, their freedom could not be taken away. It shifted my understanding of individual rights and the imposition of values not necessarily common to all. This was righteous. Broadened and empowered, I stood ready to face the next challenge.

ABBY

My next win was not as sweet and continued to haunt me for a long time. Coming on the heels of the first, I expected it would feel as triumphant. But that was a severe misapprehension, as I learned the hubris of success.

I prepped the file and visited my client the day before the hearing. There was a chance to prevail. But it depended on how my client behaved at the hearing and whether he wanted to testify.

My client, Len, a middle-aged man and a professional, was composed, but his eyes were deep pools of regret. After suffering misfortune, a business failure, and a divorce, he drank heavily and attempted suicide. Desperate to rejoin his family, he tried putting his life back together. Another setback occurred, and a second drinking binge and suicide attempt followed.

Len accepted medication in the hospital but denied having a mental illness. He admitted feeling depressed but blamed it on his circumstances rather than a mental condition. Len believed his consumption of alcohol triggered his desire to end his life, and he vowed to pursue sobriety.

At the hearing, Len was resolute. "Your Honor," he said, "I've made many mistakes, most of which I attribute to alcohol. I won't deny I tried suicide, but it was only when I was intoxicated. I've learned my lesson. I'm determined to stop drinking and have already contacted residential programs. If you release me, I swear I will go directly to treatment. If I'm not drinking, my behavior will no longer be dangerous. Please release me so I can kick this and get back to my family." Len sniffled and stumbled over the last few words.

Good performance, Len. Was it enough?

I knew by law that alcoholism was not considered a mental illness to support involuntary admission, and I made that argument before the judge. Len's testimony sounded sincere; so much so that I almost believed him. But even with my limited experience, I feared his good intentions might be overwhelmed by circumstances beyond his control. Despite any misgivings I might have had, Len wanted to leave the hospital, and my job was to zealously represent him.

So we won, I suppose. I wanted to believe it was not a pyrrhic victory, and for a long while, I monitored the local news and obituaries, afraid this client would take the wrong path. Another suicide attempt, a DUI, something terrible that harmed him or others. Not that I would have been responsible; I fulfilled my obligation as his attorney to pursue his liberty. The rest of his life was in his hands.

But it still unsettled me, and I suspected I was not alone. Long after the hearing, every time I encountered her, the judge who released Len asked me how he fared. I had no information and hoped that was good news.

ABBY

Life drifted on in steady rhythm. Milestones abounded as Jordan approached his first birthday. He crawled, cruised, and took his first steps in progression, accompanied by his giggles of pride. He made sounds constantly as David and I awaited his first words. Before long, he wouldn't be a baby anymore.

As promised, Ted and Raoul bought him his first car. It was kid-sized, sizzling red and brilliant blue, with a horn that beeped and bumpers that scraped every wall in the house. The cat and dog smartly stayed out of Jordan's way as he whizzed by, squealing with delight.

Spring came, and all Jordan wanted to do was play outdoors. By summer, he was running through the grass as we chased him from behind. David bought him a little baseball cap and tried playing catch with a whiffle ball. Everyone clapped whenever he threw it and wherever it landed.

One afternoon, around our anniversary, Ted and Raoul came by for drinks, and Ted revealed we had inspired them. He and Raoul were investigating becoming parents through surrogacy. David and I expressed our surprise and joy. Maybe next year there would be another child in our unconventional family.

I checked in regularly with Nina. She and Bill were planning on coming to D.C. in late fall and wanted to visit. There was also good news from Miri. She started university and was in a pre-medical program, hoping to become a psychiatrist. Miri had no further episodes of anxiety and was inspired by her experience and the treatment she received in Baltimore.

David, contacted by his publisher, painstakingly put the finishing touches on his biography of Erdős. It had been a long time coming, and the book often fell by the wayside.

I had some concerns about the number of projects he was pursuing and the amount of time David worked. Constantly, it seemed. But it was his nature and ordinarily, he fit everything in, including us.

Marta considered giving me a tougher assignment at one of the massive state hospitals. Many of the patients housed there had been abandoned by society and hospitalized repeatedly. Some had serious criminal records and were subject to court review.

I asked for a little more time, and Marta agreed to let me have one full year under my belt before undertaking this challenge. I was grateful for the brief delay.

The routine was comforting. I treasured the stability I lacked growing up. But I was also wary. Everything had been going so smoothly, I began to get edgy. That is my nature.

By mid-October, David sent his final draft to the publisher, but the effort took a toll on him. Many evenings while reading, he fell asleep in his chair not long after we put Jordan to bed. I hated waking him but didn't want him to spend the night like that. Usually, I was the one worn out from the day. For the first time, he seemed tired and overwhelmed. Snappish, even. So unlike him. David dismissed it and promised things would ease up now that the book was essentially done. By the time he received the galleys, David's energy level returned.

Or so I thought.

ABBY

We usually woke early. I tried to leave the house by 7:00 when Sandy arrived. Around 5:00 one morning, David got up to use the bathroom. When he didn't return after several minutes, I called to him. No answer. I became jumpy and ran in to see if he was all right.

He wasn't.

David lay slumped on the floor; his skin clammy and pale. I froze. I shouted his name and his eyes fluttered open, then closed again. Oh my God oh my God oh my God. His chest rose faintly with breath, which gave me some assurance, but not enough. David is so much larger than I, there was no way for me to move him, much less take him for help. Besides, Jordan was still asleep in his crib. My knees buckled, and I almost fell on top of him.

I ran for the phone and dialed 911. David's eyes opened but he still did not speak. The operator asked me questions about our location, his condition, and other details. As best I could, I described the situation and told her David was only forty-four years old. Then I remembered—my mother died at forty-three. This could not be happening. I knew things were too good.

I wiped his forehead and held his hand until I heard the paramedics. Fortunately, Jordan remained asleep. By this time, David, still dazed, was able to slowly rise as they checked his vitals. The paramedics recommended taking him to the nearest hospital for tests to rule out anything serious, like a heart attack or a stroke. Hearing those words, I panicked all over again. In a voice I could barely hear, he told me I should wait until Sandy came, then meet him at the hospital.

As soon as Sandy arrived, I filled her in and sped off. It's a miracle I didn't get a speeding ticket or crash the car. Sprinting from the garage to the emergency room, I dropped my purse and its contents spilled onto the road.

I had to wait what seemed hours before I could find someone with any information. David was admitted for testing and taken to a room. It took even longer to find out exactly where he was and how to get there. Thoughts ping-ponged through my brain. The worst thoughts. Calamitous thoughts. The end thoughts.

After wandering down the wrong corridor more than once, I reached the right hallway and entered the room. David, wearing only a flimsy hospital gown, was the only occupant and looked to be asleep. His glasses sat on a table by the bed. I was glad I remembered to give them to him before he left with the ambulance crew. He would have been lost without them.

But the sight of him! I collapsed into a chair as my chest caved and sliced my heart. His pallor was as gray as his hair and ashen stubble framed his face. I had never seen him like this. David was my strong and stalwart partner and here, he looked so vulnerable and frail. I stared, stricken, and may have even started to pray.

After about fifteen minutes, David began to blink awake. I eased over, helped him sit, and handed him his glasses. He fumbled with one of the earpieces at first and soon looked more normal.

"I'm so sorry," he whispered.

What was he apologizing for? I found a spot and perched on the side of the bed, facing him. I started to choke, and he patted me.

"I'm all right; it was a fluke," he said. "I'll be fine."

Considering what brought us here, I had my doubts. But, as a few minutes passed, he was more like himself. A flush returned to his cheeks, and he took a sip of water from the cup by the bed.

"I've been working too hard, and it caught up with me. It's not fair to you or Jordan. I'm going to let up, I promise. It's not worth it anymore."

"This is not your fault. Do not blame yourself," I admonished him. But he didn't seem convinced.

A doctor entered and stood at the foot of the bed. He read from his notes, not looking at David or me.

"Mr. Armacost, as we suspected, this was an episode of vasovagal syncope, a brief loss of consciousness due to hypotension, probably the result of what we discussed in the E.R."

What did that mean?

"Your blood work looks good; no evidence of a cardiac incident or stroke. Your cholesterol is slightly elevated, so I'm prescribing a low dose of a statin. And is there any history of diabetes in your family? Your blood sugar is a little high, too."

David's voice deepened. "My mother was diabetic. Am I?"

"No, at least not yet," the doctor answered, not reassuringly. "But it's not high enough to medicate. Watch your diet and get some exercise. You should get it tested again in a month."

I piped up as forcefully as I could. "He will."

The doctor peered at me over his half-glasses. "Are you his daughter?"

If only I could have shot icicles from my eyes. Sharp and lethal ones. I gnashed my teeth.

"His wife."

The doctor cleared his throat. Was that a laugh? What a jerk. It wasn't funny anymore.

"Let's get out of here," I urged as soon as the doctor left. "Where are your clothes?"

David pointed to the narrow closet. I stepped toward it, then turned to him.

"Wait a minute. What did you discuss with the doctor in the E.R.?"

David glanced at the foot of the bed, sheepish. "There was this stuff I was taking."

"What stuff?" I glared at him, incredulous.

David kept his eyes down, avoiding my stare.

"I'm not sure, an herbal mix. I bought it at a health food store. Some supplement for energy. I was stretched so thin, I wanted to make sure I could get everything done."

"You idiot! Is that what made you pass out?"

"That's what he thinks. That it caused low blood pressure, and, well, you know the rest."

I shook my head. How could someone that smart do something so stupid? But seeing him look so miserable in the bed, I softened.

"Sorry, you are not an idiot. But please do not ever do that again. I was scared shitless. If anything ever happened to you . . ."

A waterfall doused my cheeks with brine. My nostrils bubbled, cutting off air. I grabbed balled tissues from my pocket to stop the flow.

"I know, I know. Come here." David beckoned to me, and I squeezed beside him. I fit my head beneath his shoulder, my ankle dangling off the side of the bed. He cradled me until he rose to get dressed, and we went home.

The remainder of the day and the evening were quiet, except for Jordan's babbling and laughter. David sat with Jordan on his lap for a long time, reading him book after book until Jordan fell asleep in his arms. I transferred Jordan to his crib and mouthed another silent prayer, to whom or what, I did not know.

ABBY

David slept in the next morning. Not even the smell of coffee roused him. Still wiping sleep from his eyes, he plodded into the kitchen as I gave Jordan a mid-morning snack.

"I can't remember the last time I slept this late," he said, eying the clock on the wall. "What did I miss?"

"Just breakfast, two dirty diapers, spilled juice, and three puzzles. Not much."

I handed David a mug of coffee and a plate with buttered toast.

"No jam?" he asked.

"We're cutting back on sugar, remember?"

David groaned.

"Don't worry, I'm not the food police. We ran out," I admitted.

Later, as Jordan napped, we shared our thoughts. Yesterday was as tough on David's psyche as it was on mine. Maybe more. David had been driven for so long; it never occurred to him that it might take a toll. He was the one who always took on the extra work, pursued every idea, and completed each task. Limitations were a rude awakening to him.

"Did I squander my youth? I didn't appreciate it, did I? All those years, going, going, going."

"Don't be silly." I waved him off. "You're still young. You have a lot more to contribute. You need to prioritize and say 'no' once in a while. It's not just you anymore—it's us."

Our roles reversed. Usually, it was David assuaging my doubts and fears. Now he needed a boost, and I didn't know quite what to say.

"You finished the book. That's done and off your plate. The Gleanings is functioning like a well-oiled machine and The Numbers Game is thriving. The Warfield School is off the ground and certified by the state. For once, you can teach to your heart's content. Isn't that enough?"

"I suppose." He nodded. "But I was thinking about a writing program and was talking to someone from Brown . . ."

"Aaah!" I gagged. "Really? Another one?"

David looked straight at me. "Abby, this is who I am. I'll cut back, but I can't stop."

I shifted away from him and tried not to snarl. "Please promise me you'll take care of yourself. We need you—I need you."

David covered my small right hand with his two large ones, securing it in warmth and care. "I love you, and you and Jordan are my priorities. I will never jeopardize our family. You are the most important part of my life. Please believe me."

I did. If anything, David was the most sincere person I had ever known. I loved him for all of the qualities that made him who he was. I simply had to try to reign him in a little if he went overboard, and knew he would do the same for me.

DAVID

What a fool he was. He had no recollection of passing out. All he remembered was lying on the floor and Abby standing over him, frantic. It was a scare; he couldn't deny it.

He knew he had too much going on. Maybe the pressure to publish the book was the factor that pushed him over the edge. He wasn't used to feeling worn out. In the past, he could always keep working and needed little sleep.

On a whim, he stopped in a health food store. He hadn't been thinking of taking anything medicinal, but walking by, he thought they might have a natural pick-me-up. If it was organic, it must be safe, right? He didn't even think of any potential side effects. Stupid.

How could he have frightened Abby like that? He kept replaying it in his mind. He had never seen her so scared—she was terrified. And for him. For something dumb he had done. Unforgivable.

One thing alarmed him. When the doctor mentioned elevated blood sugar, his radar pinged. He watched his mother suffer from diabetes. It affected her vision, her circulation, and ultimately, her heart. He did not want that to happen to him.

He had put on a few pounds the past couple of years. The last time he stepped on a scale it read 215, a little high for him. Easily blamed on his sedentary job and creeping middle age. And a sweet tooth. He would have to be more careful, maybe up his exercise. The thought of his mother's insulin shots made him shudder.

His knee was bothering him, but that was another subject he wanted to avoid. He smashed it to pieces in the last game of freshman lacrosse. That ended his college athletic career, for what it was worth. But it healed and was fine for a long while. At the time, the surgeon told him it might cause him trouble when he got older. Funny how that crept up on him, too.

But, for everyone's sake, he would take it easier. The writing project was only a consult, a few phone calls, and would be done soon. The book was finished, thank goodness, and teaching was always a pleasure.

Of course, he hadn't mentioned to Abby his conversations with Bill Soresman. It's not as if he were keeping a secret from her. He wouldn't do that. There were no set plans yet, anyway, simply discussions. He should keep it quiet a little longer. If Abby knew, she would probably flip.

ABBY

Life drifted back to normal. David was less burdened with work, and I proceeded with my new career. I wholeheartedly bought into the mission and kept clear the line between an emotional attachment to my clients and my professional responsibilities. So far.

In mid-November, Nina and Bill visited. They had been in D.C. for Bill's work and to spend time with their son, Michael. I was excited but also anxious. Our humble home was nothing like Bill and Nina's not-so-humble abode, and I wanted to make a good impression. David tried to talk me down. He knew neither Bill nor Nina would care.

I prepared brunch and served shakshuka, pita, fruit salad, and homemade scones. David mixed mimosas with fresh orange juice and prosecco. Bill and Nina couldn't get over the view, and David took them on a brief tour of The Gleanings. When they returned, Bill gave David a pat on the back and nodded to Nina. A good sign.

Nina and Bill doted on Jordan, who was his most adorable self. He advanced to two and three-word sentences and named every object in sight. They brought him a gift, a doctor's bag filled with toy medical gear. Jordan proudly wore the stethoscope draped around his neck all day.

Nina smoothed Jordan's hair. "Who does he look like? You or David? Do you have any pictures of yourselves as children?"

"Let me see," I said. I stepped into the study to look for a small box David brought when he moved from Boston.

I had no pictures or mementos of growing up. When Eileen died, I tossed everything, but I probably shouldn't have. Now and then, I wished I had something to recall her face other than my fading memory. Mostly, though, pictures sadden me. Time gone by, experiences ended, reminders of those I loved I'll never see again. Sentiments I can't afford to summon.

The box, a red and gold tin from an old Baltimore candy store, sat on a shelf behind David's desk. There weren't many pictures inside. I sifted through them for Nina. She smiled at one of David as a young boy, dressed in a cowboy shirt, boots, and bandana. Jordan inherited his light brown hair and blue eyes. In another, David held an infant Maggie on his lap. David stared at the camera with a nervous smile as if he were afraid he might drop her.

It was another picture that most touched my heart. It must have been his college graduation and taken by a friend or passerby. David stood in his graduate's gown, flanked by Maggie and his parents. His hair already started going gray. He resembled his father, a tall man with thin lips and a firm jaw. David's mother was reedy and fragile, her frame overwhelmed by a puff of pale hair. I recalled she had been ill for a while by then. Maggie flashed a huge smile and tightly held aloft her bouquet of celebratory balloons.

Nina tilted her head with a sympathetic air. "Your family—is anyone left?"

"No," David said. "They're all gone."

"So both of you were truly alone in the world."

I held my hands out toward Nina and Bill. "We were, but not anymore."

Bill changed the subject. "We're off to Israel soon. I'll be consulting at the Technion, in Haifa."

"They honored Erdős in 1983," David said.

"That's right," Bill confirmed. "How's your bio?"

"It's with the publisher now. It should be out in the next few months."

Nina chimed in. "Congratulations. We can't wait to read it."

I didn't expect it to be a best-seller, but here was one copy accounted for.

Bill turned to David. "I'll need to talk to you about what we had been discussing. Let's get in touch after we arrive."

Oh no. Here we go again.

"Sure." David quirked a smile. "Call me anytime."

ABBY

Marta kept her word and, after my first anniversary, handed me a new assignment. I would represent clients at Summervale State Hospital, an aging public site for psychiatric patients and defendants deemed incompetent to stand trial.

Marta warned it would not be easy. "Look, I'm not going to lie. The place is a shithole, and the clients are the toughest in the state. But you're ready for it."

Summervale's current public defender was contemplating retirement, and Marta wanted him to train me so I could take over when he left.

"You'll be fine," Marta said. "Just make sure not to wear your Louboutins."

I was afraid to ask Marta what she meant. She picked up on my puzzlement.

"Oh, I forgot. You're more the Birkenstock type. But don't wear those, either. Make sure everything's covered. You won't want your feet touching any of the crap that falls on the floor."

I wasn't sure whether I should feel grateful or insulted. I settled on grateful; my fashion deficit was beyond insult. After learning about Birkin bags, I dropped my inquiry. I didn't even know what

Louboutins were. Maybe I'd wear my L.L. Bean duck shoes. With thick socks.

Marta tapped her index finger on her upper lip. "Once in a while, you might have clients at Rosemont, too. No one wants to work there, but someone has to go."

People spoke of Rosemont in hushed tones, as if its existence could be forgotten or wished away. It was another antique that mostly housed developmentally disabled youth. In an unguarded moment months ago, I overheard Marta call it the worst of the worst.

I shut my eyes. Maybe I should rethink this career choice.

No, Abby. You wanted this job. Remember, the greater the challenge, the greater the reward. How bad could it be?

During the ride home, I abandoned my reservations, convinced myself of the righteousness of the cause, and celebrated my new assignment. I could be a warrior for liberty, too.

I bounced past the front door. David was already home, and I couldn't wait to tell him. His eyes glowed until I mentioned Rosemont. Instantly, his expression grew dark.

"I can't believe that place is still open," he sputtered. "How could they send anyone there anymore?"

His jaw set so tensely I thought his teeth might crack.

"What's wrong with it?" I asked.

"Everything—it's a terrible place. You don't want to go there."

"Well, it's my job. I might have to. What do you know about it?"

"I know enough." David's stare could have lasered my eyes. "Someone told my parents to send Maggie to Rosemont." He hissed the name of the dreaded institution.

"My mother visited that horror one day, and it almost killed her. She was a stoic Scot; I had never seen her cry. That day, she was beside herself. She told my father she saw children wandering around filthy, emaciated, and unkempt. It was a medieval asylum, the hinges of Hell, and she would die before taking Maggie there."

"Whew," I said, "that's pretty strong stuff. But that was a long time ago. Don't you think it's changed?"

David's face flamed.

"No."

He took a deep breath and streamed it out. "Not at all. There's always something horrific about it in the paper, an exposé or new scandal. It should have been closed years ago."

I opened my mouth to respond, but he stopped me and turned away. "Sorry, I can't talk about this now."

He strode past and slammed the door to his study. My mention of Rosemont struck an unfathomable chord. This was a side of David I had never seen, and it made the sparse hair on my arms stand on end.

As strong as his reaction was, it couldn't deter me. I had taken the job, warts and all. Besides, if Rosemont were so awful, maybe Summervale would look good in comparison. I had heard nasty things about Summervale too, but not as bad as that.

I hoped.

ABBY

My gut churned as I drove toward Summervale. The entrance, off the main road, bore a simple sign which at one time must have read "Summervale State Hospital." Some of the paint had since faded. The "v" in Summervale was missing, as were the "o" and "a" in Hospital. The word "State" was completely obliterated. A demonic laugh vibrated in my head. Welcome to "Summer ale H spit l."

Did this whisper or scream bad omen?

At the crest of the hill sat a handful of rickety cottages and at the bottom, immense faded brick buildings. Crumbling red structures, ghostly with boarded-up windows, dotted the sprawling campus. Overgrown, twisted shrubs surrounded the abandoned wards.

Other buildings, single-storied and spare, sprouted farther down the road. My office would be in one of them, the Nice Pavilion.

Nice? I found the name bizarre, considering its setting, until someone explained that it was named for a governor of Maryland in the 1930s. It still reeked of irony; nothing at Summervale seemed nice.

I parked close to the structure, a box with an impersonal 1950s faux-modernist vibe. As I expected, there were strict security measures. I pressed a buzzer to be allowed to pass through the locked outer door. After entering, I had to walk through a metal detector and have my briefcase examined.

When I passed muster, a guard unlocked a door leading to a walkway, and I followed, gazing up and down and from side to side. I shifted from the flaking ceiling to the speckled linoleum floor and sniffed. Something hard to precisely identify assaulted my nose. Sweat, urine, Lysol? I avoided a puddle in the middle of the hall, and the guard led me to yet another locked door. He spun a key to the final inner sanctum, and we reached our destination—the office of the public defender.

ABBY

Waiting for me was Gene Reilly, who had manned Summervale's public defender's office for about ten years. Everyone's favorite, Gene rode to work on a Harley Davidson, wore a Stetson hat and alligator boots, and told a story like no one else.

I met Gene several times but never worked with him. He was legendary. Laconic in hearings, privately, Gene could go on for hours about the history of the hospital, the array of erratic clients, and his madcap experiences outside of work. Gene, a world traveler, had gotten into trouble in more countries than I could name. He played several musical instruments and sang in an Irish band. I didn't even mind that he called me "hon." It was part of his aura, a pussycat masquerading as a tough. Or the other way around. Maybe both. I wanted to learn as much from him as I could before his planned retirement in a few months.

I paged through the pile of folders for the next docket. Gene had taken notes from the patients' charts the day before and wanted me to review them. The recertifications were for chronic patients entitled to a hearing every six months of their confinement. Some of these clients had been at Summervale for thirty years or more.

Gene expected most, if not all, of these patients to be retained. Patients confined for so long seldom improved and were simply maintained. Every so often, one would be released but would soon return, unable to cope outside the institutionalized world.

My thoughts flashed to Mark. Had this been his life?

Gene echoed Marta's words about the dilemma of knowing a client needed treatment but refused to accept it. No matter. The public defenders were obligated to represent their client's interests, despite their personal misgivings. These were always the hardest ones, especially at Summervale, with the most severe cases.

Summervale was the polar opposite of Good Shepherd, which Marta deemed the crème de la crème of psychiatric hospitals. You needed a flashlight to navigate Summervale's halls. Hissing radiators spewed little heat in the winter, and after April, every building baked into a sauna. The walls shed enough green and black mold to support a penicillin factory. Our offices, filled with discarded state furniture, were the bare exception, with windows that provided a glimmer of light from the outside world. If you could see through the grime. Nevertheless, a substantial step up from Summervale's sunless, crowded wards.

While we were talking, the phone on Gene's desk rang. My first Summervale case, scheduled for 9:30, was about to begin. Gene grabbed his briefcase, and I followed the tap-tap-tapping of his cowboy boots down the hall.

ABBY

The hearing room, a windowless rectangle, reverberated with the hum of a faulty intake vent. A young woman in a business suit already positioned herself at the table. She rose as we entered, and Gene greeted her with a smile.

"Terry, this is Abby Fischer, the newest addition to our fold. Abby, this is Terry Newman. She'll be presenting for Summervale."

"Hi Terry," I said. "Nice to meet you."

Terry held out her hand. "Welcome to the funhouse."

Gene pointed to the paper Terry had been holding. "Hon, how's the docket look?"

"Not too bad, only two hearings," Terry said. "I don't think either patient wants to come, so we'll have to go with the judge to waive their appearance."

The judge stepped into the room, dragging a rolling briefcase. She unpacked her recording equipment, and Terry led us to the patients. Gene introduced me and joked with the judge, a woman he once worked with in the public defender's office. She pointed her index finger at Gene. "Abby, don't listen to a word he says."

We walked over to an adjacent building to see the first client. At each door, Terry picked through a large ring of keys to find the right one. Drab green cinderblock walls closed in on us. In this wing, the rooms had no doors, only entryways. Terry led us to a room at the end of the hall. Our client sat on his bed, unclothed from the waist down.

Gene maintained his distance and asked, "Sir, we're about to begin your hearing. The judge will decide whether you'll stay in the hospital. Would you like to come?"

The client said nothing and reached for his genitals. Gene and the judge exchanged a glance; this one was waived.

To reach the next client, we had to walk through a common room filled with other patients. Some wandered about, engaged in conversations with themselves or unseen companions. Others stared blankly at a mounted TV screen, and one poor soul sat in a corner screaming. The windowless room reverberated with fluorescent lights that periodically flashed on and off.

Gene knocked on the door of the next client's room. He announced who we were and why we were there. No response, so we peeked into the unlit room. The client rose from his bed.

Gene repeated his query. "Sir, would you like to attend your hearing?"

The client shuffled his foot. "Hey man, call me Paul. Shit, yeah. I'll come," he said, raspy and low.

In the shadow, I saw that Paul was young, slight, and fortunately clothed.

An aide brought Paul to the hearing room. Gene briefly described the process and said I would be representing him at the hearing. Paul spat a wad of gum onto the floor. The aide grunted, picked it up with a scrap of paper, and tossed it into the trash.

When all were seated, the judge began the hearing. Everyone identified themselves. Paul's voice was faint, but he remained still. His long, greasy hair straddled the shoulders of his torn tee shirt, and he smelled like he hadn't bathed in a month. I was glad the aide sat between us.

The psychiatrist read from her notes and shifted her eyes between Paul and the file. The police brought Paul to the hospital after he threatened his mother with a knife. Paul had a longstanding history of auditory hallucinations and violent delusions. Since arriving at Summervale, he taunted and assaulted other patients. Aides were forced to place him in restraints and subdue him with medication multiple times.

I raised a few questions on cross-examination, but there was little I could summon to refute the doctor's testimony. I had no doubt it was true.

When it came time for the patient's presentation, I faced Paul. "Is there anything you would like to tell the judge?"

Sometimes patients offer cogent testimony. I suspected this would not be the case with Paul, but didn't he deserve a chance?

Big mistake.

At first, Paul mumbled something about the CIA.

Then, hollow-eyed, he stared straight across the table at the doctor and said, "Let me the fuck out of here. I hate myself and the whole fucking world. I wish I had a goddamn gun to kill myself. I hate happy people. I'll fucking kill them, too."

I had no further questions.

There wasn't much of an argument I could make after that. Unsurprisingly, the judge ordered Paul's involuntary commitment. When the aide led him from the hearing room, Paul shot me a dagger glare and a skewed, gap-toothed smile. I shuddered from the top of my head to the tip of my toes.

After that, the next case was simple. Arthur, the client with no pants, had been at Summervale for twenty-seven years. He came from an institution in New York, hospitalized since he was fifteen. Intellectually challenged and frequently self-injurious, Arthur mostly sat impassively in his room and took his medications without complaint. But he never improved. I couldn't say much on his behalf, either.

After the docket, Gene and I returned to our office. We sat opposite each other for a few minutes before Gene raised his eyebrows. "Well?" he asked.

"This is no Good Shepherd, that's for sure," I said. "We had some tough clients there but not on this level."

Gene nodded. "That's the difference between a state institution and a private hospital. We get the poorest of the poor with no health insurance and scant community support. But ours is an important job and a good one. Every day can be a struggle. But once in a while, someone comes along and makes it all worthwhile."

Even if that day never came, I appreciated that this was hard-core. Our clients, society's discards, mostly forgotten and systematically reviled, might only occasionally prevail. Like Gene, I could live with that.

If anyone ever needed a lawyer, it was the residents of Summer ale H spit l.

ABBY

I routinely told David the basics of my days but occasionally left out some of the gorier details. David had a mild protective streak, and I didn't want him to worry. I never felt unsafe. Security guards always escorted me on the wards, and competent aides accompanied the patients at every hearing. I learned to keep my distance and remain alert for a weird vibe.

On one occasion, Marta assigned me to Rosemont. There was only one case on the docket, a developmentally disabled teenager charged with aggravated assault. I neglected to mention it to David.

From the parking lot, Rosemont looked like a mini-Summervale, without the charm. The smaller campus contained flat-roofed red structures spread apart and connected by broken sidewalks and patchy grass. As I approached the main office, a bird flew into a dirty window and spiraled down, stunned or dead.

The case did not go forward. When I entered, a staff member said the hearing was postponed and reset for another time. Walking back to my car, I spied a playground behind the building. A young child, holding a teddy bear, stood alone by a rusty slide. He shifted foot-to-foot, rhythmically rocking back and forth. After every few rocks, he smacked his head on one of the steps leading to the slide. Two other children sat on the ground with an adult who looked away. It was November, but neither child wore shoes.

    Not long after that, Rosemont became enveloped in scandal, and I never returned.

DAVID

David stewed about Abby's current assignment. He did not like seeing himself as paternalistic, but he wished, just this once, he could tell Abby what to do. Oh boy, he could hear her now. That would never fly.

Whenever he thought about Abby going to Rosemont, heartburn fizzled his gullet. That godforsaken hellhole symbolized all that was wrong in the world. He was grateful his parents resisted the advice to send Maggie there and admired them for their resolve.

He hoped Abby liked this area of the law. Her stories were interesting, but even Abby, tough as she was, could burn out of such challenging work. He didn't expect her to admit it, though. She hated giving up.

DAVID

After psyching himself into acceptance, David coped well enough with Abby's new job. If one could define coping as dreading every time she went to Summervale but keeping his mouth shut. Immersing himself in the mundane helped.

David still patronized the barber who gave him his first haircut when he was around Jordan's age. Mr. McCord, the barber, was now assisted by his son, Craig, one of David's lacrosse teammates in high school. Now it was Jordan's turn.

Except for the year after Maggie died when he didn't come back to Maryland, he reserved time during his visits home to see Mr. McCord for a trim. There was something comforting about the experience. The scent, the talk, memories of his father, and the way it brought him back to a world that was gone.

He mentioned the idea to Abby. She shot him a sideward glance with conditional approval—don't bring him home with a crew cut. She still wanted Jordan to look like a little boy. He chuckled. Once when he was about four, his father let Mr. McCord buzz him. When they came home, his mother was appalled. Must be a maternal thing.

Jordan whooped, his feet bouncing off the floor when he heard they were going in the truck. They pulled up to the shop in Hampstead graced with an old-fashioned red and white striped barber pole. To prepare Jordan for the experience, he billed it as an exciting event. He had seen kids scared and squirmy in the chair. Not much fazed Jordan, but a little encouragement couldn't hurt.

The McCords greeted them warmly as he and Jordan entered the shop. Mr. McCord commented on how much Jordan looked like David when he was a boy. Not sure why, but hearing that made him feel proud. Jordan looked around cautiously as Craig lifted him into the big leather-seated chair.

David decided to ask Craig to do the honors. He didn't want to insult the elder barber but noticed Mr. McCord's shaky hands the last time he trimmed his hair. He wanted to avoid any possible trauma for Jordan and everyone else, too.

Craig wrapped Jordan in a blue cape and softly spoke to him, asking about his pets and favorite foods. While Jordan was distracted, Craig snipped around Jordan's ears and the nape of his neck. No trauma, all smiles.

When he finished the cut, Craig dusted Jordan's neck lightly with a fine powder, as Mr. McCord had brushed David's many times. Simply the whiff of it, eucalyptus and mint, evoked sweet memories of his youth.

Craig removed the cape and helped Jordan down from the chair. Jordan grinned and spun around to give everyone the full view. Abby was right. He does look like a little boy, no longer a baby. Mr. McCord handed Jordan a safety pop as David paid the bill. Leaving the shop with Jordan, hand in hand, he gazed back and pictured himself with his father many years ago. How comforting that not everything had changed.

Once home, Jordan ran to the front door. Abby was waiting for them with a wary eye. Jordan, giggling, showed Abby the safety pop that David asked him to save until they got home. Abby kissed him, wiping the little pieces of hair from his cheek, and gave David a thumbs-up. No buzz cut and he still looked like her little boy.

ABBY

The phone rang and interrupted my turn at Candyland.

"Hey, Abby." It was Ted. "Raoul and I want to come by. We have something important to discuss."

"Okay," I said. "We're home all day." Important? What was so important on a Sunday?

About an hour later, they arrived, worked on a puzzle with Jordan for a bit, and then sat down to talk. Ted fidgeted with his car keys and kept clearing his throat.

Raoul started. "We think we've found a surrogate. We want to interview her and have you come with us."

Really? I didn't want to discourage them and said, "That's great, but why me?"

"I . . . I . . . you know us, you're a mother, and you're a lawyer who works with, umm, unhinged people," Ted stammered. "You can tell us if you think she is, umm, okay."

He bit his lip and avoided my stare. "We were also thinking about asking you to donate your eggs but thought that might be too much."

I glared at him. "Are you kidding?"

"No, but . . ."

I counted on my fingers. "First of all, you want someone younger, and second of all—that's nuts.

You're going to have a baby who is Jordan's half-sibling? How do we explain that?"

Raoul nodded. "That's why we didn't ask."

"Good move."

"At any rate, we found this woman. She lives in New Hampshire, has her own child, and has been a surrogate twice. She seems on the level, and we want to check it out. We're hoping to go up and back sometime next week. What do you think? Will you come?"

"I guess. Let me check with David and my work schedule. I'll let you know right away."

The more I considered it, the less weird it sounded. Why not? I should be flattered they thought so highly of my judgment. I could lend an objective eye.

Ted and Raoul left before David came home. When he returned, I gave him the whole you're-not-going-to-believe-this story.

David snorted. "So, they want to borrow your crazy-person radar?"

"David, that is not a very nice way to put it. But, I guess so."

"I'm sorry." He didn't look that apologetic, but at least he stopped laughing. "I'll try to use a more sensitive term in the future."

"Please do," I sniffed. "They are my clients, after all."

He could reshuffle his schedule whenever they wanted to go. I called Ted to tell him to make the arrangements and let me know the details. Another strange twist for us. But we were used to it by now.

ABBY

A week and a half later, David dropped me off at the airport, where I met Ted and Raoul. We booked an early flight to Manchester, and Janell, the potential surrogate, lived about thirty minutes away. Throughout the flight, Ted couldn't stop bouncing his knee, and Raoul's brow bore a thin film of sweat. I suggested they nix the alcohol until the flight home. They wouldn't want to fail the sniff test.

After landing, we headed to the rental car counter for the vehicle Raoul ordered in advance. The attendant led us to a Volvo station wagon.

I glanced at Raoul, disappointed. "Didn't you tell me you always rent a Maserati when you travel?"

"Yes, but we wanted to look more family. Besides, the Maserati only seats two."

Okay. So now we're your everyday suburban threesome. Very impressive.

Janell Pierce, her husband, and their young son lived in a small rancher in a tidy development. Did each driveway have a blue Toyota Camry and a black Silverado? Maybe it only looked like that—Stepford cars. Janell waved a greeting when we arrived. Ted explained to her earlier that his former wife would accompany them.

We gathered around her dining room table as she served muffins and pastry warm from the oven and passed mugs of steaming coffee. The aroma brought me back to New England more than the flight. After I savored two bites of my muffin, Janell rose from her seat at the head of the table. She loomed over us like a CEO commanding the board. Janell may have been domestic, but she wasn't reticent. All business, to the point, and detailed, a cross between Betty Crocker and General Patton. Very un-Stepford.

"I've done this three times, once for us and twice for others. I love being pregnant. I'm in great shape, have no problems with my pregnancies, and every kid turned out fine."

About twenty-eight or so, with an athletic body, luxuriant chestnut hair, and deep-set blue eyes, Janelle would stand out in any crowd. She laid down the parameters in no uncertain terms. There would be no money exchanged. Prospective parents had to pay her medical expenses and anything else related to the baby. She had a superb obstetrician whom they could consult if they wanted. Boom, boom, boom.

She surveyed the room and focused on Raoul. "Did you have an egg donor, or do you want mine? You know, don't you, that I was Miss New Hampshire and first runner-up for the crown."

The crown? Oh, Miss America. Sure.

Raoul glanced at Ted but avoided my stare. "We'll go with yours."

"Good," Janell said. "Mine are great."

"And, how about you?" Janell's eyes shifted from Raoul to Ted and back again. "Whose seed are we using?"

Did Janell deliberately avoid the word sperm or simply like the biblical connotation of seed? Weird.

Ted pointed to Raoul.

Janell eyed the two of them again. "Good choice."

Ted shot me a what-am-I-chopped-liver? look. I wanted to say, "looks like it," but held my tongue.

She left no detail uncovered. They would arrange for Raoul to return on the optimum day. Janell would send explicit instructions about his visit and was adamant about precise timing.

Janell's eyes widened. "I like using fresh seed."

She would keep monthly appointments with her doctor and invited Ted and Raoul to join her. Both would attend the birth, and, after any necessary legal proceedings, they could bring the baby home.

"What do you want, boy or girl?" Janell asked.

Was she giving them a choice? Strange.

Janell raised her hand, her digits forming a W. "I've had three boys so far. It's time for a girl."

"Umm." Ted quirked his mouth. "Either would be fine."

She looked at me. "Have any kids?"

"Yes," I said. "A little boy."

Janell pointed to Ted. "His?"

Ted flushed from his Adam's apple to the crest of his scalp.

"No." I tried to ignore Ted's squirm. "With my current husband."

Janell nodded. "See, boys, boys, boys—we're gonna have a girl."

Janell produced a contract. Unexpected, but an interesting touch. I told Ted and Raoul earlier they needed to find a family lawyer since I had no experience with anything having to do with this type of law. Besides, I was too close to the situation.

The contract had kick-out clauses with timelines should there be any problems with the pregnancy. Janell would undergo routine testing, but there was no backing out after twenty weeks. This commitment was a giant step for Ted and Raoul.

Their eyes gleamed like first graders showered with candy from a struck piñata. I tried to calm them down and suggested they take the contract to their attorney and get back to Janell as soon as possible.

Janell stood, her feet separated like the Colossus of Rhodes. "You'll be satisfied; I guarantee. Let me know and we can get started. We are going to make one beautiful baby."

ABBY

The flight home was crowded, and Ted and I became separated from Raoul. After the attendants served a second round of drinks, Ted placed his cup on the tray and turned to me.

"You're still Fischer. How come you never changed your name?"

"I don't know," I said. "Primarily laziness. After we split up, I wasn't going back to Robins since I still hated my father. By the time I married David, I'd been Fischer so long it was part of me; it was my name. It didn't seem worth it to make the change. David doesn't care. How about you? You don't mind, do you?"

"No, not at all." Ted was high on baby love and two vodka tonics. "I'm glad you're a Fischer, Abby. I consider it our family name."

Ted opened the foil pouch tossed to him at the beginning of the flight and popped a few pretzels in his mouth. "Raoul and I decided the baby will be Fischer-Lin. What do you think?"

"I like it. Fischer-Lin. Nice."

Ted finished his drink and kissed me on the cheek. Not the oddest day of my life but . . . close.

ABBY

At home, David asked, "Well, did she pass your sanity test?"

I raised an eyebrow and debated my answer. "Questionable. But unquestionably fertile. She's looking for good seed."

"What?"

"Not what you're thinking, farm boy. Seed, like the biblical kind. Raoul's, of course."

"You're kidding."

"Would I kid about that?"

"No, I guess not." David, always more circumspect than I, tinged pink.

I heard from Ted more in the next weeks than in the past few months. He and Raoul squared the contract with their lawyer and sent a signed copy to Janell. Ted rigorously kept me up-to-date on all things baby. David would simply pick up the phone and hand it to me. Ted.

Janell delivered the news that she would ovulate on Wednesday or Thursday of next week and ordered Raoul to arrive promptly, ready to produce. She was a baby-making drill sergeant, and they hopped to her command.

Raoul returned home exhausted, and he and Ted spent the next weeks on pins and needles awaiting the results. One night the call came—success.

Janell warned them it could be a shaky few months ahead and not to count on anything until at least twelve weeks. She sent them a calendar with her regularly scheduled OB appointments. They tried to contain themselves, but I knew they were barely holding it together. Every time I called, one of them breathlessly picked up on the first ring. I don't know how they slept at night, as wired as they were.

After the first trimester passed without incident, Ted and Raoul eased up enough to plan. They decided to sell the row house. A child needed a proper yard for play. Neither wanted to leave the city, and they found a three-story brick Georgian home in Guilford, one of Baltimore's toniest neighborhoods. Perfectly landscaped, four-car garage, the works. They could move in before the baby came and prepare a nursery for his or her arrival.

Out with them for brunch, I asked Ted, "How did your parents react to the prospect of becoming grandparents? Are they excited?"

Ted was an only child; this would be their first grandchild. I only saw them once over our entire nine-year marriage. Ted's parents were notoriously absent from his life and purchased affection rather than bothering to show up. Maybe they softened with age.

Ted shrugged and rolled his eyes. "Abby, what do you think they did?"

"Sent a check?"

Ted nodded.

"Was it a big one?"

"Of course."

"You don't know, Ted," I said. "Maybe they'll change when the baby comes."

"Them? I doubt it."

Raoul hadn't told his parents yet. His mother lived in London, and his father's last known address was in Singapore. Ted met Raoul's mother briefly in an airport and thought Raoul might be mildly estranged from his father, who was on his fourth wife.

I shifted my eyes from Ted to Raoul across the table. "No matter what, David and I will always be here for you. We will never fail you."

Ted sniffed with a tight-lipped smile.

"Remember," I said. "I'm a Fischer, too."

ABBY

I shared the Summervale docket with Gene, who untethered me, simply giving advice when needed. Once in a while, he came to my rescue, like the time a patient started to strip naked as the hearing began. Gene's soothing voice calmed her, and she remained quiet and covered with his suit jacket for the rest of the case.

No real victories yet, even if there were victories to be had. Despite the high bar, the hospital managed to prove its cases by clear and convincing evidence. With too many of our clients, it wasn't hard.

I took the blame for my first injury. Trevor, a nine-year-old who looked no more than six, had been shuffled between foster homes and residential placements since he was three. Diagnosed with multiple disorders, he frequently lashed out at any authority. I thought we had a good rapport, and when he asked me for a notebook, I happily complied. The fact that he wanted to record his thoughts encouraged me.

I teased David about being a notebook hoarder. He constantly wrote notes and recorded ideas in his collection of all sizes and types. I raided his stash and brought a small spiral-bound one to Trevor. He squealed to see it and sat for most of the hearing quietly drawing.

Until I felt a sting on my cheek and saw blood drip on my file. My hand clasped the side of my face. I lowered it, and a red Rorschach blotch covered my palm. The aide seated next to Trevor grabbed him. Through his tears, Trevor grasped my arm. "I didn't mean to hit you! I was aiming for the judge."

"Take him out." The judge pointed to the door, and the aide dragged Trevor from the hearing.

"He can stay," I said, trying to catch my breath. "I'm okay—really."

"No, he can't." The judge stood at the head of the table. "We're taking a break. You need to get that looked at."

Someone brought tissues, and I blotted my cheek. Trevor's notebook lay on the floor, one of the spirals extended like a needle. After a few minutes, the bleeding stopped. Terry took me to the nurses' station, where an older woman cleaned my wound, applied ointment, and centered a square bandage below my eye. After that, any rhythm I may have had dissolved into a puddled dud.

I considered removing the bandage before David saw me, knowing it would spur his worry, if not his ire. But what if my bleeding resumed and I walked in looking like the night of the living dead? Hobson's choice. So, I kept it, a glaring reminder of my naiveté and guilt.

David beat me home and I knew I would have to deal with him. When I entered the house, he greeted me with a smile, but it dissipated as he came close.

"What happened?" He bent down to examine my cheek and removed his glasses for a better look.

I brushed it off. "War wound," I said and breezed past him to put my briefcase aside.

"Not so fast, Counselor. Let me see it."

"Not now."

David approached, yet remained at a respectful distance.

I had to offer some explanation. "There was an incident, but I'm fine. It's my fault. I gave my client a notebook and he threw it at the judge and missed. I got caught in the crossfire. It's just a scratch. Don't make a big deal of it."

"Hmmph," David grunted and pursed his lips. "Be careful, Abby. I don't want you to get hurt."

"Well, neither do I. But that's the work we do. All of us take the risk—we have to."

"No, you don't." He turned on his heel and clomped away.

ABBY

After Trevor, I tried to be more strategic and sensible. No more gifts; keep a safe distance. Once Gene was gone, I would be on my own. Detach, detach, detach, I told myself. Grow the shell. Do your job, but stay safe.

David refrained from further comments, either to placate me or shield himself. I limited my work stories to amusing anecdotes and observations. I'm sure he knew it was a ruse, but he played along. Whether motivated by fear or acceptance, it worked. Our truce mellowed into renewed domestic satisfaction. Kissed and made up. The love and care we shared were stirred, not shaken.

The next month, one of my fellow public defenders, Cindy Fairchild, planned a retirement party for Gene at her home. She invited everyone in the unit and their significant others. I was pleasantly surprised when David agreed to come.

Not that David wasn't friendly. To the contrary, he was, to a fault. But David and I didn't go out much since we left Jordan home with Sandy every workday and were generally unwilling to sacrifice any more time with him than necessary. I guessed David wanted to match the faces to the names I spoke about, particularly Gene and Marta.

    Camaraderie reigned. Everyone was able to shed their legal roles and enjoy the food, drink, and each other. After meeting David, Marta gave me two thumbs up. David engaged in lively conversation with everyone, especially Gene. Toward the end of the evening, Gene delivered a short speech. He and his wife were moving to Wyoming and he would miss us all. Someone handed Gene a mandolin and he started to play, singing in a clear, hardy voice:

> *Of all the money that e're I had*
> *I spent it in good company.*
> *And all the harm that e're I've done,*
> *Alas it was to none but me.*
> *And all I've done for want of wit,*
> *To mem'ry now I can't recall,*
> *So fill to me the parting glass,*
> *Good night and joy be to you all.*
> *So fill to me the parting glass,*
> *And drink to health whate're befall,*
> *And gently rise and softly call,*
> *Good night and joy be to you all.*

    Several of the guests joined in, and to my surprise, so did David. He resonated a rich baritone and knew all the words by heart. How could I have not known this was one of his many talents? He loved music. We tuned into the local classical station whenever we were home, and sometimes David stretched his skills on the old Knabe grand piano I inherited from Jack Warfield. We both sang lullabies and ditties to Jordan, but somehow, I never noticed this gift.

When the party ended, everyone congratulated Gene and wished him well as we straggled out. Walking to the car, David placed his arm around my shoulders and continued to hum.

We stopped under a streetlight and our eyes met. Illumined by the halo of the lamp, the creases aside his mouth deepened in pleasure. Desire overtook me. Between a lower throbbing and my racing heart, I had to have him. Tonight.

"Do you know how much I love you?"

David smiled and softly brushed my cheek with his palm.

"So much," I whispered, inhaling the warm scent of his hand. "So, so much."

ABBY

Ted shouted on the line, but the background noise almost drowned him out. They were celebrating at the Owl Bar—he and Raoul got the go-ahead. Janell passed twenty weeks and she and the baby were tip-top. Yes, Ted confirmed it; that's exactly what she said. Unlike us, they wanted to know the baby's gender in advance, and, of course, Janell was right. They were having a girl.

Beside themselves with expectant bliss, Ted and Raoul already had a buyer for the row house and planned to settle in a month. Meanwhile, they were busy packing up and planning for their new home. Raoul decided the bathrooms and kitchen needed updating and the whole house should be painted. Ted oversaw the renovations and made sure they met his and Raoul's specifications. It would be a showplace.

Ted and Raoul held close their deliberations on the baby's name and their design for her nursery, waiting for the big reveal. Each had accompanied Janell to her monthly appointments and both were in the throes of the legal work and logistics for the baby's birth.

Their attorney was adept at navigating Maryland and New Hampshire family law. All was set, except the exact timing of the baby's arrival on the scene. Janell assured Ted and Raoul all of her births had been within a week of her due date and she expected no difference with this one.

This was in contrast with my experience. I had been so immersed in studying for the bar exam, I nearly forgot I was pregnant. Except for those tiny reminders like constant kicking, weight gain, and a craving for oranges and popcorn. Together.

I guess that's when it started again. My biological clock. Tick, tick, tick.

ABBY

My solo Summervale routine took shape. Review files, visit patients, prepare hearings, and then the show.

The severity of the Summervale patients' illnesses and the intractability of their conditions far exceeded those in the private hospitals. Surely economics affected this disparity. Private hospitalization was funded by insurance. My clients at Summervale were often public wards. Sad but true that money bought comfort.

In contrast with Good Shepherd's light-filled ambiance, Summervale was crawling with vermin and pungent, its walls filmed with decades of grunge. The antithesis of antiseptic, each month it fell further behind on the bearable scale. I could grudgingly bear it. I was a temporary feature, who flitted in and out at will. For the patients, not infrequently prisoners of their own tortured minds, Summervale remained their only home.

One morning as we awaited the judge, Terry had some news. Over the past several months, Terry and I had become friendly. Although we were ostensibly adversaries, ours was a civil war.

"Hey," Terry called to me as I entered the empty hearing room. "I've got some good gossip. Rosemont is going down."

"Really?"

"Yeah, and it's about time. Apparently, there was a federal audit, and someone forgot to hide years of doctored records, all sorts of financial shenanigans, and mistreatment of patients. The Baltimore Sun is preparing a series of articles and civil rights groups are clamoring for it to be shut. This will be the end."

"Will it affect Summervale?" I asked.

"It actually helps. Can you believe it?"

"How's that?"

"So," Terry said, "the state wants Summervale to avoid getting caught in the crossfire. The board hired a new director and CEO. Wait until you see him."

"You've met him?"

"He's been around to see everyone. Smart and very charismatic. And gorgeous, a George Clooney lookalike. Zoltan Nerovitch, M.D., Harvard Medical School, with a sexy European accent. He's supposed to be some kind of hospital administration wunderkind. He's bringing in a batch of new psychiatrists, too."

"That wouldn't hurt," I said. "The current crop probably preceded Freud."

Maybe the bosses at Summervale weren't as dumb as I thought. Even they saw the writing on the wall. So many of the doctors were visibly bored with the work and lackluster at hearings. A dose of new staff could only improve the place.

God knows, Summervale needed something or else it was certain to be the next Rosemont. Terry heard good things from the other staff members and was encouraged. As an advocate for the patients, so was I.

ABBY

I pumped the air when Marta asked me to sub at Good Shepherd. She had an appointment in the morning and needed backup until she arrived around noon. A respite from the Summervale experience would be welcome.

I was almost finished, winding down with postponement requests, when Marta arrived. Marta and I had not talked for a while, and she suggested we catch up at lunch. We headed to the hospital cafeteria and huddled in a private corner.

Marta looked up from her salad. "So, how are you doing at Summervale?"

I was honest. I had to be—it was Marta.

"It is challenging, but I'm learning a lot. The patients are so different there. The impact of poverty and deprivation on mental illness is overwhelming. The Summervale clients have far less family and community support than the patients here, and they're much more likely to remain chronic than acute. Sometimes protecting their rights against a system that seems weighted against them makes me feel like Sisyphus."

Marta nodded. "That's a good way to put it. Constantly pushing the boulder, seldom getting far."

"But," I said, "if we don't do it, who will?"

Marta agreed and complimented me on my purchase of the mission. Wow, quite a confidence booster.

Marta asked about Miri and was delighted to hear about Miri's success at school and her ambition.

"You know," she said, "I'm not a doctor, but I never really thought she had a mental illness. She was homesick and anxious. If we had gone to a hearing, I think she would have been released. But, it's never a sure thing. At least as a voluntary patient, she avoided the entanglement of an involuntary admission. So, the system worked."

Marta mentioned she belonged to a long-standing club comprised of lawyers and judges and asked whether I would be interested in joining. The group, the Bench and Bar Law Club, met every other month and was always looking for members, especially newly-minted lawyers. They sponsored lectures on a variety of topics and had lively dinners. I was honored to be asked.

After the first meeting, I couldn't wait to come back. A former police commissioner who wrote a tell-all book came to recount his exploits and hawk his memoir. A number of the members were current or former prosecutors and public defenders and had lived through his tenure. I was too awe-struck to ask questions, but most did not hold back. And the food! Rare roast beef, velvety mashed potatoes, salads galore, and too many desserts to choose only one. Plus wine, a choice of red or white. I signed up on the spot.

I couldn't believe I finally found a reward for being a lawyer. So far, the strain of work outweighed any personal satisfaction. If my fellow club members could sustain legal careers, maybe I could too.

ABBY

I couldn't wait to tell David about the venue. Surely he was familiar with the exclusive Johns Hopkins Club. He worked on campus every day.

I asked him why he wasn't a member and he chuckled. "I am."

"You are? Do you ever go?"

"Only occasionally. Mostly for lunch meetings."

I gaped in awe and anticipation. "How about dinner next week?"

He kept laughing. "Abby, I think a lot of older folks dine there. You might feel a little out of place. But, if you really want to go, we can."

I did. The antique sideboards, period décor, and tuxedoed waiters all conveyed the aura of a storied past. Plus, I was dreaming about the signature ice cream sundae with real whipped cream, homemade fudgy chocolate, and caramel sauce. And a cherry on top.

He kept his word. We mounted the steps to the second floor of the club and I scanned the room. David was right. The clientele resembled the residents of Pleasant Ridge, albeit slightly more alert. I would never live this down.

David edged me an I-told-you-so look, with a smirk. I forged ahead, refusing to confirm his satisfaction.

A wabbly voice floated through the room. "Dr. Armacost!"

David led me to an elderly couple dining by a window. "Professor," David greeted the gentleman and turned to me. "This is Professor Garner, who was my math professor when I was a student."

"That was a long time ago, David." The older man's hand shook as he reached for David's.

David smiled. "Yes, it was, Sir."

The couple gave me the once over and the professor queried, "David, is this your . . . daughter?"

"This is my wife, Abby."

The professor's wife raised an eyebrow. "Oh, your wife, how nice. Lovely to meet you, dear."

I returned the pleasantries. So politely. Seething inside.

Seated at our table, I unceremoniously choked on my first sip of water. "They looked at me like I was a child bride you bought off the back of a truck."

"Well," David snickered. "You do look fifteen."

"Jesus! I'm forty."

"Okay, maybe sixteen."

David swallowed, unable to suppress a laugh. "Well, young lady, what would you like tonight? We have mashed potatoes, pureed peas, pudding . . ."

I was dying. "Quit gloating! You're going to make me fall off the chair and break my neck!"

"That's not a problem," he said.

David sputtered—he was about to lose it, too. But he kept going.

"I'm sure they have 911 on speed dial."

"Stop, just stop!"

We dissolved into giggles. I put my finger to my lips, shushing us so we wouldn't disturb the other diners, but no one stared. Was it courtesy or hearing loss? Either was a relief. We were already the anomaly in the room; we didn't need to be the main attraction.

A waiter came to the table and I asked for a glass of Chablis.

"See," I said when he left to fill our drink order. "I didn't get carded."

David shook his head. "This is a private club. They'd probably serve Jordan."

"No, they wouldn't," I protested. "It's illegal."

"You're such a lawyer, Abby."

That deserved a smug smile. "Thank you, Professor."

Though filled from dinner, I savored every spoonful of the sundae of my dreams and thanked David for indulging me. On our way out, I surveyed the remaining crowd. It had thinned considerably and the staff was already breaking down the room. I clutched David's hand as we navigated the stone path to the car. Maybe someday we would be one of those older couples, habituating a familiar place, sharing memories and wine.

ABBY

Only four more days until our week-long getaway up the coast. I lived for a time in southern Maine as a child and loved the scenic oceanside towns nearby. It was close enough to drive, and we could stop in New York to see Bill and Nina along the way.

I called Nina to confirm. Her voice rose two octaves and proceeded at three times her usual speed. Their son, Michael, who seldom had time to visit, would also be there that weekend. Caren, Ben, and the kids, too. Don't forget our bathing suits. What did we like to eat? I visualized the wheels spinning in Nina's head.

A month earlier, I purchased a new car. I was still driving the Honda from when Ted and I were together an eon ago, so it was time. It reached its 250,000-mile limit, and I wasn't about to replace the air conditioning a second time. I'd be ribbed about it, but I liked the Volvo that Raoul rented in New Hampshire when we met Janell. The seat lifted me a little higher and let me see the entire road. Maybe I could ditch my silly pillow.

David teased me. "Isn't that a little stereotypical, Counselor? I didn't know you were ready to join the establishment."

"Don't worry," I said. "We're socially insulated by your red pickup." David was probably never going to drive my car anyway if I could help it.

David left a plastic object on the kitchen counter. I picked it up and held it between my thumb and index finger as if it were toxic, and glared at him.

"What is this?"

"They're sunglasses. I bought them for our trip."

"Sunglasses? This looks like Darth Vader headgear. Are you serious?"

"Of course," David answered as if he had no idea why I objected. "They go over your eyeglasses. I didn't have time to get a real pair, and I thought these would work."

"Please tell me you're joking." Incredible. He still looked clueless.

"David, this is the kind of thing my best friend's grandpa wore at the beach. You can't go out with these."

"Are you afraid I'll embarrass you?"

"Yes. You'll look ridiculous."

"No one will know me. Or you. Who cares?"

"Uhh!" I stormed out as David chortled.

He called out to me. "You can always bring a paper bag to put over your head, if you feel that way," choking on the last word.

I closed the door to the bedroom; not a slam, but with enough force to be heard. Then I started laughing, too. Maybe Marta could find me a designer bag.

ABBY

Not a bad ride up. We deliberately delayed toilet training Jordan to avoid stopping at every gas station or McDonald's along the way and hoped it did not make us terrible parents. I was able to tolerate the kid-friendly music to placate Jordan while David, as usual, read and snoozed.

This would be a welcome interlude for all of us. I had to get away from Summervale; no further explanation needed. David dialed back some of his work, as promised, and he was better for it. As agreed, David monitored his blood sugar, and although not appreciably lower, it did not rise. He was aware of his risk and had obvious reasons not to ignore it.

We also looked forward to a planned stop in Boston to see Bob and Joanie, David's friends and former tenants who bought the house he once owned. The last time we were all together was at our wedding three years before.

I woke David in time to find Bill and Nina's house in Westchester. I had been there twice but didn't quite remember the twists and turns of the neighborhood. Michael was already there and Caren, Ben, and the boys were on their way. As soon as they arrived, Jordan took off with his older cousins.

Nina basked in the delight of her family and shared some good news. "Danny and Li in Vancouver are expecting a baby in April. Bill and I are already looking for a place nearby."

Bill nodded. "I expect we'll be spending more time there. Ever been?"

"No." I said. "But I've always wanted to see it."

"Without question," Nina offered, "it's the most beautiful city I have ever seen. It's spectacular, wedged between the mountains and the sea. You'll have to come."

I flashed a smile at David. Someday.

Michael's job as an assistant attorney general for the DOJ dwarfed my limited legal niche. I couldn't believe how interested he was in what I did. That lifted me a couple of notches. He was a real lawyer; usually, I felt like an imposter.

For a while, David and Bill huddled in Bill's study. I had no idea what they were discussing but suspected something was brewing from their expressions when they joined us outside.

Dinner was divine. I wasn't sure whether it was the repast, the company, or a splendid combination of both. Ostensibly, it was a simple cookout. At one point, David pointed to what appeared to be a prosaic burger.

"Nina, what is that? I've never eaten anything like it. Best I've ever had."

Nina beamed. "Organic kosher bison. The butcher said it was flown in from Montana."

David eyed me with anticipation. "Can we get this at home?"

Good question. Maybe in Baltimore. Probably not in Hampstead.

The boys slipped into the pool for a last swim and David joined them, balancing Jordan so he could kick and splash. Dusk descended, bathing the sky in rosy bands of light. I swirled the last pieces of fruit floating in my goblet of sangria, enjoying the extra splash of brandy Michael passed around. Soothing buzz; glorious night.

ABBY

Onward and upward. After leaving New Hampshire, we crossed the short steel bridge into Maine. Passing Wells and Ogunquit, I pulled into a roadside stand where we munched luscious lobster rolls at a worn picnic bench covered with penknife carvings. Amy hearts Steve. Jimmy hearts Beth. Jordan wasn't keen on the lobster but chomped on the buttered roll. He'd learn. We ended up in Kennebunkport, one of Eileen's favorite towns.

David checked us into Austin's, a weathered inn on the wharf, and after unloading we toured the town. We stopped by a white clapboard library with green shutters, full of books with local lore. A shop with a red and blue awning sold homemade candy and fudge. Had to get some of that. Later, we indulged in another lobster dinner overlooking the Kennebunk River.

For the next few days, we explored coves and rocky beaches. Jordan loved skipping over the rocks and chilling his toes in the ocean. I desperately wanted to laugh at David; he rolled up his khakis and waded in with Jordan. With his silly old man wraparound sunglasses, all I could think of was Prufrock, without the peach. But I didn't have the heart to tease him. Besides, he was the opposite of a sad, lonely man.

Jordan squealed when we spied a ginger cat precariously balanced on a fence post. He skipped through fallow fields with abandon, unfettered. David hoisted him onto his shoulders as we hiked nearby trails; Jordan grasped the leaves above his head. Those he accidentally plucked landed on the ground, like breadcrumbs leaving a trail.

I treasured the quiet of the place, the scent of salt water, and the cool, rustling breeze as we walked on the strand. And the sweet memory of Eileen, her auburn hair streaming in the wind, gazing at the horizon in peace.

ABBY

Tooling down Route 95 into Massachusetts, we stopped to see Bob, Joanie, and their daughter, Emmy. Emmy was now fourteen and a budding teenager, all sarcasm and sass.

Bob glanced at the car and frowned at David. "When did you get all bougie on us?"

"I confess," I said, raising my hand. "It was all my doing. Mea culpa. Sorry, I forgot we were entering the socialist republic of Somerville. David's completely absolved. You know he would never make such a bourgeois purchase."

To soften the blunder, I pointed at David. "But get this. He went all country boy on me and bought a pickup. Only the dog will ride with him."

Bob asked, "Cab or bed?"

David grinned. "Cab, of course. Safety first."

After buying the house, Bob and Joanie renovated and converted the upstairs apartment where David lived into three bedrooms and an office. David complimented them. It was far more than he had ever done with the place.

We strolled over to Inman Square for an early dinner at a Thai place David used to love. David scanned the menu. "Everything looks good. I'm glad it's still around."

Bob said, "If you miss Boston, you can still come back. Except you'll have to find another house."

David gazed afar, with a cocked smile. "No, it's so different for me now. I have no regrets. Boston's a great town, but it can never compare to our Arcadia."

The next morning, I climbed into the driver's seat and we headed home in one fell swoop. The trip was a sweet diversion and a chance to refresh. It was so good, so right. But as soon as we reached the Maryland border, little hammers started pounding in my head. Pain, pain, pain. It wasn't about going home; that was my sanctuary, my haven.

I knew exactly what it was. Tomorrow, it was back to the circus.

ABBY

Cindy Fairchild, who hosted Gene Reilly's retirement party, handled the Summervale docket while I was away. Cindy had been the assistant public defender there before Gene, so she was well aware of the Summervale experience.

I called Cindy to see what I missed. "Nothing at all," she said. "I even recognized some of the chronic patients from before. Not that they remembered me, or much of anything else."

Even after working there for less than a year, I understood.

"But some things were better," Cindy said. "A few buildings were less disgusting. I didn't have to hold my breath as much. Someone planted some shrubs outside, too. That's an improvement. Not much has been done to improve the wards, but I'm not surprised. Probably because no one from the outside sees them, and the patients rarely complain."

Sad but true.

Cindy continued. "But unquestionably progress. I met some of the new staff hired by Dr. Nerovitch. I don't remember the name, but one of the new psychiatrists testified in a hearing. Quite stylish;

blonde, soft-spoken, with a British accent. Very un-Summervale. Especially the shoes—Louboutins."

Now that I knew what they were, I snickered. Brave soul.

"As usual, sad cases all," Cindy said. "One patient swore she was pregnant and refused to take the meds, afraid they would harm the baby. Negative pregnancy test, though. I've seen these before, even with older patients. From what I've been told, claiming a non-existent pregnancy is a common delusion. They'll probably take her to a med panel next week."

What Cindy meant was a Clinical Review Panel, where the hospital would determine whether a committed patient who refused treatment would be forcibly medicated. These patients could also request hearings to contest the findings of the panel but were not entitled to representation by a public defender. We didn't attend them.

"It's awful, too," she said. "I once saw someone forcibly medicated. He was cursing and flailing, then they strapped him down and injected him, like something out of a B-movie. I knew deep down the meds would help him, but it was still a horror show."

On my next day at Summervale, I asked Terry about the non-pregnant patient and whether there had been a panel. Terry looked up the patient's file; no med panel was held. The patient was discharged shortly after the hearing. Terry speculated the patient decided to take the meds, improved some, and was deemed sufficiently under control. That would be good news.

If it were true.

ABBY

Janell was a pro and lucky as well. She had an uneventful pregnancy and suggested Ted and Raoul come to New Hampshire a week before the due date, in case the baby arrived a little earlier than expected. They bought their tickets and gave me the assignment of retrieving them from the airport on their return, car seat in place.

Two days later, as I was fixing dinner, the phone rang. At first, I thought it was a crank call but soon recognized Ted's voice between the chokes and gasps.

"Abby, you won't believe it. It was incredible. She slipped out, so tiny and beautiful . . ." I grasped the receiver, afraid Ted's heaves would vibrate it from my hand.

"Where's Raoul?" I asked.

"Still with Janell in recovery. We'll probably stay about three or four more days or until the pediatrician says we can take her home."

"Well, congratulations, Dad!" I said. "I'd love to see a baby being born. With Jordan, I was too busy participating to see much."

"Believe me, it was life-changing. I never felt this way before." His sniffling resumed.

"Her name? Can you reveal it, or do we still have to wait?"

"No, we're good. Raoul gave his permission. Her name is Tatiana Elise Fischer-Lin."

"Beautiful. More details, please." I wanted it all.

"She is seven pounds, five ounces, and twenty inches long."

"And exquisite," I said.

"Abby, you can't imagine."

Knowing Raoul and Janell, I easily could.

At the designated time, I pulled up to the arrival deck at the airport. After 9/11, only ticketed travelers could go to the gate, so I was limited to the limousine line. I searched the airport doors for their arrival; so far, no two men and a baby. I didn't have to wait long. The automatic doors closest to me soon parted and they exited, laden with the accouterments of their new life. Ted struggled, wheeling a bulky suitcase, and Raoul clung to a baby carrier.

I stepped from the car and waved. They found me and loaded Tatiana into her new car seat. The baby was as beautiful as I expected. Tiny and delicate, with a café au lait complexion and tufts of straight, dark hair. Her newborn eyes were blue, and since both of her genetic donors had blue eyes, I suspected they would stay that way.

Ted and Raoul recently moved to their new home. Ted directed me to Warrenton Road, where I pulled into the driveway of a sprawling brick manse. Raoul unloaded Tatiana and the car seat (to be placed in Ted's new Porsche SUV) and gave me a brief tour.

Tatiana would be sleeping in a gingham-skirted bassinet beside their bed for the first few weeks before moving into her carefully curated nursery. The room was House Beautiful worthy with its bleached pine crib, dresser, changing table, glider, and hand-crafted Beatrix Potter mobile that played "Peter Cottontail."

"What can I bring? What do you need?" I asked.

"We have everything covered," Raoul assured me. "Just be her best auntie."

"That is a given." I flushed with self-conscious envy.

I offered to pick up dinner, but Ted said they would order in. He and Raoul arranged for a baby nurse to come for the rest of the week to help them set up a routine and assist at night. Of course, they had—they always thought of everything.

I couldn't wait to tell David all about Tatiana. Maybe I would leave out the part about the pangs of baby lust drumming me when I saw her since I wasn't sure how David felt about adding to our family right now. But Jordan was almost three, and if we were going to try . . .

ABBY

Work hobbled along with a mix of chronic and acute patients. Once in a while, I secured a patient's release, but more often my representation consisted of trying to counsel a client to cooperate with treatment in hope of eventual discharge.

The saddest cases were those of abused children, like Trevor, whose stress exploded into full-blown mental illness. Unwanted by their families and society, they floated between residential placements and social service institutions. God only knew what their lives would be like as adults.

It wasn't all depressing; sometimes moments of humor crept in. One client, dressed to the nines in a flowing gown and costume jewels, proclaimed she was "stable as a horse." If only. All of the professionals indulged in some comic noir. You couldn't survive the sadness otherwise.

It wasn't just the patients who raised the absurdity quotient. One morning on the way to work, I stopped for a red light on Route 26, only yards past the Baltimore County line. The light must have turned green while I was deep in thought, but it couldn't have been that long. The jerk in back of me sat on his horn.

It was still early in the morning and it blared. My head threatened to explode.

I almost gave him a one-finger salute but thought better of it. I was an officer of the court now, wasn't I? I should exhibit better behavior. At least in public.

But that wasn't the end of it. As soon as my foot hit the gas, he passed me on the right, squealing on the shoulder. He barely missed a sideswipe and sprayed my new car with mud. Before he sped away, I was able to fix my sights on the red sports car, so low-slung it skirted the road. And it bore a most memorable license plate, which I easily caught. GOD. Not a Maryland plate, but with only three letters, those three letters, it was a cinch to recall.

Who would do that? I soon found out. Not long before, Summervale assigned designated parking spaces for staff and regular visitors, such as the assistant public defenders. I had space number 72, not far from the not-so-nice Nice Pavilion. The big shots parked at the Warfield Administration Building (yes, I know—Jack's grandfather had been governor of Maryland way back when). It was there I spotted the car. It was unmistakable.

I didn't want to be obvious, but my curiosity consumed me. I tried to drive by nonchalantly, just passing through. Damn! It was the director's spot. So Dr. George Gorgeous Clooney Nerovitch was the dick on the road. And I thought doctors thinking they were God was a sloppy and unfair cliché. Not this time. Damn! God at Summervale? More like Lucifer. And everyone made him sound so good. No wonder Gene called Summervale the Shrine of Perpetual Disappointment.

Then there was the screamer. Never absurd, but emblematic of Summervale. He was a chronic patient who had been there for decades. The poor man was older than most of the Summervale staff and had been confined before many of them were born. Daily, he would abruptly start to scream, unprovoked. It became so routine that no one responded anymore. I once had him as a client for recertification. He lay in his bed, unresponsive, and the judge presumed the man waived his appearance at the hearing. I concurred. As the judge, the hospital representative, and I left the room, the man's scream penetrated the hospital's foul air. Other than the three of us, no one seemed to notice or respond. The Summervale symphony—the sad soundtrack of shattered souls.

ABBY

My hardest task was to leave the burden at the hospital door. The drive home from Summervale or any other hospital had to be cleansing to shift from work mode to home. It was a persistent struggle, and some days it was impossible.

I sought the brightest light for the cure. Seeing Jordan's smile as I returned home evaporated my concerns of the day. He was growing and learning so quickly it challenged my conception of time and amplified my desire to slow it down.

By Jordan's third birthday he could read some simple words, and David taught him a few rudimentary math concepts. Jordan chattered constantly about everything: his day, our aging pets, Bongo the cat and Ridgely the dog, and the chickens Pete was raising for eggs at The Gleanings. Jordan was ready for preschool, and we had to start thinking about plans for the fall.

We visited Ted and Raoul several times over the winter but Jordan mostly kept his distance from the baby. By spring, Jordan shed his hesitation and actively sought to play with her. He sat with the baby on the floor and handed her toys and books, which she accepted with glee. He called her Tati and soon everyone followed.

David, with Ted's help, assembled a playset behind our house. Surprise, surprise—Jordan loved it. Whenever Jordan saw Ted or Raoul drive up, he would race to the door asking, "Where's Tati?" He understood Ted was Tati's Daddy and Raoul was her Baba, and we were all interconnected. Jordan's affection for Tati fed my desire to give him a sibling to love as well.

ABBY

How should I broach the subject with David? I alluded to it once in a while, but the conversation never developed. Was it deliberate or incidental? I couldn't tell. It weighed on my mind and I watched for an opportune time to raise it.

One evening after putting Jordan to bed, I decided to gingerly approach the topic. David was sitting on the couch reading, as he often did in the evening. I recently noticed he was taking his glasses off to read and asked him about it.

He shrugged. "I guess I need a new prescription."

"Bifocals?" I asked.

David narrowed his eyes and nodded. "Probably. Don't laugh."

"I'm not laughing. I'm sure I'm not far behind."

"Not you."

"I found a gray hair the other day!"

"Not a chance," he said, with a soft smile. "My love, may you stay forever young."

That was sweet. Recently, he had taken to calling me affectionate names.

"Okay, Bob Dylan," I teased. "Nice try."

This was a good moment.

I sat beside him and he shifted to face me. I rubbed my finger over his sleeve. "How about trying for another baby? I think Jordan would love a sibling and I'm ready, too."

David's smile melted and his eyes dimmed to steel. He replaced his glasses, squinted, then stared downward at his hands.

"No."

Audible anguish surged from his gorge and he spat it out like a burning chunk of coal.

Wham.

I did not expect that. I could not have been more stunned if he smacked me in the face. It must have shown.

David pressed his lips together and closed his eyes as if he had anticipated this conversation and was reaching to remember the words he prepared.

"Abby, the older we are, the greater the risk of having a disabled child."

"But last time, we agreed it wouldn't matter."

"You were already pregnant then," David reminded me, which was true.

"But even so, we said we could handle it."

David held up his hand to signal he had more to say and would prefer I not interrupt. His shoulders slumped and it took more than a minute for him to resume.

"After Maggie was born, my parents spent the rest of their lives worried who would care for her after they were gone. When that happened, it fell to me. I became her parent. I would have left school to do it, but before my mother died, she made me promise to go back. I kept my promise, and I'm glad I did, but the responsibility was always there. I made sure Maggie was in a safe place and I like to think she thrived. I loved her. Everyone did. If Maggie lived, I would happily be doing it still. But I don't want that for Jordan."

A wash of shame showered me. "I never thought about that."

"I understand," David said. "It wasn't your experience; it was mine."

I stared at him as warm rivulets snaked down my cheeks.

David took my hand. "Please know, I am not complaining. It was my obligation and I chose to fulfill it. And we had good times. I came down, and when she was well, I would take Maggie to the zoo, the aquarium, movies, parks, or wherever she wanted to go. I tried to do everything she loved."

"Like going to Baugher's," I interrupted, and he smiled, remembering her favorite place.

"Yes, Baugher's. But for ten years, between her medical care and my monthly visits, I clocked a lot of time on the road. My lifestyle accommodated it. So absolutely, no complaints or regrets. But it is not a responsibility I want to pass on to Jordan. Knowing the price . . ."

"I'm so sorry," I said. "It never occurred to me. I get it now."

David wiped away my tears. "Maybe if we were younger, I would feel differently. But not now. We have a perfect family and I could not be more satisfied. Let's not push our luck."

That would have to be enough. David held me, and after a few minutes, he resumed reading and I went to bed.

DAVID

That was the conversation David hoped to avoid. Abby barely looked at him before turning in. His left hand shook, and he poured two fingers of Jameson into a glass. The golden balm warmed his throat and made him numb enough. It had been a long time since he needed one. Don't make it a habit again, he warned himself. Tonight, though, it might help.

Maybe grading a few papers would refocus his mind. No such luck. He tossed the files back into his briefcase and crept down the hall to the bedroom.

Abby was curled on her side, as usual. He lay beside her, flat on his back. Fear and regret blocked his sleep. After about an hour, he traipsed to the study with a book. Maybe that would do the trick. It didn't work, either. He resisted the pull of another drink and sat staring at the wall.

He had noticed Abby with Tati and expected the idea of another child would surface. He thought he planned a considerate response but when the time came, he failed.

Did it sound like he resented having responsibility for Maggie? That was not what he intended but feared that was how it came out. Unless he really did, hidden behind his willing façade. That caused him even more shame.

He hated saying no to Abby, especially when she wanted something so much. He saw her point about having a sibling for Jordan. She had been an only child. He loved Maggie and was grateful for her devotion to him. But he and Abby were older now like his parents had been. He did not want to take the risk. He couldn't.

He remembered his years in Boston when he tried to fill his time with non-stop work. Relationships went nowhere. It would be wrong to blame that on anyone but himself. For so long, he carried an emptiness he could not shake. Too many nights like this, until Abby came along. He wanted Jordan to have a full life, with infinite choices and no obligations. Was that wrong?

How did one know what was right or wrong in this world? He always strove to be good—a good son, a good brother, a good student. Was he a good husband and father? He wanted that more than anything, more than money, success, or acclaim. What if he wasn't as good as he thought he was? If only he could live up to his ideal.

If he had failed Maggie, he would have never forgiven himself. He owed it to her and his parents to make her his focus. David comforted himself with the belief that it was right. Now he had a responsibility to Abby and Jordan—his family. He hoped he was doing right by them, too, and in time, Abby would find it in her heart to understand.

ABBY

For the first time in our relationship, David and I barely talked. We passed in the hall, mouthing only the most necessary words, ate meals rushing to return to our respective corners, and slept back to back. Neither of us would look the other in the eye. Not from anger. My inner gnawing was a humiliating, regretful shame, like wanting to hide from an unforced error. I suspected he felt the same; his actions mirrored mine.

I pummeled myself. How could I have been so dense? I admit I'm low on empathy, but this was a misread like no other. His halting speech and flickering eyelids haunted me. Besides not being able to face him, I couldn't even look in a mirror, afraid my shallowness would render me invisible. I desperately needed a path to repair the rift but was immobilized.

It couldn't go on, and I didn't know how to fix it. Words, even those I could conjure, were insufficient. Neither of us could bear living this way. I was as desperate to help David as I was to help myself.

To his credit, as a far more evolved person than I, David found a way. One Saturday morning as I cleaned up after breakfast, David sauntered into the kitchen with Jordan on his shoulders.

"Let's go down to the pond." He crooked his finger toward me as Jordan swung his leg, barely missing David's first rib.

"Come on, Mommy. Maybe we'll see a fish."

I was cornered. He knew I couldn't turn Jordan down. "Okay, give me five minutes."

The warming breeze brushed my face as soon as I opened the door. Lilacs bordering the patio bloomed, and their perfume suffused the air. I inhaled to magnify the pleasure of their scent. Every tree bore leaves; winter fully left behind. Good riddance. Lacy green fans sprouted from renewed branches and fluttered up and down. If April is the cruelest month, May must be the most kind.

Ahead of me, Jordan's chunky thighs clung to David's shoulders and his little tush bounced in rhythm to David's steps. Long steps. I sped to keep up.

At the pond, David eased Jordan down. Upon release, Jordan ran to me and grabbed my hand. "Dad said to find rocks."

Jordan filled his pockets with them. I snatched a handful from the ground and scraped off the dirt. We met David at the water's edge. He raised his arm and released a rock that almost hit the center of the pond.

"Look, Jordan." David pointed to the pattern forming on the surface. "See the ripples?"

"They're like circles." Jordan, on his toes, stretched his neck to see the spreading diameter.

"That's right." David tossed another one.

Jordan followed the path of the second stone. "Another circle!"

David tapped Jordan. "Buddy, you're next."

Jordan dug in his pockets; small rocks spilled from his hands. He grasped a few and heaved them into the pond. Tiny rings formed, intersecting and radiating to the edge.

Jordan bounced with glee. "I did it! Mommy, your turn."

I flung one. It hit the water between their tries.

"Now let's all do it at once," David said. "Ready?"

We wound up our pitching arms and, on David's call, hurled our collections into the pond. Circle upon circle formed, from the center to the shore.

"See how the circles touch each other?" David asked. Jordan nodded, his eyes following the expanding rings.

"They're like a family. All in together. On different paths, but connecting." David cleared his throat.

Jordan was too busy digging for more rocks to reflect on the message. Not sure it was for him.

"And they all end up in the same place, on the bottom?" Cynical me.

David shifted a side-eye. "What counts is that it's the same place, together."

"Our little pond? Did I get the right metaphor?"

"Exactly." David reached for Jordan's hand and placed his other arm around my waist. "Our little pond."

He turned his head in my direction. "Forgive me?"

"Forgive you? Nothing to forgive. Forgive me?"

"Nothing to forgive."

"Dad, lift me up!" Jordan raised his arms to David, stretching for a boost.

David mounted him above his head and pivoted towards home. I jogged ahead of them, then spun around. Jordan's muddy sneakers stained David's shirt and bounced off his chest. Mini-thuds. Where had I heard them before? Like father, like son; solid as rock.

ABBY

After that clever bit of reconciliation, life was full enough to provide diversion, and my pain dissipated over time. David and I remained busy throughout the summer. He made an occasional work trip to Washington and often suggested we take Jordan. He was entering a dinosaur phase, and the Museum of Natural History on the mall beckoned.

One Sunday in August, we rode the MARC train to Union Station and took the Metro to the mall. It was wilt weather. David patted his brow with a handkerchief every few minutes. Spreading pockets of sweat accreted under my arms. Even Jordan's steps stalled. Escaping the outdoors, we ducked into several museums, always hitting the water fountain first.

The guys' clear favorite was Natural History. Jordan's eyes nearly popped from his head when he saw the huge elephant in the rotunda, and he could have stared at the dinosaur bones for hours. My choice was the National Gallery, so we made our way over after sharing ice cream bars from a cart.

As we approached the entrance, I thought I recognized Michael Soresman. I took a chance and called out his name. I was right. Michael turned around and returned my greeting with a wave. He walked over, hand in hand with a taller blond man, whom he introduced as his partner, Joel Silverstein. We spoke for a while and since it was so scorching, David suggested we move to a cooler spot, like the gallery cafeteria. Starting to sweat again, I led the way.

The air conditioning revived us and though we just snacked, fresh squeezed lemonade hit the spot.

Michael chewed the ice in his cup. "Damn, it must be a hundred degrees."

Joel clipped Michael's shoulder. "This is nothing. I grew up in Florida. At home, this is considered balmy. Even the humidity here is less."

"True," Michael said. "I'll never visit your parents in the summer again."

"Do you live near here?" I asked.

"We have an apartment in Georgetown. We both work in D.C.," Joel said. "Michael's with Justice, and I'm an assistant U.S. Attorney for the District. We've been in our place about three years."

"We love Georgetown," I said. "How's your family?"

I last spoke to Nina a few months before, when she called to tell me that Danny and Li's baby was born. Nina's voice soared on the call. After Caren's two boys, they had a granddaughter, Alicia.

"My folks? Doing well, I'm sure. I think they're in Vancouver with my brother and his family. Did my mother tell you about her new crusade?" Michael asked.

"No, she didn't. What is it?"

Lucky crusaders. Who wouldn't want Nina on their side?

Joel guffawed and Michael smirked. "Marriage equality. You know, same-sex marriage."

"Really?"

"Yup. Massachusetts made it legal in 2004, and now my mom is clamoring for it in New York."

Joel chimed in. "She loves me, but we think she just wants to plan a wedding."

Michael rolled his eyes. "Nina lives for the big occasion, tasteful but abundant. You should have seen my sister's wedding. It was the event of the century. And my brother's—Jewish and Chinese combined. Oh my God. Besides, my mother would give anything to see me married, even to Joel."

"How about your dad?"

"He's cool with it. You know, anything Nina wants. They're a pair."

This I knew.

"My dad comes to D.C. occasionally for business, and I saw him last month. He always has more going on than anyone else I know. He's working on another venture, of course. He's never going to stop."

David slid a smile. Hmm.

We gabbed some more until it was time to catch the train back to Baltimore. I invited Michael and Joel to come to Arcadia to escape the D.C. heat.

Jordan fell asleep on David during the ride back, and David had to carry him to the car. Jordan was getting to be a big boy, and my days of being able to lift him were ebbing. Jordan was plumb worn out from our busy day and so was I.

ABBY

Raoul called for David that week, and I picked up the phone. Maybe he would be interested in our conversation with Michael and Joel.

"Do you know anything about same-sex marriage in Massachusetts? We ran into my cousin in D.C. and he told us about it. Apparently, making it legal in New York is my aunt's latest crusade."

"Yes," Raoul said. "I've read about it and did some research. We discussed it, but if it's not recognized in Maryland, what good is it? We're not moving to Massachusetts."

"When do you think it might be legal here?" I asked.

Raoul snickered. "I don't know. Maybe when pigs fly."

I wasn't sure. Sometimes things change quickly. I hoped so if that was what they wanted.

A few days later, I spoke to Ted. He was jazzed. "Hey, Abby. We haven't gone on vacation yet. Want to rent a house on Cape Cod?"

"You want to go to Massachusetts?" Was this a result of my conversation with Raoul?

"Yeah. We changed our minds. Even if it's not valid in Maryland, why not get married? Someday it might be, and we'll already have a few anniversaries under our belts. Think about it, Abby. We'll all celebrate. It'll be a blast."

It would. And why not? Perfect timing. It might be the perfect tonic for David and me, too.

Ted and I drove in tandem, with frequent stops for the kids. Well, my kid. Tati mostly slept. Raoul secured a four-bedroom house in Chatham. Ted wanted Provincetown, but everything there was booked. Once we arrived, it took us nearly an hour to unload and tote in all of the baby/child paraphernalia—cribs, strollers, toys, and more toys.

A roomy porch with a wide, planked floor girded the oceanfront, gray-shingled house. Each of us took turns on the glider, snoozing or gazing at the view. David's ideal vacation was stretching out on a lounge surrounded by beautiful scenery and reading. He brought a satchel full of books in the car, and I suspected he would read them all.

Jordan gleefully romped in the sand and surf, and Tati, passed among the four adults, cooed and smiled. We gave new meaning to family vacation and for that matter, family. But we were, and for this we were grateful.

By the middle of the week, Raoul and Ted procured a license and found an available justice of the peace. We piled into his chambers and amid papers and ledgers, Ted and Raoul were wed, at least in Massachusetts.

Raoul made dinner reservations at a swanky oceanside boîte. Fresh lobster and scallops for all. And crème brûlée, torched tableside, for dessert. David toasted our celebrants and I raised my flute of champagne, focusing on the man I married twenty years before.

"Ted, my wish for you is that your second courthouse marriage be more enduring than the first."

Ted inched a knowing smile. "It was a practice run for both of us, wasn't it?"

"It was," I replied, and unplanned but in unison, Ted and I blurted, "Practice makes perfect."

Everyone laughed, and our spouses winked at each other and lifted their glasses, joining in the toast.

By the time we left, the light of day was fading, and the outline of a crescent moon hung high in the sky. Full and not a little tipsy, we ambled back to our temporary home. The children bedded, we joked some more, told stories, and quietly continued our celebration.

Before long, we couples, newly and not so newly wed, repaired to our respective rooms. My eyes followed our companions as they entered their suite down the hall. I shut our door and appreciated the oddness of sharing a house with the two men who shared my life. I loved them both still, in very different ways.

David sensed my wistfulness and teased, "Just because it's their wedding night doesn't mean we can't . . ."

"Oh, Professor." I beckoned him from the bed. "You don't know how right you are."

A night breeze from the ocean chilled the room, and I pulled David on top of me, partially for warmth but mainly with desire. I carefully drew him into me, rhythmically lifting my hips to fit his breath. He released and we rolled, still bound, resting on our sides. Face to face, we kissed, our union secured. From the corner of my eye, through the narrow casement, I caught an ambient, peaceful sliver of light.

ABBY

I was not eager to return to work. The unremitting sadness of my clients was getting harder and harder to absorb. I questioned my ability to detach and my skill at providing them with focused representation. The psychology of the patients was fascinating on a clinical level and the work legally challenging, but so many nights I came home spent and unsure.

My spirits brightened after my next trip to Summervale. I was sure I had a winner, one that would make it all, despite the doubt and the heartbreak, worth it.

The day before the hearings, I tried to meet with all the clients I would be representing the following day. At least the ones who could communicate. As I entered the locked ward for my pre-hearing routine, I asked the desk nurse to point out my client. The nurse directed me to a small lounge area, where a young woman sat at a round table reading a book.

I strode in and identified myself as the young woman's assistant public defender. The woman confidently stood as if she were anywhere but a rundown psychiatric ward and smiled broadly.

"Hi, Abby. I'm Agnys DeSilva. Please remember to spell it correctly—Agnys with a y."

"I will, Agnys," I said. "Tell me a little about yourself."

"I'm from Providence, Rhode Island, but my parents came from the Azores. They're islands off the coast of Portugal."

"Really? I lived in Pawtucket. I knew lots of Azoreans. Where did you go to school?"

"Providence Country Day. How about you?"

"Lincoln," I said. "But that was a while ago."

Agnys looked about twenty-five, or even younger. With her dark, penetrating eyes and wavy espresso locks, she resembled my school friends whose parents immigrated from the islands.

"So, Agnys, what brought you to Maryland?"

"I'm an artist and a student at the Maryland Institute. I prefer mixed media, but my major is painting. I've taken a couple of writing courses at Goucher, too."

Goucher was my alma mater; another coincidence. Agnys was chatty and relaxed. Not my typical Summervale client. She laughed easily and spoke more like a friend than a patient. There was a familiarity that struck me. Maybe she reminded me of Miri, too.

"How are you feeling?" I asked. "How did you get here?"

"Other than being pregnant, I'm fine," Agnys said. "But I really need to leave. I'm afraid the meds they want me to take will hurt the baby. So you've got to get me out. I don't want to talk about how I came, if that's all right with you."

I needed to know but didn't want to push. Our conversation had been going so well. Her file should contain enough pertinent information, and I'd look through it as soon as we were done. After another twenty minutes, a nurse came by to tell Agnys it was time for a group session, and she left the room with a wave.

Agnys' presence at Summervale puzzled me. Nothing Agnys said sounded delusional or odd. When I picked up her chart, it was unremarkable as well. The only thing blinking on my radar screen was Agnys' claim that she was pregnant. Agnys did not elaborate on the origin of her pregnancy or her plans. But she was adamant that she should not remain in the hospital and was reluctant to take medication because of the pregnancy.

Something about Agnys' story rang a bell. Then I remembered my conversation with Cindy Fairchild after she covered my docket the year before. One of her clients made a similar claim, and Cindy said pregnancy was not an uncommon delusion. But maybe this time it wasn't a delusion at all. Agnys' chart contained no mention of pregnancy. It was possible she hadn't been tested yet. Summervale wasn't exactly on the cutting edge of up-to-date medical records.

So, I planned a simple defense—there was no credible evidence of a mental illness, dangerousness, or need for institutional care. Unless the hospital could prove Agnys needed commitment by clear and convincing evidence, she had to be released. I went home that night invigorated, certain of my victory the next day.

ABBY

But it was not to be.

After a few recertification cases, an aide brought Agnys to the room. Unlike the day before when she was lively, Agnys dragged her feet and made no eye contact with anyone at the table, including me. When Terry, the hospital presenter, brought the psychiatrist into the room, Agnys gasped, rapidly inhaling and exhaling with a wheeze. Her eyes flashed to the door. Not a good sign.

The hearing began with the judge's introduction. I identified myself and Agnys, indistinct, mumbled her name. Terry called the psychiatrist as her witness. I had heard about this doctor but this was my first encounter. She was one of the newer psychiatrists who came when Dr. Nerovitch took over. Dr. Priscilla Knowles was fit, probably younger than I, with shoulder-length blonde hair. She spoke in a soft, British-accented voice and carefully chose her words. Dr. Knowles alternated between facing Agnys and gazing doe-eyed at the judge when she spoke.

Dr. Knowles leafed through the chart and stopped at several points to read parts of it aloud.

"Ms. DeSilva was found wandering and disheveled on the street in Westminster. She weaved in and out of traffic and shouted at cars and anyone passing by. A concerned bystander called the police, who brought her to a local emergency room where she was certified. When she arrived at Summervale, Ms. DeSilva begged to be released, claiming she was pregnant. After a negative test, she tore up her room and had to be placed in a quiet area with restraints. She refuses to take medication and is completely uncooperative with treatment. Ms. DeSilva has no insight into her mental illness and requires institutional care."

None of this had been included in the file given to me yesterday.

The muted woman who sat beside me was certainly not the Agnys I interviewed the day before. Breathing hard, Agnys rapidly opened and closed her fists as if ready to pounce. The aide who accompanied Agnys to the hearing placed a light hand on Agnys' arm.

Agnys exploded.

She shot up, sobbing, and pointed to Dr. Knowles. "You are a liar! You were there when he did this to me. You lying bitch—I hope you die!"

Agnys raised her hands, grasping at something unseen, and emitted an inchoate yowl. The aide leaped behind her, ready to apply restraints if needed.

No one uttered a sound. Dr. Knowles glared at Agnys and straightened the papers in her file. She clicked the top of her ballpoint pen in tempo, her thumb rhythmically pushing and releasing it like a metronome.

The judge broke the silence. "Ms. Fischer, can you control your client?"

Agnys crumpled in her chair, murmuring. "I am pregnant. You did it. You know you did."

Dr. Knowles resumed her stare, her mouth upturned on one side. That unnerved me as much as Agnys' outburst. My shoulders shook as a chilly spasm jolted my spine.

The judge wisely suggested a break. I followed Agnys and the aide out of the room and into the hallway.

Agnys remained inconsolable and panted between sobs. She spilled to the floor and pounded the cold, hard tiles. I was afraid she would fracture her hands. The aide stood over her, gasping. I guess she didn't expect this either. Usually, I could predict who would fall apart in a hearing, and nothing Agnys said or did the day before remotely suggested this turn of events.

The judge and Terry exited the room, motioned me over, and asked whether Agnys wanted to or would be able to continue in the hearing. I returned to Agnys, who remained sitting on the floor in tears, and asked what she wanted to do.

"I want to go home," Agnys repeated between sobs and gasps.

I was close to breaking down, too. "Agnys," I whispered, "do you want to go back into the hearing?"

Agnys shook her head back and forth. "No, no, no."

I signaled to the judge that I would return in a minute or two as the aide led Agnys away.

When I reentered the hearing room, the judge noted on the record that Agnys chose to leave the hearing and directed us to proceed. The doctor continued her testimony and offered more of the hospital's evidence to prove it had met the criteria for Agnys' involuntary commitment.

I put as much effort as possible into cross-examination, but Agnys' outburst rendered it ineffective. Agnys' absence obliterated any evidence I may have been able to present in her defense. My arguments at the end of the hearing were similarly fruitless. Maybe I could have done a better job, but by the time it came for my closing argument, I had little to say.

The judge's decision was a foregone conclusion. The hospital prevailed, having proven every element of its case by clear and convincing evidence. No surprise.

I sat speechless as the judge handed me the decision to deliver to Agnys. Terry shot me a sympathetic look as she and Dr. Knowles left the hearing room. I searched for Agnys on her unit, and an aide told me she was asleep. I left the decision with the charge nurse and blindly made my way to the parking lot, grateful it was my last case of the day. I was no good to anyone after that.

It was the worst hearing I ever had. It came out of the blue like the wrath of God. And struck me down, slain.

My mind was a cobweb of confusion. I drove home on autopilot, trying to unthink the day. It was so painful, and I wasn't the one who had to stay at Summervale. I could go home to my family and comfortable life. As much as I wanted to believe I was providing my clients a valuable service, I remained shrouded in doubt.

I surely failed Agnys. A better lawyer would have known what to do. I wasn't up to this. Maybe it wasn't for me.

ABBY

I welled with relief to see David's truck when I drove up to the house. I was in no shape to care for Jordan or do much of anything else.

I entered like a zombie. David must have heard me and called, "How was it?"

Last night, I told him about my upbeat meeting with Agnys and how I was sure things would go our way.

"Horrible," I said. "I need a drink."

I slumped, my body desiccated, and David sat me down.

"Where's Jordan?" I asked.

"Puzzle Town." Good—that was his favorite game and could keep him occupied for at least an hour.

"That bad?" I could tell David was deciding how deeply to probe.

"The worst."

I drew my lips together so hard my teeth raked my gums.

"It was as if she were another person." My eyes bore through the floor.

"An evil twin?"

He was trying to lighten things, but his effort fell flat.

Not now, David. Not now.

"I don't know what in the world happened," I mumbled. "Yesterday, Agnys was so rational, so smooth, no indication of mental illness. And today, she completely fell apart. I couldn't believe it. Someone with more experience would have been able to predict her meltdown. She deserved a better lawyer."

"I'm sure you did the best you could." David reached out; I flinched at his touch.

"I feel like a fucking idiot. I should have been more prepared."

"Look, Abby," David said. "Quit beating yourself up about it. Talk to Marta. I'm sure everyone in your office has had this happen at one time or another."

David also suggested a short break from Summervale to a more manageable hospital. That wasn't a terrible idea, but I didn't want to wimp out now. I tried to process the utterly weird feeling I had about this case. Something about it felt off, even more so than usual. An eerie vibe. But I was wounded, and maybe it was my imagination run amok. Surely Marta would offer some wisdom in the morning.

ABBY

Marta's pep talk boosted me. As usual, David was right.

"Abby, every one of us has had clients unexpectedly sabotage their hearings. I'm surprised this was your first patient meltdown. Usually, it happens much sooner. You're lucky it took this long."

I clasped my hands. "I have such a creepy feeling about the whole case—the empty file, the accusations, the disconnect from my meeting with Agnys and her crack-up at the hearing. Something isn't right, I just know it."

Marta shook her head. "You'll have to take it in stride. Summervale is like that. Up and down, and mostly down."

"All right," I said, resigned. Yeah, mostly down.

She closed the file I gave her and switched to a crafty smile.

"This ought to help. I have some juicy gossip. Knowles and Nerovitch are an item. Cindy saw them canoodling at the Prime Rib downtown."

What a picture. Dr. Gorgeous and Dr. Perfect smooching over cocktails and filet mignon. Did she know what an asshole he was?

I couldn't help myself and blurted, "The Barbie and Ken of Summervale."

Marta spurted her tea. "Oh my God. I'll never get that image out of my head."

But that didn't help Agnys. Independent of Dr. Knowles' dating status, I hoped the psychiatrist had the skill to properly treat her. It was obvious that Agnys was bright and engaging. It would be tragic if something could not be done to preserve those traits and enable her to function in the world.

At my next docket at Summervale, I discovered Agnys had been discharged with no forwarding address or contact information. I was probably too personally invested but desperately wanted Agnys to be the one patient who never returned.

.

ABBY

Ted and Raoul usually came to us for Thanksgiving, but this year they wanted to host dinner at their house. Tati was toddling everywhere, and it would be easier to keep her occupied at home. Perfectly fine with me. It was a good year for a break.

I asked them for assignments, and so far, the list included bread, salads, and a dessert. Ted and Raoul would supply the wine—much appreciated since their taste and budget far exceeded mine.

Jordan bounced up and down in his car seat the entire trip. He clutched the bag of books he brought to read to Tati, who recently turned two. In the blink of an eye, Tati budded from a baby to a little girl. She met us at the door in a cerise chintz dress with a matching headband, patent leather Mary Janes, lace-trimmed tights, and a giggly smile.

Before dinner, we sat in the family room in front of a massive stone fireplace, one of three in the elegant home. We were sipping drinks when Ted asked, "Guess who called?"

I couldn't imagine. "You know I hate to guess."

"Go ahead," he said.

"Your mother?"

Ted snorted. "No way. It was Janell."

"Really? What did she want?"

She couldn't want Tati back, could she?

I didn't have to say anything. Ted could still read my mind.

"Not what you're thinking, Abby. She's ready for another one."

Raoul heard us from the next room and shouted, "She said we were her favorites and made the most beautiful baby. She's giving us the right of first refusal."

I was incredulous. "Is that what she said?"

Ted nodded. "Verbatim."

"Well?" I asked.

Raoul entered the room, looked at Tati, and shook his head.

I looked up at him from the couch. "Not ready for another?"

Oh no—what made me say that?

"Not yet," said Ted. "How about you?"

I froze and stammered, "No, not…"

I asked for it, and it hurt. I thought I had gotten over it. Obviously not.

Raoul quickly changed the subject to something inconsequential. Thank God. David offered to gather the kids for dinner.

Filling up on brioche, turkey, scalloped potatoes, squash soufflé, seared green beans, and chocolate pumpkin ganache distracted me and the two glasses of Riesling didn't hurt. I even let David drive home. He put Jordan to bed, too. I lingered in the car a few minutes, then walked down the drive and back a few times until my fingers turned blue. As soon as my head hit the pillow, I willed myself to sleep.

ABBY

The week after Thanksgiving, things began to go even further south. Ridgely and Bongo, our dog and cat, had been with us since we moved to the farm. Ridgely used to belong to Sam Scarborough, a lawyer I worked with when I searched titles. When Sam retired and moved to Florida, Ridgely became ours. I'm not much of a dog person, but David grew up with animals and was happy to gain a canine friend.

My former roommate, Mo Fox, adopted Bongo as a kitten. I inherited Bongo after Mo had a breakdown and left to live in Pennsylvania. Although Bongo had strictly been a house cat, when we moved to the farm he thrived outdoors.

Jordan loved the dog and cat, particularly Ridgely. The Golden Retriever let Jordan climb him, roll over him, and generally treat him as a pillow or a lounge. Bongo was more aloof, but still had a thing for David and followed him everywhere. Neither animal was young when we acquired them and by now, both were at least thirteen years old. Maybe older.

Each had slowed down considerably. Ridgely walked stiffly and Bongo couldn't jump the way he used to. Neither of them ate as much or gobbled their food as before. They were aging, and we knew what would inevitably be in store.

One night, Ridgely had a seizure in the living room after we put Jordan to bed. It was frightful. The poor dog shook and writhed, with labored breath. David was particularly distressed. Ridgely was his driving buddy. Every time David set out for his truck, Ridgely was at his heels, begging for a ride. David had been around animals enough, though, to know when it was time to let go.

Ridgely recovered sufficiently to hobble and sleep in his doggy bed. The next morning, David carried him to the truck to see the vet. When they returned, David's heavy steps betrayed his heavy heart.

David carried Ridgely in and laid him on an old remnant of a shag rug I placed on the floor. Ridgely sank into the soft pile, oblivious to his surroundings. David shook his head. There was nothing more to do.

"What did the vet say?" I asked. Part of me wondered why David brought him home; another was glad he did.

"Heart failure. He's not going to make it. I asked whether it would be harmful to bring him home one last night, so Jordan could say goodbye. What a nice man. He said it might ease everyone's pain, including Ridgely's, to give him a final farewell. I'll take him back in the morning."

"I'll go with you. You shouldn't have to do it alone."

"Thanks." David slumped onto the corduroy pad on the kitchen chair and placed his chin in his hands, more hangdog than the dog. "You know, we went through this many times growing up, but it's never easy. We'll have to decide how to tell Jordan."

"Sorry, but this is totally out of my repertoire. Can you do it?"

David drew his mouth tight. "Sure."

We slogged over to the garage, both of us focused on the ground. David found a wooden box he saved from a delivery of some machinery and carried it out to the truck. He thought Ridgely would fit.

That night, we surrounded Ridgely where he lay on the shaggy mat. Jordan perched on David's broad lap. David secured him by the waist as Jordan stretched to pet Ridgely's silky coat.

"Ridgely's very sick," David said, "and he's not going to be living with us anymore." Tears formed in Jordan's blue eyes. "Tell him how much we love him, Buddy."

Jordan bent over and whispered into Ridgely's floppy ear. David held his hand as they stroked the sleeping dog's side. I found explaining death to a four-year-old unbearably difficult. David, whose father probably had the same talk with him at that age, was better equipped. I didn't envy the task and admired him as he delivered the sad news.

The next morning after I dropped Jordan at preschool, David and I wrapped Ridgely in a large towel, placed him in the truck, and grimly drove to the vet. In the examining room, David lifted the barely conscious dog onto the table. We stood together stroking Ridgely's soft fur as the vet administered the lethal dose.

The vet let us spend a few minutes alone with Ridgely. We held each other and kept our free hands on Ridgely's stilled flank. I never thought I would weep for a dog, but I did. David brushed the single tear trickling down his cheek. An aide entered and offered to help David return Ridgely to the truck. David smoothed Ridgely's ruff and enveloped him in the towel. I followed behind as he and the aide carried our beloved pet and carefully hoisted him into the wooden box. We drove silently home.

DAVID

While Abby picked up Jordan, David dug a grave for Ridgely in the far corner of the yard facing The Gleanings. He strained as he shoveled mound after mound of dirt to accommodate the coffin. The ground was not yet winter-hard but was firmly packed and dotted with rocks. It was a harder task than he expected. His back would not soon forget.

Abby promised that on the way home with Jordan she would explain, as best she could, what would happen next. He gave her some suggestions on how to break the news. When they arrived, he watched Abby take Jordan's hand and lead him to the gravesite. David had already, with a struggle, lowered the wooden box into the grave.

He knelt to face Jordan. "Buddy, we all loved Ridgely. And now, he will always be with us at our home." He regretted the stance when he felt a sharp snap at his knee, but not his words.

He took a few extra seconds to stand, then faced the grave. "Ridgely was an important part of our family. He was a friendly dog and a loyal companion. I'll miss him and our rides together."

He flexed his palm to Abby as a sign to continue. Abby gave him her quirked-mouth, eyebrow-raised look. "Hmm . . . I haven't prepared a full-blown eulogy. Let me think. Okay, I knew Ridgely for a long time, before we became a family. He was very helpful in the Court House when my friend Sam brought him to work."

He turned to Jordan and cupped his shoulder. "Now it's your turn. Tell us, Buddy, what did you love about Ridgely?"

Jordan sniffled and, after a quiet cough, said, "He was a good dog. He was always happy to see me when I came home from school."

Abby looked away from them as if afraid she would start to weep again. David kept it together, barely. He had not anticipated such an emotional reaction. He didn't remember his father getting all torn up over a dog.

He announced that in the spring they would plant a tree nearby to mark Ridgely's grave. It would be Ridgely's tree and, year by year, Jordan could watch it grow. Abby asked whether it would be a dogwood. Was she serious? Sometimes he couldn't tell.

He began filling in the grave and handed Jordan a small shovel he brought down from the garage. He guided Jordan as the boy thrust the shovel into the mound of dirt and tossed the contents into the grave. After Jordan filled a few shovelfuls, Abby led him to the house as David completed the job. His arms ached as much as his heart.

After Jordan went to bed, Abby patted David on the back. "Good job, Professor. Well done. I'm grateful for what you said. You know, you're a born teacher, and you teach by example. I would have never thought to eulogize a dog or encourage Jordan to help bury him. You showed him what to do for a pet out of loyalty and love. Your father must have taught you this, and now you're passing it down to our son."

He did not expect accolades but did not contradict her. Reflecting, he visualized his father performing the same ritual when David was a boy. Perceptive of her to point it out. She also said it meant more to her than Mark's funeral, but he didn't believe that.

That night, Bongo wandered around the house, adrift, as if he were looking for Ridgely. He uttered plaintive meows and searched in corners and empty spots. In another two weeks, he would be gone, too. He wandered off, and no one could find him. Abby put out Bongo's favorite food, and David searched everywhere he could imagine. He remembered, though, it was not uncommon for cats to leave their homes to die alone. Abby said she thought Bongo may have suffered a broken heart.

To soften Jordan's doubled sadness, he promised when they planted Ridgely's tree, they would also plant one for Bongo. Jordan would come with them to the nursery and help pick them out. Abby suggested they could get a kitten then, too. Jordan's eyes brightened. He'd be fine.

ABBY

I had to tell Mo about Bongo. He'd been in my charge ever since she did her balancing act on the balcony of our condo before I met David. So, he'd been mine for a long time. But I still thought of him as my former roommate's cat, since she had been the one to adopt and name him. She deserved to know.

Mo and I didn't see each other often, but once in a while we met halfway for lunch, usually around the Lancaster area. She lived in the Philadelphia suburbs and I was in Arcadia, so that seemed a fair compromise. Mo loved Amish food and usually chose Yoder's, where she raved about the chicken pot pie and apple schnecken. I mostly stuck with some cabbage salad. Although I live on a farm, I'm not much for country fare.

I wanted to believe Mo was happy now. A few years before, she married husband number four, the veterinarian dreamboat she brought to our wedding. So far, only good news from Mo. She was surrounded by small animals and her adoring vet. Even though the news about Bongo might sadden her, she would want me to call.

"Hi Mo, it's Abby."

"Hey girl, what's up?"

"Sorry to tell you, it's about Bongo. We had to put Ridgely down, and soon afterward, Bongo disappeared. We think he missed him so much that he couldn't bear to live without him."

"Oh, I'm sorry. He was a sweet boy. Animals do that sometimes. They have deep emotions, just like us."

I didn't necessarily buy that, but Mo styled herself as a pet therapist, so maybe she knew better than I.

"Well," I said, "I thought you would want to know."

"Thanks, Abby. We'll meet him again on the other side of the Rainbow Bridge."

"Where?" I had no idea what she was talking about.

"You know, Abby. Across the Rainbow Bridge. Pet heaven."

Uhh, no. I didn't know.

"Sorry, Mo," I said. "I'm not familiar with that location."

"It's a beautiful place. It has meadows and hills and room for all pets to run free. They're happy there, with all of their companions. I know I'll see him there someday."

"Okay, Mo. I hope it's not too soon."

Mo chuckled. "No, I have lots of pets to go until then. Hey, Abby. One of my tabbies just had a litter. Want one?"

"Thanks, but no. I don't think we're ready yet. Maybe in a few months."

"Okay," Mo said. "Anytime. There's always a new litter around here."

"How many cats do you have now?" I was almost afraid to ask.

"Right now, thirty. Twelve are mine, ten are adult rescues, and eight are kittens. Our place is huge. Plenty of room for them. I'm thinking of calling it Maison Meow. What do you think?"

"Hmm," I said. "French—sounds classy."

"I thought so. If you know anyone who wants a cat, this is the place. I can send you pictures."

"Why don't you do that? That'd be great. Jordan will like them."

"Sure. Sorry about Bongo, though. But let me know when you're ready for another. We always have more. Hell, we're practically overrun. Hey, did you tell Sam about Ridgely?"

"I tried calling him, but the number I had must have been wrong. Do you have one?"

"No," said Mo, who at one point had been Sam's daughter-in-law. "I heard he got married to a filthy rich widow. They're living on some luxury island off the coast of Florida."

"Not bad." I always thought Sam Scarborough was ruggedly handsome, but not the gigolo type. Maybe it was true love.

"Not bad at all. But we're all doing pretty well, aren't we, Abby?"

"Yeah, Mo. We are."

"Let's meet in a few weeks," Mo said. "Yoder's?"

"You bet. See you soon."

Rainbow Bridge. Only Mo could make me smile about stuff like that. I'd have to remember; it softened the loss.

ABBY

"It's too quiet," David said when he walked in. He missed Ridgely's eager greeting. Even as the dog grew older, David's entry never failed to rouse him to the door. Bongo would meow as soon as he heard David turn the key.

It didn't stay silent long. Jordan ran in, clomping like his father. "Dad!"

David lifted him and smiled. "That's better."

Released, Jordan rushed back to his room to resume whatever he was doing before.

"I told Mo about Bongo," I said. "Did you ever hear of the Rainbow Bridge?"

"Isn't it near Niagara Falls?"

"No. Mo mentioned it. It's where animals go when they die."

"To Canada?" David had no clue. Of course, neither had I.

I laughed and offered Mo's explanation. "Stop being so literal. It's not a real place. It's like pet Valhalla."

"Not in my cosmology, Abby. Never heard of it."

"Do you think animals have any concept of life and death?"

"I don't think most people understand it, let alone animals. I, for one, don't. Speculating about the meaning of life is generally not in my wheelhouse."

"Right," I said. "You're a numbers guy."

"I am. But numbers can have a spiritual quality. I'm just not the one to ask about it."

"Okay, Professor." I nodded. "That's enough philosophy for today."

ABBY

For someone who grew up in New England and should have been used to it, I loathed winter. Dark when I woke, dark going home, dark unremitting. And snow. Maybe it was lovely for about a minute, then the rotten concoction was only cold and wet.
    I hated everything about it. Walking in it, driving in it, shoveling it, and after the first flakes, looking at it. Evil squeezed into one hard icy ball. I had ursine envy. If only I could hibernate and wake in the spring.
    Of course, Jordan loved it and only wanted to make snowmen, snow angels, and watery ice cream from the white terror that covered the earth. David reveled in winter's frozen glory. "It's invigorating!" he exclaimed. "How can you not like this?"
    "Easily," I said, my fingers, toes, and nose numb simply from trekking from the car to the house. The pièce de rèsistance was when I slipped on the front step and landed on my ass, braced by my wrist. At first, I feared I broke it (my wrist, not my ass), but it was merely sprained, which entailed wearing a brace for a month. Better than a cast, I suppose. That finished any lingering tolerance of winter I might have had. My bones were small to start; all I needed was for them to shatter. I told David if he laughed at me when I walked

on ice as if I were a hundred years old, I would stab him in his sleep.

David glanced at my narrow, still-bruised wrist. "Abby, you know I would never do that."

"You'd better not," I warned. "Because I will."

Winter put me in that kind of mood. Homicidal.

ABBY

Weeks went by without sun. The two-shade sky hung flat over the valley, day and night, gray or black. The evil snow turned to dirty slush that refroze each night and never melted. Every so often, we lost electricity during an ice storm. We huddled under layers of down and brought Jordan into our bed to keep him warm.

While I shivered in misery, David thrived. In that way, we were so different. For me, it was sheer torture; for him, it was the expectation.

David sustained his spirit with seed catalogs, planning gardens for the spring. Last year's crop was a bounty. He grew three varieties of tomatoes, huge cucumbers, far too much squash, green beans, red and golden beets, and purple cabbage. Roses, hydrangea, and lilacs surrounded our house, and, for the first time, David's cherry trees bore fruit. We savored the sweet-tart crimson flesh when we could keep the birds from eating it first.

David was a natural farmer. His thumbs, plus his hands and wrists to his elbows, were green. Meticulous in most things, David was even more particular in the garden. He calculated the precise amount of water, plant food, and fertilizer and made sure everything that could be fenced and protected from wildlife was secure. His talent was in stark contrast to my horticultural deficits. Where David could create the Garden of Eden, my landscape would have resembled the apocalypse. There was no plant I couldn't kill. I was relieved to absent myself from this enterprise and leave the cultivation to him.

Jordan inherited every bit of his father's love of soil. Last year, as a gag, I bought David a straw farmer's hat. He loved it. Jordan insisted on getting one, too. Watching them squatting together, planting and weeding, David guiding Jordan's chubby fingers in the dirt, was almost more than I could bear, and it welled me with love.

From my perch by the fireplace, I spied David marking catalog pages, deciding what he and Jordan would be planting in a few short months. His anticipation was the only sight that could lift my spirits, even on the darkest days. We would survive the winter, wagering on the hope of spring.

ABBY

The world began to brighten a few weeks after Jordan's fifth birthday. Crocus buds rose from the expectant earth, and daylight lingered longer each day. My winter funk abated. Work had been stagnant and monotonous but not intolerable. Jordan surprised me daily with his curiosity and agile mind. When I looked at him, I could see David as a child. They were so much alike.

One evening, shortly after putting Jordan to bed, the phone rang.

"Abby?" It was a tentative, soft inquiry.

"Yes," I answered.

I didn't recognize the voice. Who could it be?

"Abby, it's Agnys. Remember me?"

Remember her? How could I forget? My stomach sank. If it weren't for my other organs blocking the way, it would have hit the ground, splashing its contents over my toes.

My brain flashed "be wary" like a Broadway marquee. Only seconds to decide. The devil on one shoulder shouted, "Hang up now." The angel balanced on the other prodded my conscience and I succumbed.

"Are you okay?"

"Yes and no," she said. "I need you to come get me."

"How did you get my number?"

"I called the one on the card you gave me."

My public defender card? It certainly did not include my home phone; I never gave that number out.

"Not your lawyer card, the other one."

Oh, right. The first time we met, I didn't have any public defender business cards on hand, so I gave Agnys an old card from The Gleanings I still had in my wallet. But that didn't show my home number either.

"How again?"

"I told him I was your cousin, and he gave me the number this afternoon."

Who—Pete? Clever girl.

"Where are you?"

"In a phone booth outside of a 7-11 in Westminster. On Route 140."

"Where are you going?" I hoped for a coherent answer.

"I'm not sure, but I need help." Agnys sounded rational, but she had before, too.

Are you in trouble?" I asked.

"Maybe..."

I closed my eyes, held my breath, and made up my mind.

"I'll be there in twenty minutes. Go inside and stay in the restroom. I'll find you."

This plan was the safest move. I didn't want Agnys out on the street if something went wrong.

I grabbed my jacket, purse, and keys. My hand shaking, I dropped my keys on the floor and stooped to pick them up.

David stepped from the kitchen, his eyebrows knitted with curiosity. "Where are you going?"

I debated how much to tell him. I knew he would worry, so I was judicious with the facts.

As I buttoned up, I breezed, "A client."

His mouth tensed. "What's going on?"

"It's Agnys, remember her?"

David closed an eye in thought. "The sad one?"

I quirked my brow. "David, they're all sad."

"The meltdown?"

He remembered.

David's pursed lips confirmed his memory of that disastrous day. "Are you sure it's safe?"

"Yes." I tried assuring him, though I had my doubts, too. "She sounded lucid and I'm going to a public place."

"Where?"

"The 7-11 on 140. It won't take me long to get there."

"Where are you going to take her?"

"I don't know." I had to be honest here.

"Be careful, sweetheart," he cautioned, worry written all over his face.

"I will," I promised, with as much confidence as I could muster.

I sashayed past him, trying to act nonchalant. "I won't be late," I said.

And hoped it would be true.

DAVID

David's gaze followed her as she drove away. He knew Abby was being evasive. Not that he didn't trust her. But she could be impulsive, and it worried him. His heart thumped in his chest; ba bum, ba bum, ba bum, faster than usual.

Of course, had she not been intrepid, they may never have met. That was the upside. But he could find no advantage tonight. It was already dark, she was alone, and he had no idea what she was doing.

He chided himself; he was never like this before. But before, he didn't have anyone to worry about. He shook his head—the yin and yang of family. Maybe putting on some music and trying to read would help. No, not working. Too hard to concentrate. David loped down the hall to check on Jordan, who was fast asleep. Returning to the living room, pacing, he predicted he would be watching at the window until Abby returned.

ABBY

There was little traffic. I turned on the radio and, through some static, heard the Rolling Stones. "You can't always get what you want . . ." It sounded like a message. God speaking to me through Mick Jagger? Maybe I was hearing voices now, too. As I approached my destination, my fingers trembled, and I clutched the wheel for dear life.

    I pulled into the well-lit lot of the 7-11 and parked a couple of spaces from the door. There were some other cars. A two-toned Buick, a large black SUV, and a Toyota or two. Better it wasn't deserted.

    I tried to be blasé. If I bought something first it would look more natural. I picked up a Mars Bar and asked the cashier where I could find the restroom. He pointed to the left back corner.

    No one else was in the aisle. I checked behind me and pushed open the restroom door. One fluorescent light was dim and the other randomly blinked. Of the three stalls, two doors were ajar and the third one, streaked with flaking yellow paint, was bolted shut. I squatted and peeked underneath for feet. Aha! Two small blue sneakers.

    "Agnys?" I stage-whispered.

"Abby . . ." Agnys' voice, strained, was barely audible. "You came."

The door to the stall opened and Agnys emerged, profoundly pregnant. At least seven months. Her midsection grazed the metal edge as she stepped out.

Agnys pointed to her belly. "See Abby, I was right."

"I can see that." Geez, could I ever.

Agnys wore a light windbreaker and balanced a dark green nylon knapsack on her shoulder. I handed her the Mars Bar and led her to the car.

ABBY

"Please don't take me to the hospital," Agnys begged. Her eyes darted from side to side, like a cornered fox in a field.

I wasn't planning to but remained unsure of our destination. As we drove down Route 140, Agnys proceeded to tell me a chilling and terrifying tale. Whether I believed her was another story.

"Back in September, I was having drinks with some friends at the Mount Royal Tavern, near school. Some good-looking guy started a conversation with me about music. He bought me a drink and that's the last thing I remember."

"The next morning I woke up lying on a cot in a bare room. No other furniture in there, except a toilet and a small sink in an alcove. The sheets on the bed had cartoon characters or something on them. My clothes were gone; all I was wearing was this huge men's tee shirt that barely covered my butt and these weird white underpants."

"Then, this girl, who looked like a ghost, came in carrying a tray of food. I asked her where the hell I was but she said nothing. She locked the door from the outside when she left. I screamed my head off, but no one came. I can't even tell you how scared I was."

So far, I'm listening, but it's a little too made-for-TV horror movie for me. Maybe I should take her to the hospital. But she kept going.

"So, I'm in this lame room, with these stupid sheets and this man comes in. He was handsome but icy cold, very distant. Doesn't say a word. He pulls off my flimsy pants and flattens me on the cot. I tried to fight him some, but he pinned me down. Not sure why I remember, but he was wearing a Rolex. Funny, huh? A fancy watch and no underwear under these sweatpants that had the name of some college written down the side of the leg. He did me once, turned me around, and did me again, like a dog. Fast, too. When he pulled out, I blubbered, and he smacked me. He left as fast as he came. I couldn't keep track of the time, but it happened over and over the next few days. Sometimes, other people came into the room and watched. One woman, not the ghost, took notes."

Oh Jesus. My heart sank. I had no response—what could I say? Agnys reached into her knapsack and extracted a manila file. I pulled into a gas station and parked on the far side, underneath a light. The file contained medical information, all relevant to Agnys' pregnancy. Incredible. My mouth scraped the floor. Blood work, test results, and measurements, with photos of Agnys at various points in the process. Astonishing. Believable? Agnys continued her tale.

"Someone came to take me someplace, but I escaped. I ran until I came to a bus stop, borrowed some money from another passenger, and came back to Baltimore. That was stupid. A few weeks later, I saw him, the guy who drugged me, and I tried to run away.

He was big and fast and he caught me. That's how I got to Summervale, where you and I first met."

I remembered that encounter and the next day very well.

"What I don't understand," I said, "was how you were so together that day and then so out of control the next." There were many other things I didn't understand, but that was the first one that came to mind.

"Because I saw them." Agnys panted into her palm. "In the hallway—the man who raped me. Later, he came into the room. He looked me over and called for the doctor. She entered, and I recognized her. She had been there, at that place, too. I was in shock. And when I came to the hearing and saw her again, I lost it."

"Saw who? Dr. Knowles?"

"Yes!" Agnys' voice rose. "She was there."

Whoa. Was I a dupe, or was this an even bigger scandal than Rosemont? The story sounded beyond belief, then got worse.

"So, after they committed me, they took me to this house in West Virginia. There were other pregnant women there, like me. Every so often, the two of them came, you know, the ones from Summervale . . ."

"You mean Dr. Knowles?"

"Yes, and the rapist."

"Okay, keep going," I said.

"There were other people like nurses or aides who looked after us. They fed us, but no one was allowed to leave."

"How did you know it was in West Virginia?" I asked.

"I'm not stupid. I saw the signs."

"Could you find it?" Was there some way to substantiate this story?

Agnys gripped the door handle. "There's no way I'm going back there!"

"No, no, not to go back. Could it be located by an investigator or the police? How did you escape?"

"Last night, I pried open a window and squeezed through. That afternoon, I found my file and hid it under the mattress. That was my proof. I swiped a knapsack from another girl and left. As soon as I reached the main road, I stuck out my thumb and hitched a ride back to Maryland."

"That was taking a risk," I said. "You could have been attacked or murdered."

"If I had, it would have been no worse than what I left."

She had a point.

Agnys folded her hands in her lap. "And that is my story."

"But what was it for?" I remained dumbstruck. Maybe I was naïve, but somehow, I was at a loss to understand the whole picture.

Agnys looked at me, exasperated. "They were selling the babies. They took pretty girls off the street, impregnated them, made sure the babies were healthy, and sold them to the highest bidders. You would be surprised what someone would pay for something like that. The charts confirm it—look."

I studied the chart under the lighted pole. Each month's exam had initials. Most of them were "P.K." In a section labeled "PAT" were the letters "Z.N." Oh my God. How could they have been so brazen?

"What happened to the girls after the birth? Please don't tell me they were . . . eliminated."

That would have made the story even more macabre and horrifying, not that it wasn't awful enough.

"No," Agnys said. "They didn't kill them, as far as I know. We heard someone would drive them out to the middle of nowhere, like Oklahoma, and leave them on the side of the road. But no one really knew."

ABBY

What was I supposed to do with this? Despite the mindboggling and horrendous story, Agnys kept her composure. Her breathing evened. No signs of hysteria or alarm. Despite my misgivings, her story made some sense in a farfetched way. Extremely farfetched.

I remembered how Dr. Knowles discounted Agnys' pregnancy claim when it must have been clear at the time she was expecting a child. The records given to me when I first interviewed Agnys were bare. In contrast, the patient described by Dr. Knowles and the circumstances surrounding her admission guaranteed to lead to an involuntary commitment. All of this persuaded me to begin to believe Agnys' story. The next step, of course, was a big question mark.

I headed home. Agnys asked where we were going, and I told her. Agnys could stay over, and tomorrow we would decide how to proceed.

Agnys' voice broke. "Abby, I'll never forget this."

I gazed through the windshield at the starless sky. What the fuck was I doing?

"Believe me," I said. "Neither will I."

ABBY

The lamp glowing from inside lit David's form. He stared out the window, stiff and immobile. That's where he stood when I left. Had he not moved the entire time? David opened the door for us and when he saw Agnys, gave me a knowing look.

"Hello," he greeted her. "I'm David, Abby's husband."

"Hi. I'm Agnys—with a y."

Agnys inched a flicker of her slim smile. That was how she introduced herself to me when we first met.

David bit his top lip and blinked. "Agnys," he said, "can I get you anything? Are you hungry?"

She looked at me and then to him. "A little. All I ate today was a candy bar."

We sat at the old oak kitchen table as David fixed Agnys a peanut butter and honey sandwich and a cup of tea. Agnys ate slowly as if she were savoring each sip and bite.

"Agnys," David said. "You don't hear that name much today. That was my mother's name."

"It was?" I said. "I thought it was Mary."

Was he making this up?

Agnys eyed us, eyebrows raised.

"Well," David explained. "Her name was Mary Agnes, but not many people called her that."

He crooked a smile. "My father seldom got angry, but when he was very serious, he would get this expression." David narrowed his eyes and lowered his voice. "Mary Agnes . . ."

Agnys giggled. It was the first time I ever heard her laugh.

I was grateful for David pouring on the charm, trying to make Agnys feel more at ease. We chatted, and Agnys, close to flopping her head on the table, asked if she could go to bed. I took her to the spare room and gave her a nightshirt, towels, and a toothbrush.

I left Agnys' file on the kitchen table for David to read. When I returned, he looked at me and shook his head.

"Wait," I said. "You haven't even heard the whole story," and related what Agnys described in the car.

"Unbelievable," he huffed. "So, Counselor, what are you going to do?"

ABBY

"I guess the first step will be to call Marta," I said. "We'll have to find a secure woman's shelter or some protected place for Agnys to go." I tried to envision all the angles.

"Should we call the police?" David asked.

"No," I said. "She's terrified of that, and I'm afraid, considering the circumstances, it might not be prudent. Dr. Nerovitch is high up, a real big shot. Who are they going to believe? Him or a girl who was involuntarily committed?"

"Good point."

"Here's what I'm thinking. If Agnys' story is true—and accurate—transporting someone from Maryland to West Virginia in captivity has to be a federal crime. And that's in addition to everything else—kidnapping, human trafficking, assault, rape. There are a whole host of crimes they committed. Tomorrow, I'll get in touch with Joel Silverstein. Remember, Michael Soresman's partner? He's an assistant U.S. attorney. I'm sure he'll be able to refer me to the right people to look into this."

"Sounds like a plan." He patted my hand.

"Yeah, but here's another thing that worries me. This situation is way beyond my representation of

Agnys. I'm afraid I'm overstepping a boundary and don't know what to do about it. I feel too invested to walk away, but I don't want a conflict of interest either. I'm not sure what to do."

"See what Marta says," David advised. "Then you can make a decision. Whatever you choose, I'm with you."

"I know." I kissed his large hand that covered mine. "I'm wiped out. Let's go to bed."

Before turning out the light, I rolled over and faced David. "Was your mother's name really Mary Agnes?"

"Of course it was. I would never lie about that."

Or, I suspected, anything else.

ABBY

After a fitful night, I rose early. Marta, who never seemed to sleep, would be awake to take my call. Marta's reaction was a combination of shock and delight. The terror of the story was palpable, the drama delicious. She suggested I stay home and wait for her to find a safe place for Agnys.

When I asked her about a possible conflict of interest, Marta hesitated. "I'm not sure. We'll have to think about that. It could be an issue." Marta's comment was discouraging but not unexpected.

Jordan, wearing his favorite dinosaur pajamas, wandered into the kitchen, followed by David.

"Cinnamon toast?"

"Sure, Mommy," Jordan assented, bobbing his head up and down.

David ruffled Jordan's hair. "Yum. I'll have some, too."

As they were eating, Agnys popped in, still in my nightshirt and barefoot. Jordan looked at her, wide-eyed, and asked, "Did you sleep here?"

Agnys yawned. "Yes, I did."

Jordan stared. "What's your name?"

"Agnys, what's yours?"

"Jordan," he said, then looked closer at Agnys. "Are you having a baby?"

I gave David a can-you-change-the-subject look, but Jordan quickly followed with, "My cousin Tati was a baby and now she's a big girl."

Agnys smiled at our little boy, who was bouncing on the balls of his feet. "Yes, Jordan, I am."

David stood and pointed to the hall. "Okay, Buddy, let's get ready for school."

Jordan jumped off the chair and, skipping behind David, left to get dressed.

"He is adorable," Agnys said. "Are there more?"

"No, just Jordan."

"He seems very bright and inquisitive."

"Oh yes," I said. "He certainly is."

I served Agnys some toast and tea, and David and Jordan reappeared, ready to go. Jordan could barely contain his excitement. "I get to ride in the truck today!"

Usually, I dropped him off, but because of Agnys' arrival, David offered.

Agnys asked David, "Are you a lawyer, too?"

"No, I'm a teacher."

"What do you teach?"

"Math," David answered.

"Ooh." Agnys tapped her head. "Smart."

Smarter than I am, that's for sure.

I handed Jordan his lunch, and they headed out, Jordan swinging the sack back and forth and chattering nonstop.

Agnys placed her right hand over her heart. "Abby, you are so lucky."

In general and particularly compared to Agnys, truer words were never spoken, and I had better appreciate it. I told Agnys I would make some calls to get her help. Agnys would be safe here, and I resolved to see justice done. Not sure how, but resolved nonetheless.

ABBY

Agnys was content to relax while I tried to do some research and wait until 9:00 when I assumed most federal offices would open. I reached Michael Soresman immediately and gave him a brief recap of the story.

He told me Joel should be in his office today. Michael was certain he would be interested and able to put us in contact with someone who could help.

Michael must have alerted Joel since he did not sound surprised when I called. I had the feeling both knew more about the topic than they revealed to me on the phone.

Joel quickly got down to business. "Do you believe her?"

"I think so," I said. "All of her details fit—the timing, the weird hearing, the fact that she is obviously pregnant. Nothing she told me earlier turned out to be untrue, at least as far as I can tell."

"Someone is going to want to talk to her right away. How safe is your location?"

That unnerved me. We were at my home. Had I put my family in danger?

Joel hesitated a moment. "There's more to this than you know or I can tell you. Someone will come by today, but be vigilant."

I held the receiver and stared at it after the call ended as if it were some foreign object I couldn't identify. I needed to remain calm. Agnys finished breakfast and was in the shower. Afraid of what I might blurt out when I saw her, I made some notes to prompt me. I didn't need both of us scared.

Agnys entered the kitchen as I was writing, wearing some clothes I gave her earlier. I had a pair of jeans with an elastic waist I wore when I was pregnant with Jordan. They fit, along with an old flannel shirt of David's that spanned across her formerly slim waist. Agnys' hair was still damp and fell in ringlets down her back.

"Someone is coming to talk to you. We need to get you help, and soon."

Agnys stiffened. "No police!"

"No," I said. "Not the police. These are federal investigators, Agnys. You're not the only one they know about. But you need to tell them what you told me last night."

"Don't let them take me away, please." Agnys panted and looked at the door.

"No one is going to hurt you. But we need a safe place for you to stay. My boss at the public defender's office is looking for a secure shelter. And the investigators need to find the people who did this to you and the other girls. You can help them."

Agnys bit her lip. "Okay, but you'll be here with me today?"

"I'm not going anywhere."

Not long after our conversation, a woman identifying herself as an FBI agent called and asked whether she could come by and speak to Agnys. I confirmed our address, and the agent said it would take about an hour before she arrived.

Right on time, a silver SUV pulled up and a middle-aged woman and young man approached the house. I peeked through the crack before fully opening the heavy wooden door. The agents flashed their FBI badges and IDs behind the glass storm door before I let them enter. The woman, who had called earlier, identified herself as Heather Duvall and the younger man as Chip Garrison.

I led them into the living room, where Agnys positioned herself on the couch. Agent Duvall asked whether I planned to stay for the interview.

Agnys focused squarely on the agent. "Of course, she'll stay. She's my lawyer."

"Agnys," I said. "My role is more complicated now. As an assistant public defender, I represented you in the hearing at the hospital, but this is different. Ethically, I'm uncertain whether I can act in a legal capacity on your behalf. But if you want me to remain in the room as your friend, I will guarantee confidentiality and sign any agreement in my role as a citizen for verification."

I faced Agnys. "You understand I am not acting as your attorney now, don't you?"

"I do," Agnys said. "I want you to stay."

ABBY

Agents Duvall and Garrison questioned Agnys for almost two hours. Agent Duvall, dressed in a navy pantsuit with an American flag lapel pin, appeared to be in charge. Her short, spiky blonde hair reminded me of the Statute of Liberty, with the pointed crown on its head. Her partner, Agent Garrison, looked like a young military recruit. He wore a snappy gray suit and red tie and had a ginger brush cut. My eye level barely passed his waist. Both spoke kindly to Agnys, with measured questions.

For the most part, with a few teary exceptions, Agnys kept her composure. She had amazing recall and identified the town and street in West Virginia where she was held captive. Agnys agreed to the agents' request that she submit to a medical examination. I was going to suggest it anyway and was glad they would make the arrangements.

The agents poured over Agnys' file and photographed the pages. I asked whether I could make copies of the documents before relinquishing the originals to the agents. The agents consented, and I agreed to forward the materials to them the next day.

"Where are you planning to live?" Agent Duvall asked Agnys. "We strongly urge you not to leave the area."

"I've consulted with my supervisor at the public defender's office," I said. "She's currently seeking a safe women's shelter for Agnys. She could be anonymous there."

"Can't I stay here?" Agnys asked.

"We highly discourage that," Agent Garrison said. "It would be safer for you and Abby's family if you're housed in a secure location."

"Oh, of course." Agnys' lower lip trembled. "I would never want to do anything to put Abby or her family at risk."

"Agnys," I said, "I promise to visit often and, within the bounds of safety, help in any way I can."

"I know you will, Abby. You rescued me."

"No." I touched Agnys' forearm. "You rescued yourself. I just provided the transportation."

ABBY

Agnys had arrived in the dark of night, and we whisked ourselves into the house. After the agents left, I suggested we venture outside. By mid-afternoon, warmth in the air beckoned, and I thought our vista might boost her mood.

Though most of the trees remained bare, tiny buds peppered their branches. New grass shoots peeked, and here and there, a purple crocus broke the ground. The air held a sharp scent of the promise of spring. Agnys expanded her gaze to grasp the panorama.

She turned, full circle. "This is amazing. I can't believe you live in such a beautiful place."

I pointed to The Gleanings, down the path from our home. Agnys followed me, and as we approached the building, I remembered Pete was with Raoul at our Charles Village office today. I fingered the correct key on my ring and unlocked the door. I showed off classrooms that contained pictures of the students and their projects and the larger area used as a greenhouse/lab. Agnys marveled at the rows and rows of seedlings waiting for spring to warm the earth enough to plant.

We wandered past the gardens, already staked and primed. Agnys related happy memories of gardening with her grandmother in the Azores. I admitted my horticultural challenges. The irony was that I could plan but not plant. David and Jordan shared the agricultural gene. I was a mere admirer.

Agnys asked how The Gleanings came about. I gave her the condensed version of how I discovered the title defect and then found David, who was able to reclaim his family's land. We built The Gleanings to give kids who had no exposure to farming an opportunity to create their own gardens and bring their skills to the communities where they lived. In the summer, David and I hosted parties for the students and their families, with games and awards. There was friendly competition, but everyone went home beribboned and proud.

Agnys crouched and smoothed the ground. "How wonderful it must be for a child to grow up here."

"David certainly thought so," I said. "That's why he was so happy to come back. I don't think he'll ever leave."

"Why would he?" Agnys rose and swiveled; her curls bounced in the breeze.

That evening, as we sat down to supper at the old farm table, Agnys asked, "Would it be okay if everyone held hands and said a prayer?"

"Of course," David said. "Agnys, why don't you take the lead?"

We clasped hands, and Agnys closed her eyes.

"Dear God." Her voice was strong and clear. "Thank you for my deliverance. Bless this family who opened their hearts to me in my time of need. Keep us safe and worthy of your love. Amen."

Everyone joined in the amen, and Jordan, who never experienced anything like this before, looked puzzled. I patted his hand and smiled my assurance. Admittedly, we had been deficient in his education when it came to spiritual matters. Not that I was opposed to religion. I never felt the need to practice one or choose a faith to follow. Maybe we would have to rethink that.

ABBY

Marta arranged for Agnys to shelter at Glynn's Gardens, a residence in South Baltimore primarily for victims of domestic violence. The location was a closely held secret, mainly to prevent vengeful partners from finding their prey. There was 24-hour security and law enforcement knew to patrol the area frequently. Agent Duvall was familiar with the venue and approved.

Agnys amazed me with her resilience and focus on the future. She considered returning to New England or the Azores, where her grandmother still lived.

Agent Duvall recommended that Agnys remain in the area for the present to facilitate the investigation of the case. Agnys did not protest. The baby's birth was coming, and Agnys agreed it would be prudent to stay put.

Jordan followed Agnys like a puppy. He sat, rapt and still as a statue, when she read to him. She taught him new songs and finger games. A talented artist, Agnys delighted Jordan with sketches of animals and birds. Jordan ran to show me each new one and made sure I posted it on the fridge.

David and I offered to take Agnys to the shelter when it was time for her to go. The authorities vetoed our proposal. They expressed concern about our anonymity and advised us it was safer to have Agnys transported by law enforcement. Agnys was wary, but we persuaded her to acquiesce.

David, Jordan, and I said our goodbyes as Agnys tearfully slid into the back seat of the officer's car. Jordan tried to reach in for one last hug. Agnys kissed her finger and tipped his cheek. He turned back to David, who enveloped him in his arms.

I vowed I would see Agnys soon. Jordan broke away and ran into the house to console himself. I choked up, too. David braced my shoulders, and we waved as the car's trail faded down the road.

ABBY

Still conflicted, despite my now unalterable decision, I called Dan Hutchinson. Dan would know how bad a position I was in. He would tell me, too.

"Hey, Dan, it's Abby." I tried to sound as casual as possible.

"Hi Abby," he said. "How's saving the world? Making any money yet?"

"No, but that's not the reason I'm calling. Dan, I fucked up and I'm not sure what to do."

"Tell me what happened. Believe me, there's nothing that can't be fixed."

I related Agnys' story, my impulsive retrieval at the 7-11, the FBI investigation, and the fear of ruining my legal career. Before it even started.

"Geez, Abby. How'd you manage that?"

"Innate talent?"

Dan huffed. "It's probably not as bad as you think. I've heard a lot worse. Look, you didn't steal any money or lie to a judge, so your license is probably safe. You might lose your job, but you can always find another one. My offer still stands."

"That's not it," I said. "I don't think I'll get fired. I guess I'm just questioning my judgment. I don't want to be one of your shitty lawyers who can't stay out of trouble."

"That's not going to happen, Abby. You're too smart for that. Consider this a learning experience. You got too involved this time. You need to keep your guard up in the future and not let it get personal."

"It's hard, though, isn't it?" I asked. "How do you keep from caring?"

"You can care, but at a distance. No matter where you're working, don't forget—they're your clients, not your friends. Leave them at the office when you go home at night. That's the easiest way to walk the line."

Good advice, but I was already in too deep. David was the statistics expert, but even I knew this exact scenario was unlikely to occur again. Dan was right, though. I had to set boundaries and keep them if I wanted to stay in the legal profession.

"Thanks, Dan," I said. "Just don't make me an example in class, okay?"

"Don't worry, Abby. This isn't a big enough fuck up to make it into the curriculum. Take my advice and try to stay out of trouble. I don't want you as a client."

DAVID

David thought he was used to Abby falling into unpredictable predicaments, but this one took the cake. Who could have imagined they would host a victim of a human trafficking and kidnapping ring? He used to think he lived a normal life.

Poor Agnys. He truly wanted to believe her. And, if her story were true, it could turn into a massive scandal. He wasn't wild about Abby caught up in the maelstrom. David remembered the others whose lives Abby had touched, Mo and Jack Warfield, for example. How in the world was she a magnet for such needy and desperate people? No one could accuse her of being overly empathetic. She considered herself cold. But he disagreed, mostly. She had a softer side, the part she usually tried to hide.

It must be Abby's sense of justice that put her in these situations. She found him in her quest to save their land from ruin. He surely benefitted mightily from that. Now she was seeking justice for Agnys, who was lost and alone. He would help her in any way to right those wrongs. And, in the process, protect Abby as best he could. A challenge, no doubt.

ABBY

"I'm just not sure, Abby."

Over the phone, I couldn't see Marta's face. Maybe that would have better revealed her thinking. But maybe not. I'm not a great reader of people.

Ordinarily, Marta's ambivalence would unnerve me. She said she understood my dilemma but had legitimate concerns about the propriety of the situation. I knew my involvement with Agnys tested the limits of an attorney/client relationship. But, having gone this far, I couldn't cut it off.

I understood I could not return to Summervale. That was no tragedy. Marta suggested I continue reviewing files at other hospitals, and we could revisit the issue pending the outcome of the investigation. That was reasonable. No one else in the office was aware of my situation. This break would give me some breathing room before I had to decide my future steps. Or they were decided for me.

I tried to visit Agnys several times a week. I'd call ahead, and staff would direct me to a parking space in the back. Agnys improved day by day. When I first found her, discolored half-moons ringed her eyes and her hair frazzled like an electrified mop. By the second week at Glynn's, Agnys' bronze complexion glowed, and her dark eyes were bright and alert. Agnys' soft curls cascaded past her shoulders, infused with the scent of lilacs and dew.

We spoke little about the baby. Agnys complimented the shelter's food, kind counselors, and comfortable accommodations. I brought her the books she requested, but she turned down my offer of stationery and stamps. The staff at Glynn's mentioned that Agnys made no out-of-state calls.

I knew from the file Agnys brought that the baby was a girl whose testing was unremarkable and appeared healthy by all standards. If Agnys found it difficult to offer more detail or approach the subject, I would respect her reticence. It had to be hard enough for Agnys to move forward, knowing the origin of her child. The last thing I wanted was to amplify her pain.

ABBY

"We found it!"

"Joel?"

I had no idea how long the process would take, and Joel's call not long after Agnys moved to Glynn's surprised me. The investigation only needed a final nudge. Unexpectedly, it came from FBI interviews with a young artist from Rhode Island. My former client, houseguest, and now friend.

Agnys' description and location of the house in West Virginia were spot on. FBI agents conducted a raid, collected files and computer hard drives, and arrested two men and a woman who appeared to be in charge. There were ten pregnant women on site, and the authorities were trying to locate their families or places for them to shelter.

One of the men agreed to be an informant in exchange for a plea deal. The plan was for him to record conversations with Dr. Nerovitch and others involved. A wiretap order was pending with the federal court. A task force that included state and federal law enforcement had been conducting its own investigation based on some anonymous tips and found accomplices who agreed to cooperate. The plot that ensnared Agnys was not an isolated crime; the scheme had tentacles throughout the east coast and, the agents suspected, even beyond. Joel thought things would move quickly since the government wanted to avoid alerting Dr. Nerovitch to the movements in the case and give him a chance to flee.

I struggled with how much to share with Agnys. On the one hand, I wanted Agnys to be aware of progress in the case and give her the incentive to move on without fear. On the other, I hesitated to initiate a subject that would only revive her misery.

I settled on a middle ground. If Agnys brought it up, I would be frank. If not, I could wait for a more critical moment to reveal what I knew. Not long after Joel's call, Agnys asked. She was pleased to hear that her information led to the discovery of the house and the arrests. Agnys was doubly relieved over the other victims' liberation. I did not need to go further, as Agnys changed the subject and surprised me by talking about the baby's birth.

"I saw the doctor yesterday," she said. "She asked if there was anyone who would help me through labor and stay with me when the baby's born. Abby, it could only be you. Will you be my birth partner?"

My heart leapt to the ceiling. I envied Ted and Raoul for being able to witness Tati's birth.

"Yes, yes, of course!" I shot from my seat to embrace her, and we giggled like schoolgirls.

Agnys and I clutched each other; her rounded belly scraped my midsection. Agnys thanked me, and I was hard-pressed to find the words to express my gratitude in return.

ABBY

The story broke in the Baltimore Sun at the end of the month. Because of the ongoing scandal at Rosemont, the Summervale ignominy was relegated to an inner page. But there it was in black and white, for all who cared to see.

Dr. Knowles had been questioned and, before being deported, implicated Dr. Nerovitch and many others. To save herself from further prosecution, she agreed to wear a wire. Not surprisingly, the conversations were both incriminating and hilarious.

One of the B & B Law Club members who heard the tapes told Marta, who vowed she would only tell me and urge me to keep it to myself. Knowles' "I love you, Zolt," and "How much can we get for the baby from the Wisconsin woman," along with the seized records, proved fatal to the Summervale duo. This unassailable proof allowed the feds to make an airtight case for conspiracy, kidnapping, sexual assault, and any other crimes entailing taking women prisoner, raping and impregnating them, and selling human infants.

Dr. Knowles' lover, Zolt, was held without bond, and officials from seventeen other states assisted with the investigation that involved captive women and holding facilities all over the country. The arrogance of

Dr. Nerovitch and his depraved gaggle of degenerates was staggering. Agnys' file said it all. Nerovitch and Knowles did not even try to disguise their involvement. They flouted and abused the system, leaving broken women and stolen children in their wake. They deserved no mercy from the court.

That evening, David pointed out the latest Summervale installment hidden in the recesses of the news. He hadn't seen Agnys, not wanting to inject a male presence that might disturb some of Glynn's other guests. He was sensitive that way. But he always asked about her and had me convey his concerns.

"Does Agnys know?"

"Yes," I said. "We talked about it. She's guarded, but I'm sure she's relieved."

David clapped his hand on my shoulder. "Make sure she understands we'll help her in any way. Anything she needs."

ABBY

David left early the next morning to spend the day in Washington for a meeting. Before he walked out the door, I noticed something different.

"Are you wearing a tie? This thing must be important. I didn't know you owned any."

"Can't remember the last time I wore one."

I certainly couldn't. Not since I had known him.

David shrugged. "I guess I had a couple stowed away. This one is so old it may have been my father's."

"I'm surprised you remembered how to tie it."

"So am I." David grinned and gave me a quick kiss. "See you tonight."

After dropping Jordan at school, I raced downtown to tell Agnys the latest news and that the scales of justice had shifted in her favor. The ring was exposed, and it was unlikely Dr. Nerovitch or any of his conspirators would taste freedom soon. The despicable crime rained shame on the hospital and the entire system that Nerovitch and Knowles used to hide their greed and deceit.

Agnys absorbed the news quietly. I did not expect her to be euphoric; this was a deep hurt not easily excised. She paused for several minutes before speaking and focused on her hands. I hadn't noticed before, but Agnys' nails were chewed to the quick. She moistened her index finger and patted a torn cuticle.

Agnys led me to a parlor, and we sat alone in the room.

"Abby . . ." Agnys said, then stopped.

"Are you okay? We can talk about it another time." I didn't want to rush her.

"I'm fine, but . . ."

She swallowed. "I'm leaving after the baby is born."

That didn't surprise me. After what happened, why would Agnys ever want to stay?

"That's a good idea. I'm sure your family will be happy to have you and the baby home."

"No." Agnys' eyes shifted to the floor. "I'm not taking the baby. I'm not sure where I'll go, and I don't want a lifetime reminder of . . ."

I held my breath.

Agnys paused and nibbled her thumbnail. "I'm going to give the baby up for adoption. This is the hardest decision I've ever made. I've thought and thought about it and am just going to ask outright. Would you and David adopt my baby?"

My eyes clouded with tears. I tried to speak, but no sound emerged.

Agnys reached for my trembling hand. "You're the best parents I've ever seen. Your love for each other and Jordan is so pure, and he is the sweetest, most inquisitive child. This baby would grow up in a loving family with every advantage. I need a new start, and I don't know where that will take me. With you, this baby will have a clean slate, too. She'll have the beautiful life she deserves."

"I, I . . ." I stammered, unable to articulate another word.

"The day we walked around your property, I was filled with the wonder of living in a place like this, surrounded by nature and goodness. I saw the impact of that serenity on you and your family. It was as if a blanket of calm covered you as soon as you came home. Surely there is magic there, and this baby will be loved."

Agnes stared at me, her eyes liquid and deep. "I know you'll have to ask David, but please. If you would ever do anything for me, do this."

I thanked her as if my life depended on it and dazed, drove home.

ABBY

The rest of the day blurred. David said he would be home late, so I fed Jordan dinner, and after a bath and stories, he dropped asleep. David came in around 10:00. I asked about his day and whether he had eaten. Yes, it was a good day, and he had dinner before he caught the train home. He yawned hard, and I caught his eyes droop. But I needed to tell him about Agnys' proposal. I couldn't wait another minute or I would burst.

David perused the day's mail; I stood behind him.

"I saw Agnys today."

"How did she take the news?" he asked.

"I think she took it well. Subdued, but satisfied. David . . ."

He turned around, alerted by my halting words.

I tried to calm myself and still my racing heart. "Agnys is leaving after the baby is born and does not want to keep her."

I paused for a second. "She wants the baby to be adopted."

David glanced at the ceiling, then lowered his gaze to me. His left eye twitched and the lines around his mouth grew deep.

"Do you think she would consider us?"

My knees wobbled and threatened my balance. I swallowed to clear my gathering phlegm. My heart resumed its rhythm, but my voice balked until I could manage a sound.

"Yes," I replied, seeking volume and confidence. "She asked me if we would; she wants us to. I didn't suggest it or say a word." I pressed my face against him, dampening his shirt.

David's arms encircled me and he stroked the back of my neck. "Is this what you want?"

My lower lip quivered. "I do," I said, soft as air.

I stepped back. Our eyes met and he placed his hands lightly on my shoulders.

"Then tell her we will."

We embraced again, and eventually I pulled away, dizzy with joy. All I could do was stare at him as he dried my tears with the back of his hand.

It was getting late. I was still breathless as David lifted his glasses and rubbed his eyes.

"I'm really beat," he said. "Sweetheart, we have a lot to talk about. Can it wait until tomorrow?"

Yes, it could.

DAVID

David had a notion this might happen; he secretly wished for it. Agnys struck him as bright and independent. It was not surprising that a woman in her situation would want to erase, as much as possible, all reminders of her ordeal. He still harbored vague concerns about some gaps in her story, but if the government was satisfied, so was he.

Agnys was young, with time and talent. Many opportunities lay ahead for her. He hoped he hadn't done anything, even unwittingly, to influence her decision. He dreaded being considered manipulative, a trait he despised.

What a day it had been! He still hadn't clued in Abby, but he spent the day in Washington with William Soresman and a group of investors. He suspected Bill had been leading up to something over the past year but was still stunned by Bill's proposal. It would mean an enormous career change for him.

He never expected to leave academia, which gave him an extremely comfortable life. Was he willing to trade predictability for the prospect of a position with this kind of impact? But if he were ever to pursue a challenge, this would be the time in his life to move forward. Absent disagreement from Abby, he would accept.

A new job, a new child. That was a lot of newness for a person who thrived on stability. Abby was the one who jumped off cliffs, not him.

What was it that Bill said? If not now, when?

When indeed.

ABBY

Agnys' request involved a life-altering decision for her and for us. For both our sakes, I wanted to quickly give her an answer. Not that we had to deliberate. We were all in. I raced to see Agnys in the morning.

I found Agnys at breakfast, engaged in conversation with other women at her table. Agnys waved me over and introduced me to her tablemates as "Abby, my best friend."

Agnys finished her cereal and, bouncing, led me to a private area. We sat across from each other and I reached for her hand.

"David and I talked . . ."

"And?"

"Yes! Absolutely yes!" I tried to keep my rising voice from offending anyone's eardrums and lowered it to continue.

"Agnys, we will be grateful to you for the rest of our lives. Are you completely convinced this is what you want to do?"

We had to be certain Agnys was unequivocal before we started the process, legally and emotionally.

"Yes, I am." Agnys emphasized each word. "I cannot raise her. I need to take responsibility for myself, and I will not risk not loving her enough because . . ."

Agnys broke her thought. "This is the best course for her and for me, knowing, as your child, she will be protected and loved."

"And she will be." Even with two marriages, I never made a more fervent vow.

Agnys' fingers drummed her chest. "Abby, I know this in my heart."

ABBY

Accepting Agnys' offer involved preparation as well as complications. I worried about the ethics of adopting the child of a former client. It may not have strictly violated an attorney's code of conduct, but there were surely questions of propriety.

Agnys made it clear that the idea was her own and of her own volition. I did not believe I had unduly influenced her in any way. However, there was always that implication, even if untrue, and the possible appearance of impropriety.

Deep down, I understood I could not continue my present job. It was compromised, even if unintentionally. I knew exactly what I was doing when I agreed to meet Agnys that night. Someone more prudent might have called law enforcement, social services, or another community resource.

I acted on instinct and still had reservations about whether that was correct. Not about the outcome—just the process. These doubts were enough for me to question whether my current career path was viable and my capacity to do it well.

David and I spent the next evening discussing our next steps on the path to adoption. We decided to contact the family lawyer Ted and Raoul hired when

Tati was on the way. Our situation would be different, but I had faith that the attorney, whom Ted and Raoul liked and trusted, would be able to sort it out.

We agreed to ask Agnys whether she wanted to stay with us until the baby was born. Since Agnys appeared to be out of danger, there was no reason for her to remain at Glynn's. She had several weeks to go, and we would do everything possible for her to feel comfortable and secure.

It might be confusing to Jordan, but he was a bright, resilient boy. I hoped he would be so happy to have a little sister that he would quickly be able to accept the situation. Wishful thinking? We would answer his questions as best we could.

As for my work, David always encouraged me to do what I thought was right. Bringing home a new baby was a perfect opportunity to rethink my career. It could be the law or something entirely new. Making it through law school raised my confidence. Many possibilities lay before me.

We were financially secure and lived a simple life. I could return to The Gleanings any time, maybe expanding some of the programs there. I was fortunate; not everyone had the options I enjoyed. It was a far cry from my childhood, and I treasured it every day.

Of all the curveballs life threw at me, this may have been my greatest test. I made decisions that would impact us for the rest of our days and had to be certain, in an uncertain world, that they were right. My choices would not only affect me; David and Jordan's happiness was in my hands. My heart told me to forge ahead and this time, my head concurred.

ABBY

Marta waxed philosophical when I called her the next day. I had mostly taken leave since bringing Agnys home, and quitting my job would relieve Marta from having to fire me. Maybe that wouldn't have happened; I'll never really know. But Marta did not seem displeased with my decision.

That didn't mean we couldn't remain friends, especially if she were no longer my boss. Marta was a skilled mentor and taught me everything I knew about being a lawyer. Any actions I may have taken contrary to her guidance were purely of my own making.

Neither of us wanted me to give up the B & B Law Club, either. It was a rare opportunity we had to share stories outside of work. Besides, I didn't think I would ever be able to drag David back to the Hopkins Club, so the B & B would be my only chance to bask in the club's rarefied atmosphere of a gentler time.

I needed to contact Ted to get the name of his attorney. So much happened so quickly, there had been no time to tell him anything.

"Guess what? We're having another baby."

"Congratulations! How are you feeling?"

"I feel fine, thank you," I said. "We're adopting."

"Good. I thought you were a little old for that."

"What?" That was annoying.

"Abby, you're almost forty-five."

"And how old were you when Tati was born?" That deserved a challenge.

"Entirely different," he parried. "I wasn't pregnant."

He had a point, but it didn't seem like a fair fight. We hung up, my ego bruised.

Still, I called the lawyer, Andy Hecht, and explained our unusual situation. He did not seem to think it was as odd as I did. He had unraveled much more complicated circumstances. Andy wanted to set up a time to talk to Agnys and us and review the legal records in the case. Satisfied we set everything into motion, we had no choice but to wait. We were on the baby's timetable now.

ABBY

As a child, I wondered about the grandparents I never met. Jordan and his new sister would grow up without them as well.

Uncertain whether I was pensive or melancholy, I asked David, "What was your family like?"

Maybe David was in one of those moods, too, and reminisced. "Someone once told me that children could never understand their parents. I suspect that's true. My father trained as an engineer at Hopkins. But, by the time I came along, he decided to farm. We raised corn and vegetables, had some orchards, and, at one time, chickens, cows, and goats. I'm pretty sure before he met my mother, he had been married to someone else but was widowed and maybe lost a child. I don't know much about it; I never asked. There was a depth of sadness to him sometimes, when he seemed remote and needed time alone. I never saw my father angry, but he was never overly cheery either. Mostly he was a temperate man."

Like you.

"But we had many good times. He liked being outdoors, building things, and reading history. I still own many of his books."

And a few ties, I supposed. I knew his father died in a farm accident, but David did not elaborate.

"Now, my mother had been a schoolteacher for more than twenty years before they met. One time I was shopping with her, maybe I was about four or five. It was before Maggie was born. A group of women came over, excited to see her, and called her Miss MacLaren. I was confused, and she told me that had been her name longer than Armacost. She had a whole life before I came along. They both did."

"She wasn't as reserved as my father and could be fierce when provoked. It was a less enlightened time back then. Once, when Maggie was young, someone suggested to my mother that they put her in a home. Spitting mad, my mother gave this woman this look she had."

David snickered and mimicked her stink-eye. "She said, 'Our Maggie has a home—our home,' and, I swear, if my mother had not been as proper as she was, she would have decked her."

"We were all protective of Maggie, but my mother was her warrior and guiding light. She must have been a wonderful teacher. She worked with her all the time, and Maggie graduated from high school with a real diploma. It's such a shame they never saw her thrive as an adult. My mother's health was poor, and after my father died, she faded fast."

David looked away. "I was already in Boston then. I still think I should have been home when they needed me."

"No," I said. "Don't feel that way. You did what you could." He shrugged his shoulders.

"After my father died, I asked my mother if I could have this hat he sometimes wore. It was an old brown fedora with a wide brim like men used to wear years ago. For some reason, I thought it had caché. Maybe it made me feel close to him when I wore it. I took it back to school with me, and I feel silly saying this, but I felt dashing in it."

"Then once, when I visited Maggie, I wore the hat when I picked her up. I was sure she would like it. But as soon as she saw me, she started to cry."

"What happened?" I asked.

"When I first walked in, she thought I was my father. I have to tell you, Abby, I was crushed at the thought of frightening her. The resemblance never occurred to me. But then I saw a mirror and understood. I did look like my father and realized I probably would more and more as time went on. It was eerie."

"Do you still have the hat?"

"Maybe in a box somewhere. I took it back to Boston but never felt quite the same about it."

"And," David recalled, "Maggie had a boyfriend."

"Really?" I wanted details. "Where did she meet him?"

"I think they met at work. His name was Ennis, and he also had Down syndrome. He lived at home with his parents. Maggie told me all about their outings together. He gave Maggie a necklace with a small blue stone, and she wore it all the time. When I visited, Ennis would often join us. We must have been quite a sight—the lovebirds trailed by big, clunky David."

"You're not clunky," I said.

"I am, but I can live with it." He pointed to his shoe, the size of which more than doubled mine.

He had a point; a subtle presence he was not.

"Once, Maggie asked me why I didn't have a girlfriend. I wasn't sure how to answer. I told her I was not as lucky as she and had not met the right person yet. Which was, after all, true. Maggie assured me I would find someone, someday."

"Maggie was right," I said and reached over to fondle his neck.

"Yes, she was." David diverted my hand and kissed it.

"Ennis' mother called me after Maggie died. Ennis was upset and wanted to attend her funeral, but they had plans to go away. I thanked her, saying I understood, but I suspected Ennis' parents may have wanted to spare him the sorrow of it. They sent me a lovely card, which Ennis signed. When I cleaned out Maggie's room, I found some pictures of her and Ennis. I sent a few to Ennis' house and hoped they wouldn't make him sad. I thought he might want to remember Maggie, too."

Even if these were sad and poignant stories, they held solace for David. He had been loved and loved his parents and Maggie in return. I appreciated we were the last ones who remained in our families. The lives of those we lost would live only in our memories.

"I wish I had known them." I caressed his arm.

David sighed. "I wish they had known you and Jordan, and . . ."

He quizzically raised his brow. "What are we going to call her?"

"I have some ideas," I said. "Why don't you think about some, too."

David nodded. "I will."

ABBY

Agnys readily consented to move back with us. It was not a hard sell. Jordan went wild when he saw her.

"Slow down, Buddy," I called out, afraid he would knock Agnys down as he ran headlong into her arms.

"Is Agnys going to stay?" he asked.

"Only for a little while. Then she'll be going home to her family."

He cornered me. "How about the baby?"

Smart kid.

Relying on the classic parental dodge, I could only answer, "We'll see."

Although reasonably secure that everything would work out, I did not want to promise something I wasn't certain we could deliver.

David and I met with Andy Hecht. I mailed him all of our documents so he would be familiar with the details. Hopefully, no hitches; I had my fingers crossed. Andy was the expert, and we were confident he could navigate any legal requirements or impediments.

I did some independent research. I'm no legal whiz by any stretch but found a familiar phrase in a statute. The Maryland Code contained a section about adoption in the case of a parent who committed a crime of violence against the other parent of the child.

Proving that to a court required clear and convincing evidence. The phrase struck a nerve.

Clear and convincing: not a typical standard, but one shared with the law that brought us together. It was the legal basis for Agnys' commitment, the same uncommon burden of proof. Our belief in what had happened and what was to come required reason and certainty. The connection of those words formed the unlikely confluence and bond of our lives that was now unbreakable. We would be forever joined by this experience, despite distance or fate. Agnys would reclaim her freedom, and David and I would be blessed with a debt we could never repay. No doubt each of us felt we had the better bargain, and that was good and fair.

ABBY

David and I debated how prepared we should be for the baby. We hovered between not wanting Agnys to feel like a mere vessel in waiting and assuring her we were unfailingly committed to our promise. I asked Agnys how much preparation she was willing to witness and whether our getting ready for the baby would be painful for her.

Agnys shooed away our concerns. "Not at all. Give me something to do."

"Gladly." With my limited skills, I wouldn't turn anyone down. "But no heavy lifting."

Agnys waved her hand. "Aah—I'm fine. Bring it on."

As much as she was able, Agnys pitched in reassembling the furniture we placed in storage after Jordan outgrew his baby room. She perused piles of fabric samples to pick out bedding and choose colors she deemed suitable.

When it came time to paint the nursery, Agnys took charge and asked whether we would like her to create a mural on one of the walls. It would be a lasting gift to us and the child we shared.

Agnys chose a light aqua for the walls, and on the south side of the room opposite a large window, she painted the surrounding vista. Agnys captured each hill and vale, the small cherry orchard to the east, and David's garden beside the old barn. Fleecy, luminous clouds dotted the sky, with streams of sunlight poking through. And in a wash so faint you could barely see, Agnys added a rainbow arcing above like a guardian angel. In tiny script at the end of the indigo bow, she wrote "Agnys 2007."

When she revealed it to us, David turned to me and then to Agnys, mouth agape but without words. Finally, I had to break the silence.

"Now we can never leave."

Agnys laughed. "You were never going to leave anyway."

"You're right," David said, recovering his voice. "But this seals the deal."

I understood. In addition to leaving her child, Agnys wanted to leave behind a part of herself so she would not be forgotten. Surely, our gratitude would last a lifetime, but if we ever faltered, entering this room would remind us of the young artist who gave us the most precious gift of all.

ABBY

Time, like the baby, was rapidly bearing down. Our lives would soon be irrevocably changed by our awaited addition. There were losses, too. Not equal, but altering.

My first attempt at a legal career failed miserably. I had few regrets, considering the trade, but it shook my confidence. Jordan would have to adapt to a potential rival, but David and I believed him more excited than wary.

Already in school, Jordan was beginning to develop a life outside of us that would ultimately lead to his independence. Besides, someday he might need a sibling to share joy and grief. I never had one, and David lost his. We wanted to believe that we were expanding Jordan's life rather than limiting it.

With all of these swirling thoughts, I decided to take a walk. The burgeoning spring erupted with the blossom of wildflowers and trees. A recent shower scented the air and the ground remained moist. The day beckoned.

David waved from the window and asked if I wanted company. I had planned a solitary hike but would never reject his calming presence. David had a sentimental air and took my hand, adjusting his longer stride to my smaller steps.

"Are we ready?" he asked.

"We have to be. It's happening soon."

"I know I expressed reservations about . . ."

I interrupted him. "But they were valid. I understood."

"You know this is what I want, too." David stood still. "I never want you to doubt my love for this child."

I squeezed his hand. "I would never think that. Remember, you suggested it before you knew she asked. I cannot tell you how much that meant to me."

"This is right for us and for Jordan." David turned his gaze toward our home. "The baby will make our family complete."

"So," he said, eyeing me. "What are we going to call our daughter?"

"Well, don't laugh or cringe, but I honestly like the sound of your mother's name."

"Mary Agnes?"

"I know, it sounds like a saint or a nun."

David huffed a laugh while I continued. "Since I'm half Jewish, it seems slightly inappropriate, but I have an idea."

I had been thinking about it and wrote a note to show him. I fished it from the pocket of my jeans. "What do you think?"

I handed him the small piece of paper that read "Merrie Agnys."

I looked for his reaction and tried to explain my thinking. "It sounds the same, but it's different, you see?"

"I like it." David nodded. "So, for my mother?"

"Yes, but also for Maggie and Agnys . . . and Mark."

"It's perfect, Abby."

David swept me in his arms and lifted me a few inches above the damp earth. He twirled me around like he did when he was younger and more agile.

"Don't drop me," I teased, and we kissed. I did not think my love for this special man could ever be deeper. We resumed our walk, hand in hand, surveying the land that brought us together and bound our lives.

ABBY

A week later, Agnys, wide-eyed and panting, rapped me on the shoulder.

"Abby, I think it's time. My contractions are five minutes apart."

The countdown began.

Agnys called the OB, who asked a few questions and suggested we start for the hospital.

"What do I do?" Agnys' voice, usually modulated, rose in pitch.

"First, take a deep breath," I said, and placed my arm around her. "Everything will be all right. This is going to be a good night."

"You promise, Abby?"

"I promise. Now let's get your things and go. We have a new baby to welcome to the world."

Agnys grabbed the small bag she packed, and we took off. I thought I had put on a good show. I needed to calm Agnys, but I was as nervous as I had been on my way to deliver Jordan. Maybe more.

I dropped Agnys off at the hospital entrance, parked the car, and met her at the registration desk. A nurse led Agnys to labor and delivery, and I followed behind. She installed Agnys in the bed, took her vitals, and hooked her up to an IV and all the necessary monitoring equipment. Lots of whizzing and beeping.

At one point, the baby's heart rate dropped, and the staff whisked me out of the room. My own heart rate concomitantly rose, fearful of a complication. Jordan's birth had been so simple for me; it didn't seem fair that Agnys' youth might not shield her. She had been through so much already. Of course, I couldn't deny we had a vested interest in the outcome. But for now, I only wanted to focus on Agnys. I paced the hallway, waiting for someone to tell me something, anything. Someone came, but only to lead me to a small, unoccupied office, where I sat uninformed, trying to empty my mind.

I lost track of the passage of time. The clock on the wall was stuck at 9:30, so it was of no use, and I left my watch at home. No reading material, either. I was left with my imagination, which I was desperate to disconnect.

A knock on the door. A nurse cracked it open; Agnys and the baby were safe. He led me back to the labor room where Agnys, looking only a little sweatier for wear, greeted me with a sigh. The baby's passage advanced as Agnys weathered a few hard contractions. I stood by essentially useless but did whatever I could to help her through.

When it came time to push, staff wheeled Agnys into the delivery room. I followed them, slipping into scrubs someone handed me in the hall. I stood behind the doctor at the foot of the bed and tried to subtly peek around her. With each push, a greater portion of the baby's head emerged. Agnys remained calm, breathing on cue and pushing when told. I was transfixed.

Finally, the moment for that last push arrived and out slipped a baby girl, red-faced, her head covered with tiny raven curls. As the doctor handed her to the awaiting nurse, the baby placed her miniature hands over her eyes to shield them from the glaring delivery room lights. Scrunching her mouth, the baby emitted a high-pitched wail between breaths. Agnys, her upper body still flat on the bed, waved a lock of moist hair from her forehead and smiled.

Nurses took the baby for weighing and clean-up, and Agnys proceeded to expel the placenta and get stitched. I tagged along as Agnys progressed to recovery.

Alone in the small, curtained-off cubicle, Agnys and I spoke off and on, with long quiet breaks. Agnys mostly assured me she felt fine, and I continued to express my awe at witnessing the baby's birth. For a while, we held hands, united in our exhaustion and joy.

Eventually, a nurse brought the baby and started to give her to Agnys. Agnys held up her hand and pointed to me. "She is the baby's mother. Give the baby to her."

The nurse instructed me to remove my shirt and bra. I must have looked surprised, and the nurse explained that bonding was most effective skin-to-skin. As Agnys expectantly watched, I quickly stripped above the waist.

The nurse handed the baby to me. I pressed her to my bare chest. I could feel the baby's rapid heartbeat and her body, soft, like downy velvet against my breast. She had that sweet and ripe newborn scent I did not think I would ever know again. As Jordan had, the baby wore a funny little knitted cap, this one in pink. I closed my eyes, enveloped in an aura of love and peace.

Agnys and I agreed that Agnys would breastfeed the baby in the hospital to give her immunities and vital nutrients. David and I would take over bottle feeding at home. After a while, I lifted the baby to Agnys, who put her to her breast. Our little girl rooted, easily found the nipple, latched on, and sucked away. She was a natural.

"Abby, are you sure this is okay?" Agnys' voice shook.

I nodded my approval. I planned for this scene and encouraged it for the baby's sake.

"I promise I'll give her back." Agnys flushed. "I don't want you to get the wrong idea."

"I never thought otherwise." Well, maybe I did a little, but that is my nature.

"Did you decide on her name?"

David and I hadn't told anyone yet. Not secretively, exactly. And not uncertain, either. Maybe we were mildly superstitious.

From my chair, I envisaged the two of them, Madonna and child.

"Her name is Merrie Agnys. With a y."

ABBY

As soon as I could, I found a phone to call David. He answered on the first ring.

He picked up without a greeting. "Well?"

"We have a daughter."

"And?"

"She is beautiful, as you might expect. Six pounds, twelve ounces. Perfect in every way."

"And Agnys?"

"Absolutely fine—the advantage of youth."

"And you?"

"Transcendentally happy but missing you."

A few days before, David and I decided putting together the nursery was too big a clue for Jordan to miss. We took a walk outside with him to tell him the news. Even though Agnys would be leaving, the baby was joining our family and would be his sister forever.

I thought adoption might be harder to explain to a five-year-old, but Jordan seemed to instinctively understand.

"Can she play with me?" he asked.

David tousled Jordan's hair. "Of course, Buddy. But you'll probably have to wait until she's bigger."

David was eager to see us and introduce Jordan to Merrie. I met them in the hospital lobby, having properly established Jordan's siblinghood. In the room, Merrie lay swaddled in her isolette, asleep. Agnys greeted us and stepped into the hallway. I urged her to stay, but Agnys insisted on giving us some private time.

Jordan circled the isolette, checking Merrie from each angle.

"She's so little," he whispered. "She looks like Tati."

Jordan was right; she did.

David couldn't stop staring at her, enthralled. "Beautiful. Simply beautiful."

Jordan eyed us, antsy. "When can we take her home?"

"Tomorrow or the next day."

I told David I would leave soon. I had been up most of the night and needed rest, if not a shower. I would come back later if Agnys wanted company. If all went well, we would return tomorrow, infant car seat in place, to bring Merrie home.

Jordan peeked out of the room, ran to Agnys, and threw his arms around her. He was getting tall and rested his head above her waist.

"Thank you, Agnys," he said. "I love you."

"Goodbye, Jordan." She rubbed his back. "I love you, too. Be a good big brother."

"I promise," he said amid sniffles. "I will."

ABBY

Agnys declined my offer to stay with us for a few more days. She was ready to break away and did not want to prolong the process. I bought her a ticket to Providence for the next day. I packed her small collection of belongings; she came with so little and would leave with less.

David stayed at the hospital to finish any outstanding paperwork while I drove Agnys to BWI. Music from the radio replaced anything we may have spoken. Both of us shared the fear of breaking down at the first word. I pulled into a spot in the departure lane, grabbed Agnys' bag from the back seat, and eased it down. We held each other so tightly, I was afraid we would simultaneously bruise ribs.

"I don't know how to thank you," I said, unable to release my grasp. Agnys' tears spread damp blotches on my shoulder.

"The same. Oh my God, the same." Agnys stepped back and brushed a finger over her cheek. "You are the family of my heart."

Agnys shouldered her bag and headed toward the airport entrance. She turned and we waved. After a moment to catch my breath, I drove away. To David, to Jordan, and to our new daughter. To our family.

ABBY

David and I fumbled to fit Merrie in the new car seat. She was so tiny; we didn't want to inadvertently pinch or scare her. I drove home as slowly as David's normal turtle pace. Merrie whimpered but mostly dozed. David squeezed himself in the back and gazed dreamily at her the entire ride, his thumb covering her delicate hand.

As soon as we settled in at home, Merrie downed a bottle and fell asleep in my arms. David gingerly lifted her into the bassinette that had been Jordan's, placed next to our bed. Merrie emitted a soft sneeze but didn't wake. A picture of perfection, so precious, swaddled in a flannel blanket dotted with elephants, pink and green.

David and I sat at the kitchen table, simultaneously exhilarated and exhausted. When our adrenalin waned, it would be lights out for us, too. Merrie's arrival into our family happened so fast, we barely had time to think about anything else. I wanted to start telling friends and family about our surprise addition.

Ted and Raoul knew we were in the adoption process, but not that Merrie was born. I needed to call them right away. And Nina! I couldn't believe I forgot to tell her, knowing how excited she would be.

"We've got to call Nina and Bill—they have no idea this was happening."

David winced. "I think they know."

"How?" I hadn't spoken to Nina since Agnys first came to us.

"I might have mentioned it." David pulled at his collar.

"To whom?"

"To Bill."

"When did you talk to Bill?"

"I've been talking to him a lot recently."

"Really? Is everything okay?"

"Yes, everything is fine."

"Is something going on?" I gave him a stern shift-eye.

"David MacLaren Armacost! Have you been hiding something from me?"

"Not hiding." David sighed. "I wanted to be sure I had all of the details before we discussed it."

"Discussed what?" I was totally in the dark.

"I've been offered a position."

I held my palms up, gaping like an idiot.

"Their foundation is funding several new research institutions, and I have been asked to be the director of one of them."

Did I hear him correctly? This was entirely out of the blue.

"A job? Do you want to take it?"

"I think I do." He narrowed his lips in contemplation.

"Would we have to move?"

Please say we don't have to. Please.

"No," he said. "That was non-negotiable. We are not going anywhere."

My mouth remained open, my eyelids parted as far as they could go, staring, yet blindsided.

"I thought you loved teaching."

"I do," he said. "But I've been doing it almost twenty-five years and I think I'm ready for a change."

"How long has this been in the works?"

"Well, when I first met Bill . . ."

My mouth dropped lower than I believed physically possible. "Before Jordan was born?" That was more than five years ago.

"It was nothing concrete then. Bill told me about an idea he had. Then, gradually, we started to talk more and meet occasionally."

"You never said anything about it." I had no idea. How could he keep something so important from me?

"I'm sorry, Abby," David offered, his tone genuinely contrite. "I didn't mean to be secretive. I wasn't sure it was right for me and needed time."

"You don't like change, do you?" I remembered how long he lived on his own before we met.

"No, I don't," he admitted, shaking his head. "It is not easy for me."

"But, you certainly changed your life completely after we met."

"That was different. As soon as I saw you, I couldn't imagine us being apart. I needed to be here, in this place, with you."

Whoa. How could I stay annoyed after that?

I relented. "Well, then. Tell me more."

The deal had been in the works for several years and had many moving parts. The foundation was partially funding three research institutes, one in Baltimore at Johns Hopkins, one in the U.K., and one in Israel. I was stunned.

"But you're a mathematician, aren't you?"

"Essentially, yes. But I also have a degree in biomedical engineering and my areas of concentration are computational theory and complex systems . . ."

"Okay, I get it." I cut him off and shook my head—he could do anything.

"Will you have to travel?" Maybe this was a little selfish but we did have a new baby.

David nodded. "Some, I suppose. Probably D.C. a couple of times a month and New York periodically. Possibly once a year or so to the U.K. or Israel. Maybe we can all go."

Right. Two kids on a plane for hours. Very relaxing. But on second thought, I reconsidered. We could give them experiences and opportunities we never had growing up. This prospect was getting more interesting. I wanted to be supportive, not an impediment.

"Is it a problem I'm not working right now?" Was this a bad time to give up my salary? I hoped my employment woes would not interfere; leave it to me to do something inopportune.

David barely suppressed a laugh, which raised my hackles. Was he deriding my earning potential?

"Not a problem, my dear." David looked away and coughed. "Ahh . . . they're offering me about five times what I'm making now."

Five times—even I could do that math.

That was a relief. "I guess that means there's no pressure on me to find a job."

Merrie mewed from the bedroom, and I shifted toward the sound.

"Take all the time you need." David gestured to the hallway. "I think you might be busy here for a while."

DAVID

After she put Jordan and Merrie to bed, Abby bid David an early goodnight. It had been a long day, and she would be up sooner rather than later for feedings. He offered to assist with night duty; he had been of little use when Abby nursed Jordan. Since Merrie was bottle-fed, he could help. Abby declined for the night but told him she would keep him in reserve when she needed a break. For now, she could handle it.

He looked in on all the sleepers after about an hour. The children were sound asleep and Abby was dead to the world. He stood in the doorway of their room. Abby was on her side, knees bent and hands folded together by her collarbone. The pale blue sheet pooled at her calves. He slipped in, wrapped it tenderly around her shoulders, and lightly kissed her cheek. Abby didn't stir.

He gazed at her, barely illumined by the light in the hall. Abby still looked like a child, small and lithe. Once settled in bed, she rarely moved, and he suspected she would be in the same position when she woke. He marveled at her youthful appearance, the same as when they met. Forever young.

He recalled the first time he heard her voice, bursting and bright. He didn't have a clue. Who in the world was this woman?

Now he knew. She was the air he breathed, his beating heart, his mortal soul. Before they met, he thought his life was as good as it would ever be. Complacent, he supposed. He had been on his own for a long time and had no reason to think it would change. Abby changed everything. Her single phone call altered his life and it had not been the same since.

He warmed at the memory. He was working in his office at MIT and Dawn, his assistant, buzzed. There was a call from someone about Baltimore County. Did he want to take it? Since the MacArthur award, she had been screening some of his calls. This one sounded different and the mention of Baltimore County, where he grew up, intrigued him. He asked her to put the call through.

The young woman on the phone spoke rapidly, with a nervous edge. She identified herself as a title searcher and asked whether he had family in Baltimore County. He said he did and had grown up near Arcadia. She asked about his aunt, Edwina Moore, who recently died. That baffled him. Where was this going?

She proceeded to describe a suspicious land deal and her discovery that he might be the heir to his aunt's property based on an obscure clause in a deed from 1926. Even if it were a scam, he was entranced and encouraged her to go on. Her story made some sense, in a nonsensical way. But he couldn't end the conversation. It was too entertaining, and something about the young woman's voice . . .

Later, he did some research and decided she might be right. He thought about her every day and began speaking to her every night. He knew her, even if they had never met.

The night before they were to physically meet, he was as jittery as a teenager about to go on a first date. This was so out of character for him. He was generally calm and settled and had become accustomed to a solitary existence. It had been an eternity since he had a relationship with a woman, and he feared his fascination with his phone confidante bordered on obsession. He was afraid that when she saw him, she would dismiss him out of hand. He was no prize, just a big guy whom most people thought was at least ten years older than his age. He deliberately left out details about his appearance. Maybe it was unfair, but he wanted to see her reaction to him.

On the other hand, he had a pretty good idea of what she looked like. Her description of herself was vague but there was something in her voice that created an image in his mind. He recognized her immediately at first sight. The young woman looked exactly as he envisioned. And smitten, he couldn't take his eyes off her.

They visited the property she believed he would inherit. It was as beautiful as he remembered from his youth. It was green and ripe and drew him into a vortex of memory and desire. He was not a believer in destiny but felt an irresistible pull that he was supposed to be in this place, at this time. With this woman.

It was so unlike him, usually so deliberate and cautious. The events of the day only confirmed his intuition. When that night, by a gesture, she brought him to her bed, he surrendered his solitude and reserve. And afterward, he never wanted to be apart from her. Something changed in him that day. The young woman, Abby, opened his heart in a way he never expected. Or predicted. Or dreamed.

And here they were, on their land with their growing family. What remarkable years—extraordinarily fulfilling and full of constant surprise. He faced a crossroads now. He was nearing fifty and this was the optimal time to move in a new direction. There were years ahead of him, he hoped, to produce something beneficial and worthwhile. He looked forward to the challenge, grateful for all the fortune in his life.

ABBY

I started spreading our news to friends and expectantly dialed Marta.

"Marta," I said, "it's Abby. We just brought the baby home."

"Congratulations! So, tell me all about it. Where's the girl? Did she sign everything? What does your lawyer say?"

"Everything's under control. Agnys wanted to go home, and Andy took care of all the paperwork. We don't anticipate any problems. The baby even sleeps at night. She's a gem."

"That's great, Abby. I'm happy for you."

The week before, I officially resigned from my position with a guarded apology. I did not want to leave Marta in the lurch. Marta assured me the office was under control. She recently hired some new baby lawyers and Cindy Fairchild was willing to return to Summervale, especially since the state assigned Grace Goldsmith to take over the hospital and clean up the mess.

I knew Grace from the law club. She and Marta were close. Widely respected as a resourceful manager and ingenious attorney, Grace was a natural for the job. According to Marta, Grace's mandate was to upend everything as quietly as she could and cleanse the place of Dr. Nerovitch's taint. Having the more notorious scandal at Rosemont overshadow the chaos at Summervale would undeniably help. I had no doubt Grace would succeed.

We were about to hang up when Marta added, "Don't forget, there's a box with some of your stuff in the Summervale office."

"Oops, sorry about that."

"No problem. Cindy happened to find it. She labeled it and threw it in a closet. You can pick it up whenever you want."

"Thanks," I said. "I'll drop by sometime."

The box probably contained some law books, old calendars, or journals. Nothing that I needed right away. I wasn't ready for a recap of the Summervale experience yet and needed more mileage between myself and my former office before I returned. I'd wait and find a time Cindy would be there, maybe in a few weeks.

ABBY

Spring drifted into summer and slid into fall. It was a glorious summer; only a few days of oppressive heat and roiling thunderstorms that shook the house and swayed trees slightly too far for my comfort. Otherwise, the valley bloomed.

Jordan reveled in the summer sun and couldn't wait to wade in the pond. We picnicked there almost every weekend. Jordan tossed away his shoes the minute it came into view. The water wasn't too deep or slimy, and I loved seeing him squeal and splash. Merrie sat shaded and secured in a padded baby carrier under an ancient oak. She recently started to smile and lift her small face to the sky. David, nestled next to Merrie with a favorite book, radiated bliss. Every so often, he would peer at her and lean over to plant a kiss atop her head.

Plans were being made for David's transition. The Soresman Foundation, partnering with Johns Hopkins, was busy creating the Institute for Complex Systems, and it would ultimately occupy a new structure adjacent to the campus in North Baltimore. Most of David's time was spent in meetings, consultations, and research. He exuded excitement, and I was convinced he made the right decision.

Jordan started kindergarten in the fall at the local public school, the same one David attended as a child. The five years since his birth had passed in the blink of an eye, though so many changes occurred in the interim. On the Tuesday after Labor Day, Jordan mounted the steps to the yellow bus and headed to school. We waved to him at his window seat on his ride to a new independence.

I remained ambivalent about my legal career. Maybe I would resume it one day, but for now it was on indefinite hold. I had no regrets for the actions that curtailed my employment with the public defender's office. Merrie, the product of my choices, confirmed that belief. And Merrie was still an infant and required constant attention. I was not ready to cede that attention to anyone else for now, except David. I relished the time I had to consider other options and had confidence something eventually would come along. I would simply have to be primed to recognize the opportunity when it arrived.

We received a postcard from Agnys. Before she left, Agnys confided in me that no one in her family knew about Merrie. Agnys called her "our little secret." To tell the truth, that bothered me. I hated to think of Merrie as someone who had to be hidden or Agnys' source of shame. It was unfair and wrong. But I wasn't Agnys and couldn't make that choice for her. I also didn't want any secrets from Merrie. Someday, she would ask, and we would tell her how she came to be our daughter. She was the chosen one and our precious gift. Nothing could alter that.

Something about the postcard made me uneasy. The picture on the front of the card was of Ponta Delgada in the Azores, a lush oceanside city curtained by mountains. An island paradise. Instead of a newsy message, Agnys left a poem of sorts. "On the beach, hidden away, who knows where next I'll stay. Now I'm here, then I'm gone. Like a fleeting wind or song."

Cryptic, no? I showed it to David; he dismissed it as Agnys being artsy, or something. He wasn't worried. It was a bit of doggerel, nothing else. I didn't want to think about it but didn't want to get rid of it, either. So I shoved it out of my mind into a drawer I rarely opened. As a diversion, I chose to imagine a smiling Agnys, sprinting freely on the sand, and hoped that someday she would find happiness and peace.

ABBY

Because of all the activity of the spring and summer, plans for acquiring a new pet and memorializing the lost ones went on hold. Jordan did not forget and often reminded David and me of our promises to him. David thought fall might be a better tree planting season anyway, so in September we visited the nursery to purchase two trees for Bongo and Ridgely's garden. David and Jordan planted them that afternoon and devised a schedule to monitor their care. Jordan chose a red maple for Bongo and a birch for Ridgely. They were fitting tributes to our beloved pets.

Jordan vigilantly inquired about the new kitten I had suggested. Big mouth me. David and I successfully deferred this new addition to the fall as well. I tried calling Mo, the cat keeper. Life intervened and we had missed our planned lunch at Yoder's in the spring. But the number I had for Mo was disconnected and I couldn't find another. Knowing Mo and her history, I wasn't shocked. She could be the definition of disconnected. It saddened me, though, since I thought she was settled. Maybe she was and simply had a new phone number; maybe not. Mo was changeable like that. As long as she hadn't had a rendezvous on the Rainbow Bridge, we would meet again.

Ultimately, David and I had to fulfill our obligation, and one Sunday we trekked to the local animal shelter to find a pet. David pushed Merrie in the stroller, and I tried to keep track of Jordan running down the lines of cages. One rescued cat in the aisle relentlessly meowed with a penetrating cry. I tried pointing Jordan to the kittens mewing in the other cages, but he kept staring at the one at the end of the row. I dreaded who was in that cage.

I stood behind Jordan and placed my hands on his shoulders. The cage contained a small Siamese cat, not a kitten, but young. The poor thing repeatedly vocalized with a raspy meow.

I attempted diversion. "Honey, there are some tiny kittens over by Daddy who are so cute. They look like they're wearing tuxedos."

Jordan waved me off. "I like this one."

David and Merrie joined us. I gave David a can-you-fix-this look.

David knelt down to Jordan. "Buddy, what do you like about him?"

Jordan turned toward us. "He's talking to me."

"What is he saying?" I asked. Big mistake.

Jordan shifted his eyes to me as if I were dense. "Mommy, look at him. He's saying, 'take me home.'"

The cat was handsome. At first, I wondered why someone would bring a purebred cat to a shelter. After hearing his caterwauling, I understood.

David bent to my ear and whispered. "Maybe if he weren't in a cage, he'd be quieter."

I didn't want to find out but by now, Jordan was plaintive. Not exactly whining, more like a lawyerly attempt at persuasion. Where could that have come from?

"All right," I relented. "But he has to quiet down. We can't live with this."

"He'll be okay, Mommy. I'll talk to him about it."

As if the cat would understand. Then I noticed every time the cat meowed, Merrie emitted a tiny baby laugh. I conceded, outvoted.

We left with the cat ensconced in the cardboard pet carrier included with the adoption, and David asked Jordan, "So, what should we name him?"

"His name is Spike."

"Spike?" David and I questioned, in unison.

I expected something more exotic for the delicate creature, with his slim cream body, mink points, and clear blue eyes.

"Yup!" Jordan peered into the carrier. "Right, Spike?"

Spike purred, with only the faintest sound.

ABBY

Perhaps due to our newfound tranquility, the next winter did not seem as harsh as the year before. A January thaw encompassed most of February and by March only a few cold days remained. Jordan and David lamented the absence of substantial snow. I kept my relief to myself.

Spring promised to be a busy season. Jordan's school events, David's new venture, and my consideration of a continued career filled most of our days. Nothing jelled for me yet but I was not concerned. Merrie still required most of my attention. Now that she started to walk, we entered an entirely new phase of development—the chase. As tired as I was by the end of the day, I appreciated the trade-off. No need for a gym. Running after Merrie kept me in shape.

Nina renewed her annual invitation to their Passover seder. We hadn't been able to go in the past, and this year she was insistent. David, ever eager to experience a culinary event, especially one led by the Soresmans, persuaded me to accept. I didn't know whether to expect refined dining or controlled chaos and suspected there would be some of both.

I wasn't disappointed.

DAVID

David had never experienced a Passover seder. Years ago, Abby attended one at a friend's in Vermont but said she had little memory of it other than a late night and tons of food. He could believe that. Mark's funeral repast was overwhelming. Imagine the feast at a festive occasion—his stomach was growling already. Nina warned Abby to come with an appetite. That would not be a problem.

He didn't want to arrive in total ignorance, so he asked a colleague who directed him to a Jewish bookstore on a northwest Baltimore boulevard. He hit the buzzer and heard the door mechanically unlock. He pushed it open and adjusted his eyes. Shelf after shelf obscured the light in the crowded room. Rows and rows. Stacks and stacks. English, Hebrew, and other languages. Incredible.

"Can I help you?" He peered over a table laden with volumes and saw an older man wave behind a counter.

What could he say that didn't immediately identify him as an outsider? "Yes, thank you. I'm looking for some books about Passover."

The man stepped toward him and eyed him up and down. "Not from this neighborhood are you?"

His cover was blown. "How did you know?"

The man sighed and pointed to his own head, covered with a black velvet skullcap. "No kippah. Your clothes match, though."

David looked down. He was wearing his customary white shirt, but instead of khaki pants, he wore a black pair that Abby bought him in hopes of varying his wardrobe. He noticed the older man was dressed the same, except he had two white fringes hanging from his waist in the front of his trousers.

"You're right." David smiled. "I live in Arcadia."

"Where is that?" the man asked.

"Down Route 30, just before you get to Carroll County."

The man nodded. "I see. Let me find you some books. English, I presume."

"Thank you, sir. You presume correctly."

He followed the man through the aisles. David assisted him by reaching for some shelved above the smaller man's head. The man pointed to a volume, and David added it to his pile.

After paying the bill, more than he planned to spend, but excited by his purchase, he left the bookstore with a stack of his own, curated by the man. Next time he would ask about the fringes.

ABBY

We arrived shortly before the seder began. I peeked into the dining room. The space was filled with a configuration of tables in a wide U shape, set with china, sterling, and crystal goblets for water and wine.

The guests included all of Bill and Nina's children and grandchildren, as well as some of their other local friends and relatives. Before directing us to dine, Nina led everyone to their spacious family room. Couches, chairs, and floor pillows lay arranged in a circle. A round table in the middle held snacks, crudités, and dips.

Everyone found a seat, with the kids mostly on the floor. Nina announced the seder would begin here and later resume in the dining room. Someone distributed copies of books that opened left to right.

Bill sat at the center point on the rim of the circle and held up one of the books, which he called a Haggadah. I learned that "seder" meant order. To start, the group would sing out the steps of the ordered process from beginning to end. Each guest around the circle, children included, read aloud or sang various prayers, in Hebrew or English.

Bill raised topics between pourings of wine and eating symbolic foods. He explained each part of the seder and led a lively discussion. This part took at least an hour, and the children chimed in at every step. To stave off hunger before the meal, participants passed the foods on the center table amid the discourse.

After shifting the group to the dining room, our hosts treated us to a sumptuous multi-course meal. The conversation continued as we consulted our books. More wine, more singing, and more explication followed. When we finished the meal, Bill directed the children to scour the entire house for a hidden bag containing a broken piece of matzoh. Jordan scurried around with the others as if he had done it all his life. Later, Bill sent the oldest children to open the front door where the prophet Elijah would presumably make a brief appearance. I did not see anyone enter but noticed the adults carefully watching the surface movement of wine placed in a ceremonial cup in the center of the table.

David told me he never experienced anything like it. The talk of freedom, slavery, and redemption, physically and metaphorically, left him wanting more. The ceremony, the singing, the abundant meal, and the unrelenting emphasis on tradition and memory overwhelmed him. I was impressed but exhausted. The four cups of wine had taken their toll. Jordan was still running around with the other kids. How, I could not imagine. Maybe it was the sugary fruit slices served at the end that kept his energy rolling. Merrie, blissfully, fell asleep. After assigning David the job of enticing Jordan to bed, so did I.

ABBY

Not long after Passover, the Soresman Foundation prepared a ceremony/press opportunity for the opening of the Institute for Complex Systems. David wanted me to come and bring the children. I was reluctant because of the opportunity for distraction, but he was insistent. If it were so important to David, it would happen. Jordan was mature enough to sit quietly as long as it wasn't prolonged and Nina offered to take Merrie out, if necessary.

I glanced at the proof for the program he brought home earlier. When I first read it, I asked him, "You have an MBA, too? When did that happen?"

David brushed it off. "Back in Boston. I had a lot of time on my hands."

Right, just for fun. Who does that?

It cited his undergraduate degrees in biomedical engineering and math and his Ph.D. in applied mathematics. And the MBA. And his expertise in something called systems analysis, about which I knew nothing.

Funny how you can live with someone for so long and still be surprised. He was a book with many pages still unread.

David had to leave early to attend a meet and greet with some of the bigwigs before the main event. I often teased David about his uniform of khaki pants and white shirts and tried to mix it up a bit occasionally. No tie, of course. But today, he turned my head in a new navy suit and blue and silver patterned tie that brought out the color of his eyes. I even caught him shining an old pair of dress shoes the night before.

"Oh, Professor," I called as he approached the door to leave. "Pretty formal attire you're wearing. Does this new job require a tie?"

David narrowed an eye. "I suppose, but maybe I've grown into it." He grinned, his creases more pronounced. He could still make my heart skip a beat or more.

When we arrived, David directed us to the front row where Nina secured seats on the far aisle in case there had to be a quick getaway. Nina hugged me and the kids and pointed to Michael and Joel, who came in from D.C. for the occasion. I spied Raoul in a corner with a group of students. Pete, who slicked down his blue spikes for convention's sake, even wore a jacket. Ted had a late meeting, but he and Tati would join us for dinner later.

I mentally snoozed through the first speakers. When Bill approached the podium, I was more attentive and monitored the kids from the corner of my eye.

Bill scanned the crowd. "I have always considered myself an excellent judge of talent and have had my eye on Dr. David Armacost for a long time, almost since he started at MIT. At the time, I did not know exactly what would bring us together but had an intuition that someday our aspirations would converge. So, imagine my surprise when I heard that Dr. Armacost left MIT to become a farmer. Somehow, this didn't compute."

"Soon enough, I learned although he lived on a farm, he was returning to Johns Hopkins, where he began his academic career. I understand, however, he still drives a pickup truck."

There was some light laughter in the crowd. Hmm. Not too many other pickup owners present in this auspicious group, I guessed.

"And, to add to my surprise, I also discovered that Dr. Armacost and I are related—by marriage. This was another slice of information I would have never predicted. But I am delighted by this development, as is the rest of my family, who have been blessed with the addition of David, his wife, Abby, and their children to our lives."

"Dr. Armacost, who is a MacArthur Fellow, a mathematician of renown, an accomplished scholar, an author, and the creator of innovative social enterprises, is a true visionary. Without question, he is the right leader at the right time for the Institute and we are confident that his intellect, insight, and compassion will guide us forward in our ambition and to our goals. We welcome him to our foundation family as well and look forward to many years of a productive and rewarding association with the university and our sister Institutes abroad."

Nina glowed as she patted my hand. Merrie was still smiling, and Jordan hadn't started squirming yet, to my relief.

Bill spoke a few more minutes, acknowledging the Johns Hopkins administration and their partnership in the venture, and described some of the plans for the

Institute. He then turned the program over to David, who looked as if he would burst with satisfaction.

David began by thanking the university administration, Bill and Nina, and the foundation. "Dr. Soresman is correct, in part. I did leave MIT, in a sense, to become a farmer. Returning home to Maryland was a transformative event in my life. Being able to raise our family here is a gift of immeasurable value. So much so, that when Dr. Soresman first approached me, I told him that although his vision intrigued me, my residence here was non-negotiable. I was honored beyond belief but would be unable to accept any offer that would necessitate leaving our home. I knew it was an unusual condition in this business which, at this level, often requires relocation."

"To my even greater honor and delight, the foundation was able to partner with Johns Hopkins to enable the creation of the Institute at this great university that has become my second home. This being the only impediment to my affiliation, I gladly accept the challenge and am eager to begin. The extraordinary vision of the foundation and our partners will enable us to move the boundaries of human endeavor…"

Unfortunately, Jordan had to relieve himself, and I missed the rest of his remarks. I had read David's notes earlier and knew he was about done and discreetly rushed Jordan out so we could quickly return. I predicted this would happen and told David as much. I doubted he would notice.

ABBY

We returned after all the speeches concluded and joined the assembled gathered for a brief reception. Joel pulled me into a corner. "Do you know where Agnys DeSilva is now?"

"Why?" A jolt of electricity zapped the center of my chest.

"We may have some questions for Agnys. Have you heard from her?"

"Only a postcard from the Azores. A few weeks ago. No news, just an odd little poem." I recited it from memory, its indelible impression etched on my brain.

Joel sniffed and shook his head.

"What's going on?" I asked, my voice quavering. "Should we be worried?"

"No," he said. "We found a few gaps in our investigation we thought she might be able to explain. Probably nothing that would make a difference; her recall and observations were uncanny. We received some squishy communication from overseas that might merit consideration, but also might not. We'd probably contact her if we could, and if she were readily available, ask for another interview. But it looks like she's not, so that's likely the end of it."

I shuddered.

"Our adoption—are we compromised? Is there anything we should do?" I asked.

"Look, Abby, I didn't mean to upset you. This isn't your problem. We spoke to Andy Hecht; he did everything by the book. Your adoption is secure."

He spoke to Andy? That was intrusive and creepy. Big government/big brother?

Joel must have noticed my alarm. "Andy didn't violate your privilege. He gave us just enough. We're satisfied. My guess is you'll never hear from her again. Put it out of your mind and go live your lives. All is well."

Sure, I'd forget about it. Who was he kidding?

I glanced across the room and spotted David holding Merrie in his arms. He was engaged in conversation with an older couple I didn't recognize. Everyone was smiling. The woman was playing a finger game with Merrie, whose giggle I could hear in the background.

"Please don't tell David about this," I said.

Joel nodded. "It can stay between us. He doesn't have to know."

"Okay, thank you."

Joel patted me on the back. "Don't worry and sorry. I didn't mean to spoil the party."

I headed for a stall in the ladies' room. What did Joel mean by a "squishy communication?" It was no legal term I knew. From where, from whom? What could I have missed? Had we been willfully blind? Agnys was so resolute about her story and her decision. We shared each other's trust.

I sat on the commode and held my face in my hands, trying to breathe steadily. In and out, in and out, to slow my pounding heart. After a few minutes, I ventured from the stall. The restroom was empty. I turned on the faucet and splashed my face; the cool water brought me to the present. I practiced my smile in the mirror. It looked genuine enough.

Someone entered and I stepped back into the reception. I had to leave it in there—the fear, the flaming pit in my stomach fear, quelled and flushed away.

Merrie was ours; we acted in good faith. Everything was legal and airtight. I had to erase the darkness of my dread and draw on the glow of the good. Walk into the light, I whispered to myself, a mantra with each step, forcing Joel's words to the nether regions of my mind.

David and Merrie spotted me. Wiggling, she stretched her chubby arms in my direction. I took her from David to balance on my hip. "Mama," she said, "hold me."

David excitedly introduced me to more people than I could remember. I kept my practiced smile, clinging to my wits and our child. The light, remember the light. Focus on the beauty of the present, the ineffable now, surrounded by the love I once feared I would never know. My thoughts were broken by a large hand, a farmer's hand, cradling my shoulder. I gazed upwards to my right. David's face radiated his profound pleasure, and I would do anything to make it last.

ABBY

Driving home afterward, I failed to keep my thoughts at bay. Both kids fell asleep in the car, and the uninterrupted quiet wouldn't let me rest.

Who was Agnys?

Every circumstance of our meeting was odd. I first encountered her in a psychiatric hospital, for God's sake. She was a patient committed for being mentally ill and dangerous. Was our first conversation an act or the real Agnys? Was her behavior at the hearing an aberration or her true self? The swirl of fear, disbelief, and loss of confidence in my instincts sickened me.

Had I wanted another child so much that I ignored warning signs flashing in my face? Agnys reached out to me and I embraced her. She called us the family of her heart. I bet everything on believing it, and now I had to accept I might never know.

She spent months in our home, showering love and gratitude on our family. That was the Agnys I knew, wasn't it? Would I have to gaze at her mural forever and wonder? I could never tell anyone and dreaded spending the rest of my life looking over my shoulder, pretending.

And what about the weird poem on the postcard? I hoped Joel was right and Agnys had moved on to make a clean break. He'd been doing this work for years and had good instincts. I could rely on them, couldn't I?

Yes—I could and I would. I would muster the will to believe and focus on the future. I had a family to protect and if trusting Agnys' decision was final and her motives sincere created a solid shield, I would stand behind it.

I could construct the Agnys I wanted to remember and carry that part of her forward. The good parts, her priceless gift. I could compress my fears as I had gathered Mark's failings into a shrunken compartment of my life, down a dark hallway I would never have to tread. It would do no good to dwell on a dreg of reality or speculation that could only cause me and my family pain. I had transcended worse and marched ahead. This march was my mission and it began now.

I embedded my Agnys doubts in a place beneath the surface, buried with all of the other secrets and sadness I wanted to forget. Submerged, they could not hurt me and I would move on.

The sign on the side of the road, so small you could easily miss it, signaled me home. Arcadia. The rays of the setting sun guided my path. Each streaming band of light led me closer to the arms of those I love. Message received. Splashes of gratitude cleansed me and cleared my mind. This has been a happy day, I convinced myself, in my blessed life.

ABBY

Home. My spirits boosted, my fears overcome. As best I could.

David wanted to host the family for dinner after the ceremony. Nina insisted on having it catered and well, when Nina insisted, there was very little disagreement. I had to admit coming home to the hustle and bustle of others setting up, preparing, and performing all of the other required tasks was quite a gift.

Nina ordered round tables topped with festive floral linens, real napery, and crystal. Each table held a centerpiece filled with ripe blossoms and greens. Even the chairs were swathed with matching cloth covers. The tables faced a view of the valley. As soon as I saw the room, I pictured David's delight.

Ted and Tati had already arrived when we came in. Jordan grabbed Tati's hand and the two of them disappeared into his room. I tried to subtly intervene to change him into play clothes. Tati, of course, looked as if she stepped from a children's fashion magazine. Merrie fell asleep on the ride and I carefully slid her into the crib for some semblance of the nap she missed earlier in the day.

David's truck pulled up, followed by the Soresmans, Raoul, Pete, and Sandy. Michael and Joel had never visited and from what I could see, David was pointing out the landmarks of the property. I thought he might want to take them down to The Gleanings for a tour as long as it was light. I trusted Joel would keep his promise to me.

When they walked in after The Gleanings experience, Nina turned to David, "So, you really are a farmer."

David grinned. "That is right. As I expect at heart I will always be." He glanced at me. "I guess that makes you the farmer's wife."

Who ever thought I'd fill that role? The farmer's wife with a black thumb. The irony assailed me.

Servers passed hors d'oeuvres on silver trays and handed out flutes of champagne. I spied Michael, Joel, and Nina speaking to Ted and Raoul. I overheard Nina ask about Tati, noting the child's beauty.

Michael gave Nina a sidewise glance. "Mom, are you hinting you want more grandchildren?"

Nina pinched his cheek. "Sweetheart, I never hint. Of course, I do."

Nina, in true director's fashion, gestured toward the tables. I heard Merrie waking and brought her into the room. I was happy to eat with the baby in my lap and suspected Merrie would be eagerly sought and passed around to the others. Jordan and Tati sat together, giggling. Jordan was right. Tati and Merrie could be sisters, they looked so much alike. Funny how that happened.

David gave a brief toast. I made it clear to him earlier that there had been enough speeches for the day and to keep it short. For the menu, I advised Nina on David's favorites, and naturally, Nina came through. David was an unrepentant carnivore. As long as he didn't load up on carbs, I was satisfied. Fortunately, David wasn't choosy about vegetables, especially those he grew at the farm. He raved about the tenderloin, petite haricots verts and squash, and the cold cucumber soup that preceded the entrée. Nina proposed a sorbet studded with fruit for dessert. The wine, a Cabernet chosen by Raoul, was superb.

Filled with gratitude, I nonetheless gazed about the room and considered everyone who wasn't there. My parents, Mark and Eileen, both gone. As were David's, John and Mary Agnes, whom I never knew. And Maggie, so dear to David and, I suspected, still deeply missed.

And Agnys, whose art enshrined Merrie's wall, an ever-present reminder of the young woman who played such an enormous role in our lives. I tried to hold onto the confidence I gathered on my way home. Ambivalence sliced me with a serrated edge. On the flat side of the blade, we owed so much to Agnys, whose precious gift would remain with us forever. On the other sharper side, though sheathed, I still harbored my hidden fear. I hoped someday that edge would soften, and I could retreat to my original trust. How to undo knowledge and disable doubt—that would remain my challenge. I wondered how much Jordan would remember and how David and I would be able to tell Merrie her story. We had time.

To my relief and delight, after everyone left, the staff cleaned up. I put the children to bed, their nightly reading routines abridged for their late bedtime. It would be nice for David to have some quiet time after his momentous day.

ABBY

Cleansed of errant thoughts, I diverted myself into playfulness. God knows I needed something. With two young children, our opportunities for intimacy had become more limited and tonight, whether driven by ardor or desperation, I was brimming with desire.

As David and I undressed, I teased him. "You think you're really something, don't you?"

"I think . . . I am a very lucky man."

"Well," I licked the tip of my forefinger. "You're about to get even luckier."

David pretended an ingenuous glance. "Young lady, just what are you implying?"

"I am not implying anything, Professor. Take off your glasses and come here."

David removed his glasses and carefully placed them in his bedside drawer, as he did every night. Even that aroused me.

I grabbed his bottom. "What do we have here? Could this be the ass of the great David Armacost?"

"It would," David sputtered amid a chuckle.

I flattened him on the bed and began kissing him all over.

In return, David grasped me. "God, your bottom is so tiny, but it is perfect."

"Like the rest of me?" I was on a roll.

David gulped. "Yes, like everything about you."

We held each other with an intensity that matched the emotions of the day. I maneuvered myself above him, stroking his shoulder and lightly nipping his ear. David trembled with passion as I accepted his thrusts with abandon. After climax, we slid to the side, still holding on, breathing slow and steady. I rolled onto my back, blinking in the dark. A trickle of tears trailed my cheeks.

A salty drop found my tongue and I swallowed, focused on a single thought:

And he thinks he's the lucky one.

DAVID

It wasn't hard cleaning out his old office at Hopkins. He hadn't moved much in and was usually diligent in discarding items no longer of use. He had one more box to pack, mostly the contents of some drawers, pictures, and a few books. It didn't take long.

His desk was clear except for a couple of items from his inbox. He paged through the lean stack and found the letter. No return address, the postmarked smudged, and stamps bearing the profile of the Queen. He found his father's sword-shaped letter opener and slid it along the edge of the flap.

A single sheet of paper, "Leeds Psychiatric Center" printed at the top, spilled out. The letter contained one type-written sentence. "Agnys DeSilva is not who you think she is." He blinked. His hand shook and the paper landed at his feet.

What in the world? His heart pounded as he fumbled with his Rolodex, also stuffed in that last box. He had to dial the phone three times before he got it right.

"Mr. Hecht's office."

"This is David Armacost. I need to speak to Mr. Hecht. It's important."

Click. "David, how are you? What's up?"

He described the letter to Andy. "What do we do?" He choked on the last word. "This doesn't mean . . ."

"No, no, David. You're fine. We did everything right. This means nothing."

"You know about this?"

"I am aware of some communications, but they don't affect you or your family. You don't have to worry about this. Trust me."

He would have to trust the lawyer. The alternative was unthinkable.

"Andy." He swallowed, hard. "We don't have to tell Abby about this, do we? It would destroy her."

"Not if you don't want to. She doesn't have to know."

"Okay, Andy. Thank you."

"Look, David. Tear up the letter and try to put it out of your mind. Or, if you want, send it to me and I'll file it away. I promise you—you and your family are safe."

They ended the conversation with Andy congratulating him on his new job. As if it mattered as much to him now. While the letter might mean nothing, it tarnished the shine of his day. An erosion of his isle of good fortune.

But that was life, wasn't it? He had learned the lesson many times over—treasure the good, overcome the bad. He would put it out of his mind like other worries in his life and store them in a cavern of his heart. Hard to reach, but not erased. And, if Andy was right, never to surface again.

He struggled to revive his natural optimism. As long as Abby never knew, all would be well.

DAVID

Try as he might, doubt engulfed him in a fog of indecision. What if the worst happened?

He'd kept one secret from her for years. She forgave him quickly enough, but he wasn't sure she'd do it again. She had a right to know.

There would never be a good time. They were rushed in the morning and drained at night. The kids were always around, and Jordan had big ears. As hard as it would be to tell Abby, the thought of ever explaining this to Jordan was unbearable. Out flew his confidence, giving way to gloom.

He hadn't noticed the stop sign. The passing car swerved and he missed it by inches. He tossed an apologetic wave, embarrassed by his lack of attention. The other driver gave him the finger and sped away.

Not a minute later, the flashing lights and blare of a patrol car overtook him. Oh no. His stomach dropped; he never got a ticket before. He pulled onto the narrow shoulder and the officer approached. Already shaken from the near accident, he was grateful the officer let him stay in the truck. His knee trembled and throbbed. He handed the officer his license and registration with as much remorse as he could muster. Chastened and contrite, he must have convinced the officer to only issue a warning.

There was a reason he hated driving; too hard to concentrate when so many other things were on his mind. At least he didn't have an accident. What if someone had been hurt? His fault, his own bloody fault. He hoped his luck would follow him home.

ABBY

David is a better person than I'll ever be. But I've always known that. I would have kept that secret forever. Sealed, until it flayed me raw from the inside out. And he would never know, fair or not.

David sat at the kitchen table when I came in carrying groceries. I ran out of the house when he arrived home before exchanging a word, except to ask him to put the kids to bed.

He acted as if he hadn't heard me enter. He pulled at his thumbs, staring at the clock on the wall. A bottle of Irish whiskey and an almost empty glass faced him.

"What's this?" I said, pointing to the glass.

"What does it look like?"

"It doesn't look like you." He hadn't offered to take the heavy bag from me and it hit the floor when it slipped from my hand.

"You'd be surprised. It's me."

I picked up the bag and placed it on the counter. Nothing broken.

"I almost got a ticket today," he said.

"Not a speeding ticket?" That would have been impossible. He was slower than a snail. "And, so what if you had?"

"I ran a stop sign. Almost hit a car. I wasn't paying attention."

"Nobody got hurt, did they?"

"No, but I was distracted."

Also nothing new. It had to be something else.

He poured more whiskey into the glass and gulped it.

"Something's going on," I said. "Are you going to tell me or what?" This had to be bad news.

"I spoke to Andy Hecht today." No eyes on me, just the glass.

Oh—he must know. What else would account for this?

"About Agnys?"

He turned around. "How do you know?"

"Joel. I didn't want to tell you. How about you—did Andy call you?"

"No. I received an odd letter and called him."

"A letter? From whom?"

"I don't know. It was unsigned. Someone in England. I can't imagine who."

I could. Dr. Priscilla Knowles. She had a clear interest in gumming up the works and shifting suspicion to a victim.

"Where is it?" I asked.

"I sent it to Andy. I never want to see it again."

"What did it say?"

"That Agnys was not who we think she was."

Well, maybe she wasn't. But it didn't matter now.

"Are you worried?"

"Of course, I am," he said. "Aren't you?"

"I was, but I'm not anymore." It was only a tiny lie.

He stared at his hands, placed flat on the table. "Our Merrie. I love her so much." His voice broke on the last word.

I hooked my hand around his, barely covering his last two fingers.

"I know you do. So do I."

He raised his head. "Did you tell Joel about the odd poem on the postcard? Did he think it meant anything?"

"I told him, but no, not really. He said if anything, it was her way of saying she was gone. He thinks she's out of the picture for good."

David huffed. "I thought it was just a silly verse."

"I guess we'll never know. But Joel wasn't concerned, at least for us. Was Andy?"

"No, he's confident we're safe."

"Then why are you drinking?"

"Good question. To give me the courage to tell you."

I reached into the upper cabinet and handed him another glass.

"Pour me some," I said. "We'll drown our fears together."

ABBY

Several months passed, and I remembered I hadn't returned to Summervale to pick up the items I left behind. Mildly embarrassed, I called Cindy Fairchild, who assured me she never noticed the box. I could come whenever it was convenient.

I arranged a time when Cindy was there. Approaching Summervale, a sour sear scorched the pit of my stomach. My thoughts formed a loop, circling my brain. What a failure I had been. How could I have lasted so long? Thank God I never have to work here again. Humiliation and relief—not a winning combination. I made some bad choices and could not erase missing the first mark of my legal career.

The security guard greeted me when I entered the lobby. She asked me why I had been gone so long. Fortunately, Cindy showed up before I had to explain. We walked together down the cinder-block halls, dodging the slick spots on the stained vinyl floor.

I heard the relentless screamer, the perpetual patient whose demons would never let him see the light of day. Mine had been a noble cause. I truly believed the human factor elevated it above the struggle over land. Intangibles such as liberty and due process superseded even the legal symmetry of property law, and I was grateful to have pursued it, even for so brief a time. The failing was mine, not the opposition, or the environment. That I touched it, even tangentially, made me a more complete human. My time here was not wasted. Even the screamer taught me something important about life and about myself.

The office looked the same. An old, splintered desk propped with a shim on one side, a faded poster of the Chesapeake Bay, and a brown stain on the carpet, origin unknown. Cindy had some scented oil plugged into an outlet. I guess it helped.

Cindy retrieved the box from the closet and slid it across the floor. I did not bother opening it. For one, I didn't care, and two, I did not want to prolong my visit. I was happy to see Cindy, though. Cindy shared bits of office gossip and updates on some of the patients and staff. She was optimistic about Grace Goldsmith's reforms and admired my role in exposing the corruption that led to Grace's appointment. I hadn't known it, but Cindy specifically asked Marta to be reassigned to Summervale so she could help. I was relieved that Cindy did not resent me for abandoning my post.

Cindy opened a drawer in the desk and pulled out a metal flask.

I snickered. "What is that?"

Cindy handed it to me. "It must have been Gene's. Smell this shit. That must be how he did this job for so long."

I took a whiff. "Oh my God, is that what rotgut smells like?"

We collapsed in laughter. The image of Gene taking a nip between hearings was all too believable.

My memory drifted to his retirement party where with affection, all present, including David, chimed in as Gene sang his song. *"So give to me the parting glass, goodnight and joy be to you all."* Was this my parting glass? Amid the humor, my loss of confidence remained. At least Gene completed his run on a high note, even if he needed a drop or two to make it through. A pint a day wouldn't have extended mine.

I thanked Cindy. We exchanged numbers and promised to stay in touch. I hoped we would. I liked Cindy and respected her for staying the course. I picked up the box with both hands, leveraged it on my chest, and tried not to stumble or fall as I made my way down the hall past a score of dingy wards.

ABBY

My balancing act lost me in thought until I heard it again. The screaming.

Mind-piercing, relentless screaming. Fear and fury screaming that turned my blood to bits of rusty shard. Day after day, the murky halls reverberated with the din. Once, I sidestepped a poorly paid aide as he tackled the frenzied man to medicate and quiet him. Subdued, the man's shaking limbs slackened into a quiet heap. Scream, rinse, repeat. A jarring, ungodly pattern.

I held my breath and navigated the puddles on the floor. A cloud of body fluids and disinfectant hovered below my knees. A piece of flaking ceiling tile floated in the air and brushed my nose. I held back a sneeze.

I had been an advocate for the screamers, the silent, and the unaware whose haunting delusions repeatedly courted danger and dread. And, despite my efforts, most would remain, shattered, to the end of their days.

I sought to defend the defenseless, and the journey took me here, to a gloomy, crumbling shame of a public hospital that should have been demolished years ago, searching for the elusive victory of a patient's release. No more.

The screaming. I would never have to hear it again.

ABBY

My reverie ended as the sound faded, absorbed by distance and crumbling cinderblock. The box became heavier with each step. I could ditch it in the hallway, and it might sit there for years without notice. Maybe I would chuck it in a dumpster on the way back. Or I could take it home, hide it, and forget about it until it no longer held meaning for me.

An aide unlocked the double doors leading to the lobby. I smiled at the guard who signed me in. She winked and said, "See you soon." I wanted to respond, "No fucking way." But I didn't. Too polite.

The guard hit the buzzer to unlock the hefty outer door. I rushed to shove it open with my hip, trying not to lose my balance or prolong my visit by even a second. I remembered the adage "when one door closes," as the heavy frame slammed behind me.

What, if anything, would open next? I scanned the clouds and sucked in air free of decay. Liberated, yet adrift. I had no map to guide me, simply the desire to move on and get past my failure.

Goodbye, Summer ale H spit l.

Goodbye, legal career?

ABBY

I revved the motor and whizzed down the road, seeking as much distance between myself and Summervale as quickly as possible. Of course, something remarkably good had come from my experience—the beautiful little girl who would greet me when I arrived. Maybe that was the opening door, or there could be others somewhere down the line. What was Eileen's phrase? No limits? Time would tell.

The law still beckoned, brilliant with more facets than I could count. Not all of it was bound up in tragedy and defeat. Scattered here and there, reflections of nobility lit a path, with moral guideposts to lead the way. Law brought order out of chaos—the chaos of a troubled human mind, the chaos of greed. I could be a soldier in that army and fight for dignity and grace. There would be a way, a portal, a door.

Soon I would return to our small slice of paradise. I was light-years away from where I started. The girl without a family or a home. I recalled the originals who brought me to this destination: Mo, Dan, and Jack Warfield, always Jack. How he would have roared his rare laugh knowing his box of yellowed papers led to this. That was a door I opened once, and look where it led.

The rolling hills shimmered in the distance as I turned up the drive. Off to the left, the bare fields of The Gleanings, at rest for the season, stretched as far as I could see. This was the land that David almost lost, the land I risked my first career to save. It meant more to us than wealth, success, or praise. This land was our anchor and our bond. And beyond our lives and those of our children, it would remain, as I dreamed long ago.

I once feared nothing lasted in life, but the land convinced me that something of value endures, a precious beauty that can last forever. Later, I questioned what mattered, and how I could impact an imperfect world without losing my soul. This is what I learned: everyone matters, from the weakest to the strong, from my vulnerable clients, lost in the world, to the people I love. From those unknown to the faces who haunt my dreams. Land could last until the end of time. We matter, with one brief chance to make our mark, live our lives in the service of others, and to love.

Stepping out of the car, I shivered, aware of the coming winter chill. The leaves had mostly fallen, and veined branches crisscrossed the horizon. I rushed to reach the door and enter for warmth. Before I did, I pivoted for one last look. The stark beauty always restored me, centered me, and made me whole. My chest rose as I took a deep, clean breath, my heart expanding; growing, growing, grown.

Hiding in plain sight, my salvation lay before me. Arcadia. My family, our home. A small share of the greater world that teemed with promise and hope. Revived, I peered above the landscape at the sweeping sky. Boundless and serene, it was clear as a blessing, clearer than sparkling glass, and as convincing as truth.

CODA

October 1980

"Rose, I have something for you," Tony DeSilva called as he entered the house carrying a large brown paper shopping bag.

"What is it?" Rose had been in the kitchen but glanced toward the foyer.

They recently moved into a rancher in North Providence. They were the first owners, and the kitchen and bathrooms were modern, unlike the other homes in the neighborhood. Rose was thrilled. It was the first new house they ever owned.

Tony was in the construction business with his brother, Sam. In the past few years, they branched out, buying older homes with multiple units. The rental business proved quite profitable and had given both brothers a huge income boost. They had come a long way since they arrived in the States with their parents from the Azores when they were kids. Rose could sense his swell of success and pride.

Tony handed Rose the bag. "Someone left it in one of the units in Pawtucket. The crew was cleaning up and didn't know what to do with it."

Rose peeked into the bag. "Who was the tenant?"

"No idea," Tony said. "It was a sublet. No one in the office has a record of the person's name or forwarding address. They think she might have died."

"That's sad," said Rose. "And no one else wanted it?"

"No, it's yours."

Rose pulled a wrapped gift from the bag. She checked, but the bag contained no card or name identifying the intended recipient. The gift had heft and felt like a large book. Rose carefully unwrapped it, making sure not to tear the glossy cover. It was a volume titled "History of Art" and was filled with vivid color plates of paintings and sculpture throughout the ages.

Rose beamed. She was an amateur artist and loved reading about the subject. She experimented with positioning the large book, aesthetically angling it on the coffee table across from the antique candy dish from her grandmother.

"Thank you." Rose kissed Tony's cheek. "It's too bad about the former owner, but I'm more than happy to give it a home." She sat down on the new, sleek couch, placed the book in her lap, and paged through it with enjoyment.

November 1999

Agnys pouted all the way home from school. "Mom, you've got to let me go. All the other girls are going. It's not fair."

Finally, she was accepted by the cool crowd in school, the ones who wore designer jeans and went on beach vacations in the winter. She didn't start Providence Country Day until ninth grade after most of the cliques were formed. Plus, she was an outsider, with immigrant parents who still spoke Portuguese at home. It took her two years to fit in and she wasn't about to blow it.

Emily, who lived in Barrington, was planning a trip to New York with a few other girls. Her parents had an apartment in Manhattan, and the group was going to take the train from Providence. Emily told the girls to say her parents would be there, but everyone knew they would really be in Florida for the weekend. It promised to be amazing, and there was no way Agnys was going to miss out.

"It's a lot of money for a weekend, honey," Agnys' mother, Rose, said. "Between the train, meals, and a Broadway show, it's got to be over two hundred dollars. Besides, I know you'll want to go shopping, too, and I'm sure those girls don't do discount."

"Please, please, please! You know how much I want to go. I have to go. I'll pay you back. I'll babysit. I'll do anything."

"All right. I'll talk it over with your father. As long as her parents are going, too."

"Mom! Of course, they are!"

"I understand. I know you want to be with your friends."

Agnys reached across the seat to hug her mother. "Thank you, thank you!"

"Wait a minute, honey. I didn't say yes yet."

But Agnys knew she would.

She had some time to start her homework while her mother fixed dinner. Agnys lifted the large art book from the living room coffee table and brought it to her room. She had an art history assignment and wanted to read the chapter on Titian. She aspired to be an artist like her mother and loved leafing through the book, reading about the lives and work of artists throughout history. One day, she would be famous, too. She could see it now: Agnys DeSilva, artist extraordinaire.

The book had a shiny paper cover secured with tape on the inside to keep it in place. The tape had yellowed with age and was beginning to fray. Agnys did not want to harm the book but thought the tape unsightly and peeled it away. As she did, she felt something underneath the paper cover, wedged between it and the hard cloth cover of the book.

Agnys fiddled with the object and managed to slide an envelope out with her fingertips. It was rectangular, with the initials "A.R." written in ink on the front. The envelope was sealed shut.

She debated opening it but decided there was no reason not to. The book had already been sitting on their table for as long as she could remember. She vaguely recalled her mother telling her that her father brought the book home from the apartment of someone who died.

Agnys slipped her fingernail along the edge of the envelope and, breaking the seal, lifted the flap. It contained a graduation card, a cartoonish drawing of a girl wearing a gown and mortarboard. Inside, a sappy poem wished the recipient success in the future. Above the poem, someone had written in shaky script, "Dear Abigail," and at the bottom, in the same handwriting, "Your loving father, Mark."

A flap on the inside of the card hid an unexpected prize. Agnys shook the card and five one-hundred-dollar bills fell to the floor. Even though her door was closed, she looked behind her and from side to side.

Counting aloud, she smoothed each one, five portraits of Benjamin Franklin, crisp and green.

She couldn't believe it. Not only could she go to New York, now she could do it in style. She wouldn't be the girl who only looked while the others shopped and admired each other's finds. Agnys shooed away a flash of conscience. It wasn't stealing; she'd never do that. Her father brought the book home years ago before she was born. Abigail and Mark were probably long gone. And if on the impossible chance she ever met them, Agnys would pay them back, with interest. She wasn't a thief.

Agnys folded the bills and secured them in a zippered pocket of her knapsack. Hearing her mother call, she slipped the card back into the envelope and slid it under the book cover where she found it. "Coming, Mom," she sang out, hungry for supper. Later, she would find some tape to hide the envelope again, return the book to the coffee table, and no one would ever know.

It would be her little secret. For now. And maybe forever.

About the Author

H.C. Helfand is an attorney who lives in Maryland.

The first volume of The Arcadia Chronicles, Fee Simple Conditional, is the story of how Abigail Fischer and David Armacost saved their beloved land. Look for future installments of their story, including the planned third volume, The Right of Redemption.

www.hchelfand.com

Lightning Source UK Ltd.
Milton Keynes UK
UKHW010116100123
415068UK00007B/705